KT-196-000

Paddock Wood Library
Tel 01892 832006
Fax 01892 832065
paddockwoodlibrary@kent.gov.uk

Pnw
05/11

GB

0 7 APR 2012

0 1 JUN 2011

13 AUG 2012

17 JUN 2011 WITHDRAWN
1 MAR 2018

1 5 JUL 2011

0 3 AUG 2011
2 6 AUG 2011

Please return on or before the latest date above.
You can renew online at *www.kent.gov.uk/libs*
or by telephone 08458 247 200

CUSTOMER SERVICE EXCELLENCE

Libraries & Archives

Kent
County
Council

00884\DTP\RN\07.07   LIB 7

C155299439

HIS CHRISTMAS PLEASURE

His Christmas Pleasure

Cathy Maxwell

THORNDIKE
CHIVERS

This Large Print edition is published by Thorndike Press, Waterville, Maine, USA and by AudioGO Ltd, Bath, England.
Thorndike Press, a part of Gale, Cengage Learning.
Copyright © 2010 by Catherine Maxwell, Inc.
The moral right of the author has been asserted.

ALL RIGHTS RESERVED
This is a work of fiction. Names, characters, places, and incidents are products of the author's imagination or are used fictitiously and are not to be construed as real. Any resemblance to actual events, locales, organizations, or persons, living or dead, is entirely coincidental.
The text of this Large Print edition is unabridged.
Other aspects of the book may vary from the original edition.
Set in 16 pt. Plantin.

LIBRARY OF CONGRESS CATALOGING-IN-PUBLICATION DATA

Maxwell, Cathy.
His Christmas pleasure / by Cathy Maxwell. — Large print ed.
p. cm. — (Thorndike Press large print romance)
ISBN-13: 978-1-4104-3294-0
ISBN-10: 1-4104-3294-7
1. Large type books. 2. Christmas stories. I. Title.
PS3563.A8996H57 2010
813'.54—dc22   2010040352

BRITISH LIBRARY CATALOGUING-IN-PUBLICATION DATA AVAILABLE

Published in 2010 in the U.S. by arrangement with Avon, HarperCollins Publishers.
Published in 2011 in the U.K. by arrangement with HarperCollins Publishers.

U.K. Hardcover: 978 1 408 49379 3 (Chivers Large Print)
U.K. Softcover: 978 1 408 49380 9 (Camden Large Print)

KENT
LIBRARIES & ARCHIVES
C155299439

Printed in the United States of America
1 2 3 4 5 6 7 14 13 12 11 10

For Ken and Maureen Baker.
Your friendship has been an anchor in
our lives.

Chapter One

London, October 1810

The butt of the ornate dueling pistol was saw-handled, so it felt short in Andres's grip. Obviously, the gun's owner, the duke of Banfield, didn't have hands as large as his own. However, Andres did like the spur on the trigger guard, which allowed a man to rest a finger and steady his aim. It was a magnificent weapon, truly bored and no doubt sporting the fastest, most effective flintlock that ingenuity could design and money could buy.

Andres had discovered it in Banfield's library when he'd escaped from the ballroom to avoid Carla, the lovely Lady Dobbins and a man-eater of the first order. A month ago, she'd set her sights on Andres with a ferocity that was becoming embarrassing. She was hunting him down, and even a meeting in public was no guarantee there wouldn't be a scene.

7

The moment he'd arrived this evening, she'd rushed up to him, brushing past others in her anxiousness to claim him. As soon as he'd been able, he'd freed himself of her and made his way to this safe haven.

He couldn't let Carla chase him off. Tonight was important. Banfield was not one who enjoyed the country. He had become known for the parties he hosted in the fall and winter, when often the only people left in town were those in politics, those with power and advantage. Andres, who claimed the Spanish title barón de Vasconia, hoped to make an advantageous contact this evening that could lead to a possible career in the English government. The English were at war on the Continent. They had need of a man who understood the Peninsula, or even the world. Andres had traveled much of both, and he knew that, given the chance, he could make a contribution to this new country of his.

Of course, a government career was not his first choice of livelihood. Horses were in his blood. But a man without two shillings to his name, titled or not, couldn't be choosy.

The library was obviously Banfield's personal domain. Not even the strains of music or the dizzying hum of laughter and conversation from the ballroom intruded past these book-lined walls. The furnishings were Sheraton, severe and plain to Andres's eye. The settee and three chairs were grouped before the fire burning in the grate. Beyond them was Banfield's desk, a heavy, oversized structure carved from mahogany.

The pair of dueling pistols had been displayed like prized possessions in a velvet case on Banfield's desk. Their ivory handles had gleamed in the lamplight, drawing Andres to them.

He doubted if Banfield had ever used these guns for their true purpose. The duke was far too amiable a character to find himself in duels, unlike Andres, who had participated in more than his share.

Most likely the duke kept these weapons for show or to take out occasionally for practice. They were a living symbol of his ducal honor, which was a pity, Andres thought as he raised the weapon. He tested its sight by focusing on one of those ghoulishly grinning porcelain dogs on the mantel. This pistol was too fine to not be used for its intended purpose —

His eye caught movement.

Instincts honed by years of hard living brought the gun around. He took aim — and then realized he was preparing to shoot his own reflection in a large, ornate bull's-eye mirror hanging on the opposite wall.

For a long moment, Andres stood still, fascinated by his distorted image in the mirror. His face was larger in the center, his shoulders and arms small.

Slowly, deliberately, he turned his hand so the gun aimed at his head.

How easy it would be to pull the trigger.

He stood, riveted by the sight. By the temptation.

At last he understood his father.

Death would be freeing. No more struggles to reclaim a heritage Andres knew was hopelessly lost, though he feared it had never been his to begin with. No more carrying the weight of his own mistakes, his many failures. Or the pain of living without love. He could curse Gillian for introducing him to what the word meant and then leaving him to return to her husband.

If he was going to take his own life, he'd do it right. He'd blow off this face of his, which was both blessing and curse.

Andres might have been born of the noble house of the Ramigio, but he had betrayed that royal lineage more times than he cared to remember. He was unworthy. A failure. If he had any honor at all, he'd pull this trigger, just as his father had. He wasn't enough. He never would be enough —

"*No, stop.* It's a sin."

Before he could turn, could comment, he was tackled to the ground by a redheaded force of nature. She'd caught him off guard and had easily toppled all six feet one of him.

Dazed, Andres looked up to find a young woman with an impossible mop of carroty-colored hair frowning down at him. She'd fallen on top of him in her effort to knock him over, and she now pushed herself up, her hands resting on his chest. "You would make a terrible mess in the room if you shot yourself," she said earnestly, "as well as bring a halt to the party."

Andres still had the pistol in his hand. He lifted it for her to see that the hammer wasn't cocked. "I wasn't doing what you imagine."

She tilted her head, as if his accented English had surprised her, as if discovering the gun uncocked surprised her.

"What you saw is not what you think." Actually, he was embarrassed to have been caught. Nor did he want rumors circulating that he was suicidal. That was *all* he needed. Carla would believe it was over her and he'd never be rid of her. "The pistol is not loaded."

"It's not what? . . ." A frown formed between her brows. "Why would you point a 'not loaded' pistol to your head?"

"Not because I was attempting to take my life," Andres said, raising himself to rest on his elbows and take a better look at his would-be savior . . . and finding himself pleasantly surprised.

He'd not met her before. She was strikingly different from the ranks of willowy blondes and curvy brunettes of his acquaintance. She even had freckles on her nose. He'd not seen one freckle in any upper-class English drawing room. He'd thought they'd been forbidden, banned completely with creams and hats and whatever artifices could be designed — and yet here they were.

Those freckles made her seem . . . not less refined but more vivid, more alive.

She didn't move. She sat on him, contemplating him with an expression that reminded him of a small, serious owl. "You *were* considering it," she decided, "and considering it is a sin as well."

The boredom, the disinterest that had laced itself tightly around his life of late gave way. She was such an English lamb. They always felt they knew everything, and she was so certain she'd saved him.

"Not all is what it seems," he answered.

12

"For example, if someone were to walk in at this moment, what would they think was happening between us?"

Her eyes narrowed. They were blue eyes. Common with red hair but devilishly attractive. "If you wish to point out how compromising this position is, say so. I acted as I did because I thought *you* needed help."

"Oh, I could use some help," Andres assured her as lust slammed into him with a force he'd not anticipated. He sat up, wanting to both gather her in his arms and hide the fact of his arousal.

For a second, they were almost nose-to-nose. Heat-to-heat.

She'd felt him. Knew he was hard. He saw it in those disconcerting eyes of hers and discovered something else too — she was unimpressed. Disinterested. Annoyed even.

With a very firm push against his shoulders, she attempted to rise, no easy task in the tangle of her muslin skirts. "Men are the silliest creatures," she muttered, rising halfway up. "I sought to help —"

"To help what, Abby?" a male voice said from the doorway. "And what are you doing on the floor behind the furniture?"

Immediately, his would-be rescuer froze. Her gaze said all — she did not want to be discovered with Andres.

So the lamb wasn't so naive after all.

Andres did the gentlemanly thing. He raised his fingers to his lips, promising his silence, and lay back down.

Abby shook out her skirts and forced a smile to her lips. *"Myself,"* she said. "I sought to help myself."

"Why were you on the floor?" her gentleman asked.

"You know how clumsy I am," she murmured, stepping around the settee and moving further away from where Andres lay.

Andres expected the gentleman to say something gallant about her not being clumsy. Instead, her gent agreed with her. "You were never graceful."

"Thank you, Freddie," she said with no small amount of exasperation, but then her tone lifted. "I'm so happy to finally be alone with you. What is it you wished to say to me? Wait, perhaps not here. Let us go someplace more quiet."

Andres heard the door shut, but they hadn't left. "There is no place more quiet than here," Freddie said. "And I must talk to you."

"About what?" she said, her tone now eager, warmer.

Rolling over on his side the better to listen, Andres wondered who this Freddie was. He saw Abby's skirts and a pair of male legs. It was hard to judge a man by his feet, although his footwear was of good quality.

"Sit down," Freddie ordered.

There was a beat of silence during which Abby did not sit down. "You aren't going to marry me, are you?"

Another beat of silence. Freddie shifted his weight from one foot to another in guilt. Then, in a serious voice, he confessed, "I'm going to ask for the hand of your cousin Corinne."

Abby gave a short gasp, as if she'd been in physical pain. She dropped onto the settee as if her legs could not support her, her skirts obscuring Andres's view. Freddie sat beside her, his polished evening shoes two feet from Andres's nose.

Andres knew who Corinne was. She was the duke of Banfield's daughter, one of the willowy blondes.

"Abby, please," Freddie said, "you knew there could never be anything between us. You *knew*."

"No, I didn't *know*," she confessed with the bald honesty Andres was deciding he liked. "You love me." It wasn't a question but a statement.

"I do," Freddie hurried to agree, but there was something not quite right in his tone. A hesitation, a forced sincerity. A man could hear it in another man's voice.

Women rarely did . . . and Abby was no exception. "Then why aren't you asking for *my* hand? Why, when we have a chance to be together, are you choosing another? And my *cousin,* Freddie? Have you no sensibility to how I feel?"

"That's why I thought to speak to you *before* it is announced, Abby. Please, you know Mother and Father will not agree to a match between us. We went over this three years ago. Father refuses to have someone in trade in the family."

"My father is a banker."

"And my father is old-fashioned and sets his own rules on what is what. You know he doesn't see differences in what a man does. As far as he is concerned, there are the upper ten thousand and then there is everyone else."

"My uncle is the duke of Banfield. My family lines are perfectly acceptable."

"Except for your mother marrying beneath herself."

"It's a very good thing she did," Abby returned stoutly. "Father's intelligence about money has rescued the whole family. Otherwise my uncle the duke wouldn't be able to afford this ball, let alone Corinne's dowry."

Andres now knew who Abby was. Banker Montross's daughter. Her father's business acumen was legendary. Everything the man touched turned to gold. And, yes, he was related to Banfield, but it was said he was a hard man, a coarse one. Banfield was rumored to not be overly fond of Montross although he tolerated him as his sister's husband. And Andres had heard a rumor about the daughter. Something about a marriage that had gone wrong —

"As for sensibilities, Abby, what about my feelings?" Freddie said. "How do you think I felt when you agreed to marry another man?"

"My father made the agreement, Freddie. And only because he said you would never ask. He feared I'd end up on the shelf completely . . . which it looks as if I will."

"Abby, I can't be blamed because your father chose the wrong man for you —"

"The wrong man?" She came to her feet, crossing toward the fireplace as if needing to put space between them. *"You* were the right man. I waited for you, Freddie. I believed your promises. After Father betrothed me to Mr. Lynsted, I begged you to elope with me and you said you couldn't

because your family means so much to you."

"They do," he replied, also rising. "I won't apologize for respecting their wishes."

Andres thought he sounded like a prig.

"Yes," she agreed with her characteristic directness, "and because you feared being cut off from funds as well."

"This is an old road," Freddie answered peevishly. "We've traveled this before."

"I know," Abby said, hurt etching each word. "I put off marrying Mr. Lynsted, Freddie. I did everything to delay the marriage, used every excuse I had. Most women my age have a family and a home of their own. I'm five and twenty and I have nothing, just as my father warned."

"Abby, I'm sorry. . . . but it isn't my fault Lynsted jilted you. Really, who would have thought it? The man was so morally upright he could have gone into the clergy. And here he threw you over for an actress. Shameful."

"Shameful? I rejoiced, Freddie. I wasn't going to have to marry a man I didn't love. I thought you would come for me, that I could marry *you*."

Andres leaned his head against the floor, understanding the pain behind her words. To love . . . and not have that love returned. He knew it all too well.

"I do love you, Abby," Freddie the weasel said. "If I thought there was hope for us, if I could untangle myself from the betrothal, I would."

"I have money now, Freddie. My grandmother left her money to me."

"What?"

"Yes, it's true. You know she passed away last year, and I'm her heir. She didn't leave even so much as a stickpin to anyone else in the family. Once I marry, it's mine. *Ours.* It comes to me upon marriage. And neither you nor I need worry about being cut off by our fathers."

"Why didn't you tell me this sooner?" Freddie demanded. Andres had almost believed it would have made a difference until Freddie added, "How much money?"

"Does it matter?"

"It matters. I'm dependent on Father for funds, but if you have enough, well, it would have been nice."

"*Would* have been?" she echoed, sounding slightly dazed, as if she couldn't believe he argued.

"Abby, you were jilted. Everyone knows. Your reputation is damaged. There's been a horrid amount of talk, and you know Father abhors that sort of thing."

"I'm not overly delighted with it either,

19

Freddie. This is the first time I've gone out in society since it happened. I hear them whispering. No one has asked me to dance all night. And that was fine . . . because I knew you would come for me. I've been waiting."

"I wish I could speak for you," Freddie said. "However, I can't jeopardize a match with Corinne. Her father is a duke. That trumps a banker."

"And love be *damned.*" Her defiant words, born from the pain of betrayal, rang in the air. She started toward the door. If Freddie had any honor, Andres thought, he'd let her go.

Of course the scoundrel stopped her.

Andres could feel every morsel of Abby's humiliation, her sorrow. After all, had he not played this scene with Gillian and been publicly rejected?

"Let me pass, Freddie," she said, a tremor in her voice.

"I can't let you go out there like this."

"I won't break down, if that is what you are afraid of," she answered, sounding as if she'd fall apart at any minute.

"Abby, Abby, *Abby,* you are looking at this the wrong way. My marriage won't prevent us from being special friends. Our love will not die. It can thrive. Many couples do this.

They have their husbands or wives and then have those for whom they save their *true* emotion."

"Why can't it be one and the same?" she asked.

"Because that's not the way it's done. We marry for advantages. Be honest. Your father won't let you marry just anyone. He wasn't completely pleased with me. Banker Montross thinks highly of himself."

"I believe he expected you to step forward and you haven't," Abby corrected him.

"Yes, well, he's wrong if he thinks I'm not a man," Freddie answered.

Andres didn't know if he agreed.

"Abby," Freddie said, pulling her close to him. "I do love you. But Father wants me to marry Corinne because he wants the alliance with Banfield. As for yourself, marry someone, *anyone,* Abby. A married woman has more freedom than a single one. It will be easy for us to be lovers. We just have to put up a good appearance."

"Appearances? I want *more* than appearances."

She deserved more, Andres decided. Well, she deserved anything but this buffoon. Her Freddie was enjoying his position of power. He wasn't treating her love like the precious gift it was. Only someone who'd had his love spurned could identify with how she felt.

Andres was not going to let her sacrifice her pride. Freddie could go out into the ballroom and, with a casual word here and there, let it be known she'd begged him — and the man would. Andres knew his type. Insensitive, selfish, arrogant . . . Andres had been those things and more until love had humbled him. Freddie was flattered by her admission. Bolstered by it.

"I don't think anyone will have me," she said, sounding defeated. "I'm old now. Too old."

"Abby, we'll find someone," Freddie answered, his voice warm, confiding, seductive. Andres pictured him putting his arms around her, preparing to kiss her. "Being a lover is so much better than being a wife. You can't envy Corinne, because you will always have my heart —"

Andres had heard enough.

He left the dueling pistol on the floor as he came to his feet, popping up from behind the settee. "I've waited long enough, Miss Montross. Let us forget this nonsense and go dance."

CHAPTER TWO

Abby had been so wrapped up in her disappointment, her yearning, her wanting that she'd forgotten the gentleman on the floor.

And *now* was not the time she wanted to remember him.

At last she and Freddie were talking. This gentleman's presence destroyed a moment of possible understanding, stealing Freddie's attention away from her and their love.

"Who are you — ?" Freddie started and then stopped, his eyes widening in recognition. *"Barón de Vasconia?"*

Freddie *knew* this gentleman?

And Abby realized she recognized the name, too.

The barón de Vasconia was infamous. They gossiped about him in all the papers, often referring to him as the "barón V" or "Apollo" because, like the sun god, he was inordinately handsome. The wags said that the one difference was that instead of riding a chariot across the sky, the barón cut a swath through London society, leaving a trail of broken hearts and angry husbands in his wake.

Handsome. For the first time, Abby's would-be suicide's physical attributes made an impact on her. She'd been so concerned seeing him with the pistol in his hand that she'd not taken in how tall he was, how broad-shouldered, how strikingly *handsome* he was. And she knew from tackling him how hard and lean he was.

Of course, she loved Freddie. Worshipped him. He was the most attractive man in the world . . . but honesty made her admit that when compared to the barón, Freddie came out a poor second. The Spaniard's presence was so strong, so bold, that a woman would have to be blind, and dumb, and completely without arms and any sense of touch or scent to be unaware of him.

His olive skin and thick, dark hair were what Abby supposed would be called Castilian features. But his aristocratic bearing, straight, well-shaped nose, and lean jaw would have made him a model of masculine beauty in any culture. Top those features off with straight dark brows over the most incredible silver eyes imaginable and he was breathtaking. A silver-eyed Spaniard. Who would have thought it?

Freddie turned his back on Abby. He walked up to the barón, an eager fawning in his voice as he said, "It is a pleasure to meet you, Barón. Our paths have crossed, but we have yet to be introduced. Miss Montross, would you go through the formalities?"

"The formalities?" Abby repeated blankly. Was Freddie serious? Didn't he realize the man had overheard everything they'd said?

The barón had overheard her beg.

Without waiting for her assistance, Freddie launched into introductions himself. "Lord Frederick Sherwin," he said with a bow. "My father is the earl of Bossley. You may have heard of him? I'm his heir. We're quite wealthy. Well connected." He paused, as if expecting the barón to recognize him.

"How fortunate for you," the barón murmured. He shot a look at Abby and raised his eyebrow, letting her know he was unimpressed with her man.

If Freddie had caught a hint of the barón's opinion, it didn't disturb him. "Abby," Freddie continued, taking on a lecturing tone that always annoyed her, "Brummell claims that the barón is the most handsome figure in fashion. A true original. Do you see why? Don't you agree?"

"I hadn't thought on it," Abby answered.

Freddie never complimented her appearance. In fact, she'd rarely heard him sound so enthusiastic about anyone . . . other than himself.

It was clear that Freddie wasn't actually interested in her response, because he jumped right back into his thoughts. "What I have wanted to know — and so appreciate this opportunity to speak to you in private, Barón — is how you manage to tie your neck cloth in that manner that they are calling the Vasconia? Quite intricate it is. You can see I have tied mine in my own version, but it lacks something. My friends have all assured me that I am close to it but not exact." Freddie said this while attempting to peer as close as he dared to the barón's neck cloth without actually touching it. "What is the secret? Is the creation one of your valet's? Or did you conjure it up? I mean, that is, if you don't mind telling me," he hastened to add. "I understand how you wouldn't want everyone walking around looking like you. However, I would appreciate even a hint."

The barón appeared to mull over the request and then said, quite seriously, "You need thick starch."

"Yes, yes, understandable," Freddie agreed. "You need that hard feel."

"And the secret is that just as you tie the knot, you give it a little twist right, left, right."

"Right, left, right," Freddie repeated. "But which knot do you use? The Ajax? Or is that the Corinthian?" He inched his nose closer to the barón's neck.

"The Ajax," the barón said, moving away from Freddie's scrutiny toward Abby.

"And the twist?" Freddie said. "Is it a sharp turn or do you layer the folds? Soften it up a bit?"

"I layer." The barón started to direct Abby from the room, tucking her gloved hand in the crook of his arm.

"That can't be right," Freddie countered. "I have tried that. Perhaps my valet can discuss the matter with your valet? My man may not be putting enough starch in the cloths. Of course, I have him using so much right now they take days to dry."

"Yes, yes, have the valets talk," the barón said, opening the door.

"Where are you going?" Freddie asked.

"To dance with Miss Montross," the barón said.

Abby blinked in surprise. She'd been going along with him, quite astounded by Freddie's avid interest in the barón's grooming as well as his knowledge of laundry. She knew he was a dandy, but such an intense interest was, well, frivolous.

"But Miss Montross doesn't usually dance," Freddie said ingenuously.

"I dance." Abby shook her head. "Where did you conceive the idea I didn't?"

Freddie caught himself. "I didn't mean it that way, Miss Montross. I know you dance. I've danced with you."

"But *not* this evening," the barón pointed out.

"Well, no," Freddie said, sounding confused. "I haven't."

"Why not?" the barón pressed.

"Because," Freddie said. A spot of color appeared on each of his cheeks. He was flustered . . . and she knew he had not wanted to dance with her because he hadn't wanted to be seen with her. His reluctance was more than not wanting to upset Corinne. He'd not wanted to dance with her because not only was she not fashionable but she'd also been jilted. Through no fault of her own, she'd been branded socially inferior.

"I meant you don't enjoy dancing," Freddie said as an attempt at apology — one she would not take.

"Who says I don't?" Abby demanded. At the very least, she had thought of them as friends, and friends, especially from child-hood, stood by each other. Certainly she would have stood by him if their roles had been reversed.

"You don't make an issue of *not* dancing," Freddie said in his defense.

"Do you believe I *like* being ignored?" Abby felt her temper rising. "I know I'm not popular . . . but that doesn't mean I choose to be a wallflower."

"You never complain," Freddie countered, and Abby didn't know what to say.

Once again he disappointed her, and she had no excuse for him. It was hard some-times to remember how much she loved him.

The barón gently tugged on her arm, reminding her of his presence. "Miss Mon-tross is going to dance now," he informed Freddie. "She is a particular friend of mine, and I wish to escort her onto the dance floor."

"A *particular* friend?" Freddie repeated. "Abby? What is this?"

Before she could answer, the barón swept her out into the hallway. He shut the door firmly behind them and started walking her down the patterned carpet toward the ball-room.

Abby held back. "A *particular* friend? Do

you know what that means? What Freddie will imply?"

"Do I care?" he answered.

"*I* care," Abby said, coming to a complete stop. "You have a reputation. Everyone will think —" She broke off, suddenly not wanting to put her doubts into words.

"Think what?" he challenged mildly, as if she amused him.

She supposed she did. It was the height of hubris to assume the dashing barón de Vasconia, the Baron V, also known as "Apollo," saw her as a love interest.

"Things," she finished and then repeated the sentence as if she'd meant to say it. "They'll think *things*." Dear Lord, she could feel the heat rise up her neck.

"One can hope that they do," he replied.

"I'm not that sort of young woman," she whispered.

"Miss Montross." His accent, emphasizing the second syllable, gave her name a definite flair. "After your conversation in there with that buffoon, has it not dawned on you that perhaps you want people to be thinking 'things' about you? It makes them a bit uncertain, even a little afraid."

"There is a difference between being well-considered and having my name linked to that of a —" Another dangerous word.

30

She'd almost said *libertine.* Her father would not be pleased to see her on his arm.

"You have difficulty finishing sentences, do you not?" the barón pressed, the light of a thousand devils dancing in his remarkable eyes. "Or is it that you are unaccustomed to speaking your mind?" He shook his head in answer to his own question. "No, I sense you have many opinions. You swallow them whole, forcing them back down." He motioned to her belly with his free hand. "Letting them roil inside you." He said all of this with his graceful inflection. They said that since he'd come to London, many a fop, taken by his charisma, had started lisping in a poor imitation of his accent — and here he was, so very careful, and intelligent, with his English.

The door to the library opened. Freddie stepped out into the hallway.

For a long moment, he stood there, his gaze going from one to the other, a puzzled expression on his face. Abby's hand still rested on the barón's arm, and she realized they must appear very close to Freddie.

"I thought you were going to dance?" Was it Abby's imagination, or did Freddie sound almost jealous?

"We are . . . I think," the barón answered. "Miss Montross?" He began walking toward the ballroom, and Abby had no choice but to follow unless she wished to be rude.

Still, what if Freddie had at last realized what he was tossing aside? What if he was having second notions about offering for Corinne?

She looked over her shoulder to him —

"I need the name of your valet," Freddie called out to the barón. "How else will my man be in touch with yours?"

Disappointment tasted like bile in her mouth. She knew Freddie cared for her. *She knew it* . . . but could she be wrong?

"They won't be in touch," the barón said. He had come to a halt, his impatience clear. "I don't have one."

"Have one what?" Freddie asked.

"A valet. Come, Miss Montross."

This time, Abby went with him.

They walked in silence a moment before she confessed, "That was humbling." She blinked back tears. No crying. She mustn't cry here.

"What was?" the barón said, nodding at a passing acquaintance in the hall. The music had started for the next set. A crowd milled around the doorway ahead of them, people talking, coming and going. He slowed his step, as if he was not in a hurry.

Abby knew he understood she spoke of

Freddie. She didn't want to say more. She might shatter.

She changed the subject, once again pretending to carry on, clinging to her pride. "Funny that you don't have a valet and still can be the envy of every dandy in the city."

Several women around the doorway sent covert glances in the barón's direction. And then their gazes dropped on her hand resting on his arm. Lips formed into questions. Fans began fluttering up to hide what was murmured from one person to another.

Abby suspected they wondered why he was with her. Wait until Freddie announced his betrothal. Then they could really laugh at what a silly goose she was.

Her throat tightened. She forced herself to hold on. She'd not cry, not cry, not cry —

"I don't think so," the barón said.

She had lost track of their conversation. "Think about what?"

He looked down at her, sympathy in his eyes. He'd noticed how fragile she was.

"I don't think it is funny I don't have a valet," he said.

Abby grasped for context, and then remembered. She forced a smile. "Men of your station usually do. Especially those with a remarkable knot in their neck cloth."

"Don't forget, Brummell has pronounced me a fine figure of a man," he reminded her. "Why do I need a valet?"

His dry irony helped steady her. "That was such an inane thing for Freddie to say." She paused. "He always was a bit vain."

"Most of us men are," he said. "And there is no reason to apologize for having loved. He's the one who is a fool."

Shame welled inside her. "I cared so deeply." And her heart hurt. She wanted to escape, to find a quiet place to break down. Abby started to pull away, but he moved to take her by the hand, his fingers lacing with hers.

"You can't run yet," he told her, his voice low, intimate. "You promised a dance —"

"No, you *commandeered* a dance."

Amusement lit his eyes. "I did, so you have no choice." And he led her past the prying, curious eyes and into the ballroom, a room ablaze with candles and the glittering jewels of the *ton*.

The dance set was winding down on the dance floor. The dancers bowed to each other as the musicians drew out the final note. In minutes, others would take their place for the next set — and she had to admit she longed to be one of their number.

She wanted to say that she'd danced at least once this evening. That she'd been a part of it all.

And now she would be.

Some of the tightness building inside her eased ever so slightly. Freddie was going to marry another . . . and she'd have to go on. Just as she'd had to face marrying Mr. Lynsted. What was it her father had said when he'd informed her of the marriage? "Life has its disappointments."

"Disappointments about what?" the barón asked, and Abby realized she'd spoken aloud. "I don't think I'm that difficult to dance with."

"I'm sorry, it was something my father said to me when he'd arranged my marriage with the man who is now known in our house as 'that scoundrel Lynsted.' "

"And this is the man who jilted you?"

"You heard everything, didn't you?" There was no heat in her accusation.

He shrugged. "There is nothing wrong with my ears. And I agree you should not settle for disappointments."

"Do you?"

"I have," he admitted. "But I don't think you are one who likes being told what to do."

Abby laughed. "You are right. I'm too

35

much like my father for my own good. In
fact, everyone in our family has strong
opinions. Run now while you have the
chance."

Now it was his turn to laugh. She liked
the way his teeth flashed white and even in
his smile. He was the most attractive man
she'd ever laid eyes on.

And, perhaps, the kindest.

"So why don't you have a valet?" she
asked, truly curious as he started to lead
her to the dance floor.

Such was his notoriety that the crowd
seemed to part to let them pass.

"I could tell you," he said, "that it is
because I was staying with the duke of Holburn and using his servants, and now that I
have my own apartments I have not had
time to hire one."

"Or you could tell me the truth," she
prompted.

He laughed, the sound again startling in
its richness. Heads turned in their direction, as if those around them were caught
by the sound of it.

"Yes, I would tell you the truth, *palomita,*"
he said, leaning so close that he spoke in
her ear. "I'm broke. Done up. Poor. I tie my
own neck cloth, and I don't know what
Lord Frederick Sherwin is thinking. I have

no special method."

Abby's feet rooted to the floor. "Truly?"

He nodded solemnly, and she realized he'd just given her a gift — or a weapon. The gossip she could spread . . . but she wouldn't.

And in that moment, she felt a connection to him. A very human one.

She understood him. He was like herself, an outsider. She was viewed suspiciously by their current company because of her father's self-made fortune and working roots. They had to include her because, after all, she was family.

The barón was seen as foreign. He was exotic and feted, but separate and apart.

Oh, yes, she understood exactly how he felt.

"But you cut a 'fine figure of a man,' " she reminded him.

"Says Brummell," he agreed and they both laughed, in complete accord with each other. . . .

"Oh, Abigail," a high-pitched woman's voice said. "What have you found?"

Her aunt, the duchess of Banfield and this evening's hostess.

"Hello, Your Grace," Abby said. Even though the duchess was her aunt, Abby knew she expected every ritual of her station.

"The two of you had your heads close together," her aunt said. She was tall, like her daughter Corinne, although her hair was silver instead of blonde. "What's so secret?" she continued. "Your mother will want to know, Abigail, especially since you are whispering to the one man every woman here is watching. Oh, if only I was half a decade younger." She rapped the barón lightly with her folded fan.

Abby was tempted to ask her aunt what secrets she held. Certainly the duchess knew Freddie and Corinne were going to announce their betrothal, but she'd not said a word of warning. "We are going to join this next set," Abby said instead, nodding to the dance floor.

"Oh, please do. And come join us when you are done. Corinne and I have taken up station by the Greek urn." She nodded in the direction of a bronze urn the height of most men. A table and several chairs were set up there. Abby's mother sat there, along with many of the duke of Banfield's other brothers and sisters, but Corinne wasn't with them.

Instead, she and Freddie were having a confab not far from the urn. Corinne, tall, beautiful, blonde, said something angry to Freddie and stormed away, shoving aside several guests who were in her path.

Abby wondered what he'd told her.

"We shall, Your Grace," she heard the barón answer her aunt, speaking for both of them. He nudged Abby toward the dance floor.

The other dancers had already taken their places. Politeness dictated that she and the barón should stand this one out. The barón, however, was not polite. He took a spot on the dance floor, bringing her around to face him.

She feared they were going to dance by themselves until another couple stepped from the crowd to join them.

Abby didn't recognize the couple. There were so many here this evening she didn't know. She rarely traveled with this set — only when her uncle and aunt gave parties.

The music started. It was a country dance, thankfully one Abby knew. But at that moment, as she moved to take the first step, Freddie came to stand at the edge of the crowd no more than an arm's length from her.

His expression was serious, distraught.

He looked right at her — and Abby stumbled over her own feet.

She felt herself falling, but before she made a complete fool of herself, the barón's strong hands took hers and spun her in a circle, as if he'd been improvising a step.

The movement was dizzying, and for the second time in less than an hour, Abby found herself again in the barón's arms.

"Smile," he quietly ordered, and she found herself obeying immediately. The smile on her face felt false, but she'd not remove it, not with so many watching.

Not with Freddie watching.

Abby dared not look in his direction. Instead, she placed her focus on her dashing, bold partner, and an amazing thing began to happen: she started to enjoy herself.

The barón knew how to lead. She found herself moving through the dance with an easy grace she'd not known before. He didn't do anything awkward, just a touch here, a bit of pressure there, and the two of them were moving as if they had danced together before.

The music was lively and long. Apparently, the young people had been waiting for such a robust dance and were making the most of it, their enthusiasm encouraging the musicians.

How long had it been since she'd danced?

Probably before she'd been betrothed to Mr. Lynsted. He'd not been one to take to the dance floor.

The dancing grew more competitive. Couples danced down a line while others clapped, cheered, and stamped their feet. It seemed as if everyone in the ballroom was involved now. Everyone was as caught up as Abby. She didn't even have the opportunity to hesitate when the barón took her hand and danced her down the center of the floor.

She was not graceful. The music was moving too fast for her to think, and she took a misstep here and there, but she didn't run for cover. Instead, she laughed her clumsiness away, and no one seemed to notice — save the barón.

He used her lack of grace as an opportunity to rest his hand on her waist, to give her an extra twirl and bring his arms around her. He was masterful, gallant, incredibly thoughtful.

All too soon, the music came to an end.

The applause for the musicians and dancers was deafening.

Freddie was nowhere in sight.

However, her parents watched. Her father had joined her mother by the urn. Her mother appeared a bit teary-eyed, but her father's gaze was calculating.

Abby felt her confidence waver. Once again aware of her shortcomings, she hung back, not ready to be delivered to them yet.

"What is it?" the barón asked, seemingly attuned to her every thought.

"Why did you do this?" she asked. "Why did you insist I dance?"

Annoyance crossed his face. "We are guests at a ball. I wanted to dance."

"You could have your pick of any woman. It's the library, isn't it? The dancing has to do with what I saw in the library. You are worried I know something you'd rather keep quiet."

"You saw nothing," he answered. "And are you always this distrustful? Because if you are, no wonder life has disappointments. Or did your father train you to think this way? To look with suspicion on everyone?"

His comment found its mark. He was right. Her father would warn her to be careful. And yet once she started to question, she could not stop.

"You felt sorry for me," she accused. It was the worst thing anyone could do to her.

"*Sí*, I did," he said without hesitation. "I do find it amazing that you interfered, *palomita*. Most would have opened the door, seen me standing there, gun to my head,

42

and shut it to pretend they had not noticed me at all. Or was it that my path was meant to cross yours? I think so. I think there is a strong bond between us. Something we have in common."

"And what is that?" she demanded, surprised he felt the connection between them as well.

"Loneliness," he answered, the truth of the word exposing her.

He saw. He *knew.* His knowledge made her feel vulnerable, naked. Flawed.

And it equally stripped him bare as well. She met his gaze, stunned by his honesty. He was like no other gentleman in this room —

"I have been looking for you everywhere," a woman's strident voice interrupted them, even as a gloved hand, rings on almost every finger, grabbed the barón's arm and jerked him around, which was no small feat. The barón was tall, muscular. His attacker was petite and one of the most lovely women Abby had ever seen.

She was also Carla, Lady Dobbins — a renowned poet, socially important hostess, and London's reigning beauty.

Rubies hung from her ladyship's ears and around her throat. Small stars fashioned out of diamonds pinned her dark tresses into artfully arranged curls, a style she'd set and was all the rage.

Her dress was made of a muslin so fine one could see straight through it to an undersheath, which had been dampened to hug her every curve. And she didn't seem the least embarrassed that her nipples were boldly protruding against the thin material for everyone to ogle. Then again, her neckline was so low that the whole bounty of her chest appeared ready to overflow at any moment.

Abby caught herself tugging at her own modest decollete in discomfort.

"I have been here, my lady," the barón said without enthusiasm. As he spoke, he took Abby's arm as if to walk away.

Her ladyship blocked their path. "You *knew* I wanted to dance with you," she stated, her voice low but attracting attention all the same, judging from how quickly conversation stopped around them. People made no pretense about wanting to overhear what was being said.

That's when Abby remembered what else she'd read in the papers about "Baron V." This was obviously the one they referred to as "the lovely Lady D," the woman claimed to be his lover.

CHAPTER THREE

Abby took a step away from the barón. Now might be a good time to return to her parents, with or without his escort. There was a wildness in her ladyship's eyes and a tension in her body Abby didn't trust.

But her movement caught Lady Dobbins's attention. Vivid blue eyes, the ones countless men had celebrated in poetry to her beauty, honed in on Abby with the intensity of a hawk seeking prey.

"*This* is what you think to replace me with?" Lady Dobbins murmured. Her lip curled.

"Not here, my lady," the barón warned, steel in his low voice. "We have an audience. Let me escort Miss Montross back to her family, and then we will talk."

But Lady Dobbins either didn't hear him or didn't care. "Montross?" she repeated. "The banker's daughter? The one who was jilted? Oh, I see now why she was tossed aside. Good heavens, Andres, have you no eyes? I thought you Spaniards were lovers of beauty. Or have you lost your good taste?"

Abby wasn't the only one stunned by the woman's meanness. A collective gasp went up all around them, sending a burst of heat to Abby's face — which only made her look more pathetic. The crowd's sympathy aside, she could feel their eyes dissecting her every feature. Even the musicians had not lifted their instruments to play the next set.

The barón pulled Abby behind him. "Do you think you are the only beautiful woman here, my lady? You are wrong. Miss Montross has a beauty you could never hope to attain."

"Beauty?" Her ladyship snorted her opinion. "You find beauty in ruddy cheeks and a button nose?"

The barón answered. "Also her youth —"

"She is not *that* young," the countess lashed out.

"She's much younger than yourself, but I'm talking about her spirit. It is young. She's a believer, Carla, something both you and I gave up long ago."

"Because we are realists," Lady Dobbins said in her own defense. "Sophisticated."

"And value nothing," he agreed.

"I valued you."

"And see where you are now?"

His mark hit home.

Her ladyship drew back. She glanced at those around them as if just realizing she was creating a scene. A wiser woman would have retreated.

Lady Dobbins wasn't wise. "All a woman has, all that is important about her, all that matters are her looks. You've made that very clear, Barón, with so many of us. Now it appears you have developed a taste for, well, something other than the sublime. For example, her hair reminds one of a curly, overripe carrot."

"Her hair reflects her joy in life."

"Natural or not, eh?" her ladyship said. "And, yes, I am older, but she is wrinkled. She's almost as withered as a prune."

"Those aren't wrinkles," he said with a sigh as if bored with the discussion. "They are the lines left from laughter. And who wants a blank canvas? A man needs to know his woman can think and feel. A rose opens as it ages, becoming more fragrant, more full in blossom, more lovely with time. I see in Miss Montross's face her strength of character. She meets life on her terms and doesn't need to humiliate another to make herself important."

Several heads around them nodded agreement. Most of those nodding were men.

Lady Dobbins's chin shot up. "Character?" she quizzed. "What would you, of all men, know about character? You are a pretty boy, Barón. A charm. You haven't done one meaningful thing in your life, and now you are holding up this silly, gap-toothed, flat-chested chit as a paragon for all of us to admire. Look to yourself, my lord, before you chastise me."

Abby did have a small gap between her two front teeth. It was a family trait. Her mother and her cousin Corinne had gaps as well.

She wished the floor would open up and swallow her whole. She didn't care what people thought of her chest, but that small separation between her two front teeth made her terribly self-conscious.

"Her smile is charming," the barón said. "As for endowments, not all men like over-ripe melons, my lady. Especially amply displayed ones."

"You did."

Her words sucked the air out of the room for Abby. She'd tried not to think of the two of them together. She wanted to like the barón, and she didn't like the countess . . . but he had.

Without breaking stride, he coolly an-

48

swered, "My tastes have changed."

He was defending her, but his words struck Abby as cruel. As male.

And everyone listening would infer that now *she* was his next conquest. It would be *her* name linked to his in the papers on the morrow. She could see it now. She would be referred to as "mysterious Miss Gap Tooth" — and she was ruined. She wasn't a married woman whose husband obviously looked the other way. She already had enough rumors swirling around her.

Worse, Freddie's father, the earl, could be smug in the knowledge that he'd saved his son from such infamy. Corinne would never find herself caught in such a scene as this. Corinne was perfect, sensible, dutiful.

Nor was Abby the only one hit by his words.

Lady Dobbins jerked, as if jolted with a shot of electricity. Had she truly thought she could stomp her satin-clad feet and a man like the barón would be contrite? Abby hadn't known him long, but he didn't strike her as a lapdog.

Her ladyship's venom came out in physical violence. She slapped the barón, the action short, to the point, insulting. Then, ignoring the gasps of shock around her, Lady Dobbins sailed away, head high, the crowd shuffling back to let her pass.

There was a beat of assessing silence during which Abby assumed that most people were like herself — shocked beyond belief. And then came the low, agitated hum of conversation as word of the scene was passed from one pair of lips to another.

The barón turned to her, his silver eyes somber, as if he knew the cost of this scene to Abby. But she wasn't in the mood for apologies. Her reputation — indeed, her life — was now completely in a shambles with no hope for recovery. Freddie would never marry her and her father would be hard-pressed to find *any* husband for her.

"I am sorry," the barón said, and Abby lost all sense.

Her hand flew through the air, powered by her frustration, her shame, and her fear.

Her slap was not as neat, concise, and ladylike as Lady Dobbins's. It carried the full force of her turbulent emotions. Not only that, but she was a rather strong woman. The sound reverberated through the ballroom.

For a heartbeat, the world stopped.

Shocked by what she'd just done, Abby couldn't breathe, couldn't think.

Her angry finger marks reddened on his skin. He raised a hand to his jaw, frowning, angry, confused. He'd want answers — and she didn't want to give them. Not here.

She took the only action open to her; she ran.

The crowd didn't part for her. She had to shove her way through, heading for her father, the only refuge she had in the room. He met her halfway. He must have seen all, but once he put his arm around her and started escorting her toward the door, Abby didn't care. Having him by her side gave her the bit more courage she needed to leave the ballroom.

Her mother was already standing by the door. "I've asked for our cloaks," she informed them. She took Abby's hand, and together her parents led her to the front door. Her father gave a vail to the footman, who left speedily to hail their coachman.

Abby's father was a gruff man with shaggy red eyebrows under a thatch of curly, graying black hair. He claimed he was Scot although Abby and her brothers secretly thought his ancestry was from Ireland. It was difficult to tell, since he took great pains to speak the King's proper English and expected as much from his children.

Banker Montross woke early in the morning, worked a full day, came home to a light supper and a reasonable bedtime. This ball was not his usual routine, and Abby had been both surprised and delighted he'd agreed to attend. In the past, he'd left escorting duties to her mother or one of her brothers if in town.

Her mother was an inch shorter than herself. The former Lady Catherine had been the most petite of the old duke of Banfield's daughters, and the prettiest — another reason the gossips and her suitors had been so quick to savage her reputation when she'd defied her father and married a mere banker. Her thick, honey gold hair was turning silver, and her figure was still trim in spite of her having borne four children.

Abby didn't draw a full breath until they were safely tucked in their coach and on their way home.

Her father broke the silence. "Damn them all to hell."

"Heath," her mother protested.

"I'm sorry, Cate, but this shouldn't have happened, and it has made a sorry mess for our Abby. By the way, what *did* happen?" he demanded of his daughter. "I saw you dancing, looking for all the world like a happy poppet, and then the next thing I know, you slapped a man." He didn't wait for Abby's explanation before announcing, "Once I have the two of you home, I'm returning to that ball. I'll call that blackguard out. I'll make him pay for his arrogance. Foreigners! They are overrunning London. Makes a good Englishman sick to his belly."

"No, please don't call him out," Abby said.

Her mother echoed the sentiment. "You are too old for such nonsense, Heath."

"And if anything happened to you, I will never forgive myself," Abby claimed. "Please, Father, I want to forget this whole evening. It was a terrible night. I should never have gone out."

"You can't forget what has happened," her father said, punctuating the air with his gloved finger. "I've endured slights from the aristocrats all my life, even as they ask me to manage their money and turn a profit for them. But I'll be damned if some foreign nobby is going to insult my daughter. Now, what did he say to offend you so?"

"He said I was beautiful," Abby answered. "In front of everyone."

"See, Cate? I should boil him in oil —" Her father's voice broke off as he digested what Abby had said. "He said what?"

"That I was more lovely than Lady Dobbins and that he likes the gap between my front teeth." It hurt to even think about the scene. She didn't know how she was going to appear in public again.

"And you slapped him for it?" her father asked, his confusion showing in a hint of brogue coming through his words.

"He didn't say it because it is true." Abby tried to explain the words tumbling out of her as she finally released her bottled tension. "He said it to put down Lady Dobbins, who was furious we were dancing because I think she'd wanted to dance with him but then she was rude and he was rude right back to her but it was *me* they were discussing and everyone was staring at *me* and thinking which one of them was right *about me* and Freddie was there and probably heard everything but it doesn't matter because he is going to marry Corinne —" She abruptly changed the direction of her thoughts. "Did you know this? Before we went to the ball this evening, did you know that Freddie was going to offer for Corinne?"

Her father stared at her, his brows raised, as if he'd been overcome by her rush of emotion.

But her mother understood. She'd followed every word and demonstrated her knowledge by gathering Abby into her arms. "You poor dear. You poor, poor dear. Don't worry. Please, don't worry."

"Worry about what?" her father repeated

as if nothing made sense. "There was dancing, some people talking about Abby, and then nonsense about Sherwin and Corinne?"

"Lord Sherwin is going to offer for Corinne," her mother explained patiently.

"Did you know the purpose of this evening before we left the house this evening?" Abby demanded of her mother.

"No, I didn't," her mother said. "And if *I* didn't, you know your father wasn't aware. My brother took me aside to tell me about a half an hour ago, and that was the first I'd heard of the match. I tried to warn you, but when I went searching for you, you were nowhere to be found."

"That is right," her father verified. "Your mother thought we should make our excuses and leave, didn't tell me why, but what do I care? I can't stand feeling like a dressed duck. I was ready to leave the moment we took a step under Banfield's roof. And I have news for him. He's welcome to Sherwin and that father of his. The both of them are high-and-mighty stinkers."

"Heath, your language," her mother chided.

"Cate, *stinker* is a good word. When something is a stinker, I say it is a stinker. Bossley thinks too much of himself, and you can't expect me to hold my tongue when my daughter is involved — although I'm very happy our Abby is free at last of Sherwin."

Abby's stomach tightened at the memory of her interview with Freddie. "It's *his* father who wants the marriage with Corinne. Freddie is being pressured."

"Posh and nonsense," her father replied. "If he loved you, he wouldn't think of marrying another. He'd come for you the way I did your mother."

Her parents had been a love match. One look, and Lady Catherine had been smitten by her young banker — or at least that is what she claimed. What Abby knew was that her mother had loved her father enough to defy her family and be ostracized from society. They had eloped, creating a huge scandal in the day.

Abby's grandfather, the current duke of Banfield's father, had been furious and disowned his daughter. He'd never spoken to her again.

However, the banker had turned into a golden goose. Abby's father knew how to earn money. Upon inheriting the dukedom, Abby's uncle had welcomed him into the family, and the Banfield estates had prospered from it.

Of course, that still didn't mean that Abby's family was accepted with open arms by society. There were those with long memories.

"This is my brother's fault," her mother said quietly. "He wouldn't think of pulling anything like this with my sisters' and brothers' children."

"Like what? Arranging a marriage to Sherwin?" her father barked. "I thank him for it. And you will, too, someday, miss," he said to Abby. "Yes, the earl of Bossley has money, but there isn't any amount of gold that could pay me to listen to that windbag over a family dinner. And his son will be just like him as he ages. Mark my words."

"Freddie is not like his father," Abby insisted.

"No, he's *more* wishy-washy," her father predicted.

Her mother made an impatient sound, indicating she would like him to be less direct. She turned her back on her husband and took Abby's hand, her face a study in empathy. "Abigail, I'm sorry. I know how attached you were to Freddie. But, my dear, he didn't speak up for you when we arranged your betrothal to Mr. Lynsted. That is your father's concern —"

"Freddie didn't have a chance," Abby

said. "He knows Father doesn't like him."

Her father sat back in his seat, muttering under his breath, and in that moment, Abby could almost hate her parent. He didn't remember what it was like to be in love. He couldn't and be so hard on her now.

But Abby did love her father. She loved both her parents. She changed the subject to another very real concern. "You aren't going to call the barón out, are you?" she asked her father.

"And say what?" her father answered. "You called my daughter beautiful, so *en garde?*" He shook his head. "I don't understand you, Abby. I don't know why you don't have more pride. Why you fawn over that weak, pandering fool —"

"Heath," her mother warned.

"It's true, Cate. She put off marrying Lynsted because she was waiting for Sherwin — don't try to deny it, Abigail," he said, seeing her about to protest her innocence. "Your mother and I both knew what you were up to."

He was right, and the time for pretending her parents didn't know was over. She'd made a ruin of herself this evening and all because she'd lacked the grace, the maturity to be honest with them and herself. If she'd never gone looking for Freddie, her path wouldn't have crossed the barón's. "You'll have a hard time marrying me off now," she admitted.

Her mother gave her hand a squeeze. "Please don't say that, Abby. All is not lost."

"Yes, it is. I seem to not know what is good for me," Abby said. "And now I've created a dreadful scene, and who knows what will happen on the morrow?" She didn't want to cry. She wouldn't.

"You aren't the one who created a scene," her mother said. "It was that wild Lady Dobbins. I hear the woman has been shameless in her pursuit of the Spanish baron. They say she dressed up like a valet and went parading in the streets in front of his lodgings," she told her husband. *In broad daylight.*"

"She'll blame me," Abby predicted, referring to her aunt. "Certainly the duchess will blame me."

"Lucinda won't," her mother assured her. "I will talk to her. I'll explain it all."

"When has that ever helped?" Abby couldn't stop the bitterness. "I can't believe Corinne and Freddie. Everyone in the family knew I cared for him."

Her mother bowed her head for a moment. When she raised it, her smile in the coach light was rueful. "I thought they did . . . but you know how my brother the duke is. He doesn't often consider feelings or wants other than his own."

"And his set looks down his nose at me," her father corrected.

Abby sat up, her problems forgotten. "You are better than all of them put together."

"Thank you, my girl," her father said. "But you don't have to worry about me, or yourself. There was a reason why I agreed to go this evening, and it has paid off handsomely. I doubt if your little scene will deter him."

"Him?" Abby's senses went on alert. She glanced at her mother, who shook her head, indicating she didn't know what her father was about.

Her father caught that look. His bushy brows came together in consternation. "All right, I'd best confess. I wasn't going to say anything until I talked to you first, Cate, but, with Abby all contrite, now is as good a time as any."

"As any for what?" her mother asked.

"To say that I've arranged another marriage for Abby."

Abby didn't believe she'd heard him correctly. Her mother was equally confused, because she said, "Excuse me?"

"I spoke with Lord Villier tonight. You

remember him, Cate. He is one of the Lords of the Treasury. Sharp man. Well respected and has the First Lord and the Exchequer's ear. He's been in need of a wife, and when I broached the subject to him this evening, he was delighted."

"Lord Villier?" Abby shook her head. "I do not know him."

"You will," her father said. "He'll be over to pay his respects on the morrow."

Abby looked to her mother. "Do you know this man?"

A deep frown line marred her mother's forehead. "I do. He's —" She paused. "He's nice."

That was not a sweeping endorsement. "What is wrong with him?" Abby demanded. "I mean, this is such sort notice. I didn't even know you were looking for a husband for me, Father." Her goodwill toward him moments ago was rapidly vanishing.

"Of course I was looking for a husband for you," her father answered. "Did you think I'd let you turn into an old maid? I want what is best for you, Abby, and let me tell you, Lord Villier will be an even better husband than Richard Lynsted."

"That isn't the best comparison, Father," Abby snapped, shocked that he would marry her off again.

Her mother placed a hand on Abby's arm. "Let us wait and see," she advised. "Meet him first before passing judgment."

"What's wrong with him?" Abby demanded, turning to her mother. "You know him. You have reservations. I can see it in your face. Is he ancient?"

"No," her mother hurried to insist. "He's older, but not unreasonably so."

"Then what is wrong with him?" Abby repeated.

"Nothing. *Not one thing,*" her father answered.

"Well," her mother hedged.

"Yes?" Abby prodded.

"He has children," her mother answered.

"There is nothing wrong with having children," her father insisted.

Abby shook her head. "There is something wrong when a man with a title has to have a marriage arranged with me."

"You underestimate yourself," her father said. "You have your grandmother's money and the dowry I will be settling on you."

"Ah, so he needs money," Abby surmised.

"Half the lords in London do," her father answered.

"And what of his children?" she asked again, looking pointedly at her mother, who was having trouble meeting her eye.

There was a moment of silence, then her father broke it. "All right. He has thirteen children. And, in the interest of telling all, he's had two wives, who each died in childbirth. However, that fact is *not* his fault."

"Two wives?" Abby repeated, stunned.

"You'll become Lady Villier," her father announced, as if it had been her dearest wish. "No one will look down their noses at you ever again."

"Thirteen children?" Abby was having a hard time wrapping her mind around such a number. She'd been around children before, but usually one or two at a time. "Why don't you just sell me into slavery?"

"Abby —," her mother started, but her father cut in.

"He's a good man. He'll treat you well. There are many advantages to this arrangement."

"Including for you, Father. Didn't you say he was involved with the Treasury?"

"Abigail, that is unfair." Her father withdrew to his corner of the coach. "I think of you. I want to see you safe and well-established. No more of this being prey to scenes like we had this evening."

The coach rolled to a stop as he spoke. They'd arrived home.

Home was a palatial white marble town house. The black lacquered doors opened and servants dressed in blue-and-gold livery rushed out to open the coach door and attend the family.

Abby took this one last moment of privacy to say, "What I don't understand is that the two of you were a love match. Why would you not want the same for me?"

Her father caught the door handle, holding it so the footman could not open it. "If you met a man who loved you and who had one ounce of my drive and my ambition, I'd bless the union. But Sherwin isn't the man and you've been so daffy for him, Abigail, for so long, I believe it is too late for you to find another."

He said this not unkindly but with the practicality of his nature.

And he was right. At five and twenty, she was already on the shelf in the minds of most people. She was spent, used, no longer fresh and young. Already many assumed she'd not marry. It wouldn't be long before they'd be referring to her as a spinster, even to her face. Her brothers would marry and their children would call her a maiden aunt.

Still, it was not in Abby's nature to give up. "Let me have one more chance," she whispered.

"I've done the best I could for you," her father insisted, and she knew he had. "But the truth is, Abby my girl, looking back now with the benefit of age and experience, your mother and I realize we took a tremendous risk. It could have all gone so wrong if either of us had been of a more shallow nature."

"We were very lucky," her mother agreed.

"But we want more than luck for you," her father continued. "I must know your husband will take care of you and treat you with the respect you deserve. You are more precious to me than my own life, and what was good for me is not good enough for my only daughter."

"Meet Lord Villier," her mother said. "Perhaps you'll like him."

"Yes, perhaps," Abby echoed.

Her father opened the door, considering the matter closed.

They went inside. Abby could feel her mother hovering, worrying.

Her father had no doubts. Abby knew that in his banker's mind, he considered the matter a bargain well made.

It was a relief to Abby to finally be alone in her room. After undressing and dismissing her maid, she tried to sleep and failed.

Finally, she climbed out of her bed and walked across the thick carpeting toward the window. How many nights had she sat on the cushioned window seat, looking out in the garden and dreaming of Freddie coming for her like Romeo had come for Juliet?

Those had been the days of passionate notes smuggled to each other through books at the lending library. Many a time her maid had gone out shopping and returned with a nosegay that Freddie had bought and asked to be delivered to her. No name but a gleam in her maid's eye had told Abby she'd seen him.

Everything had always been clandestine because of his father's disapproval, and it had added an element of romance.

Or had it clouded her judgment?

Tonight, after Freddie had rejected her passionate plea, Abby had to face the truth — her father was right. Freddie was weak.

Acceptance didn't make her feel better.

The October sky outside her window was clear save for a thousand stars. Pressing her nose against the glass, Abby marveled at how vast the universe was. What were her small troubles in comparison?

One star burned brighter than the others. Venus. Abby's brother Robert — the one who had died fighting with Nelson — had considered himself an astronomer and had taught her to search for it. It wasn't a star but a planet named after the goddess of love.

Star or planet, what better orb to choose for making a wish? Perhaps Robert in his heavenly life would hear her wish and grant an intercession.

"I want to be loved," she whispered. Was it such a difficult request? "I want someone who loves me *for me*." Not for money, or connections, or any of the exchanges that made arranged marriages so important.

The answer was silence . . . and the knowledge that right now, back in the duke of Banfield's ballroom, Freddie was probably happily toasting his betrothal to Corinne with iced champagne.

Abby leaned her head against the cold windowpane. *Thirteen children . . .*

She was not anxious for the morning to come.

The duke of Banfield's ball was turning into the longest night of Andres's memory.

After Miss Montross's slap and departure, he could have happily left. He hadn't deserved her anger; he'd been protecting her. However, to leave would have called attention to the incident, and he was absolutely certain that if he stayed, Carla would do something so outrageous that the gossips would forget Miss Montross had even been in attendance at the ball. If history repeated itself, everything he'd done this evening would end up in the papers, especially with Lady Dobbins involved.

He wasn't wrong.

Not thirty minutes passed before his friend the duke of Holburn sought him out in the card room.

"She's going too far this time," the duke said, coming up to stand beside Andres, who'd been watching the play at a table of his gambling friends.

The marquis of Salisbury, who was sitting at the table, overheard him. "I say, Your Grace, who has gone too far?"

"Lady Dobbins," Holburn answered.

The men at the table lowered their heads to snicker. They didn't look at Andres, but he knew they thought of her as his problem.

"What is she doing?" the marquis asked. "I've a gold crown that says she has locked herself in the Necessary Room set aside for the ladies and refuses to come out."

"That could still happen," Holburn said. "But right now she is throwing the glassware on the floor in the dining room and screaming she's not understood. Along with calling the barón every foul name known to most sailors in His Majesty's navy."

Andres closed his eyes as if blocking the

image his words conjured in his mind. "She did the same three days ago at Mrs. Drummond's musicale," he said. "And I wasn't even there."

"Well, of course," the marquis said, laying his last suit of cards down and winning the hand. "She's a woman. She shouldn't make sense."

"She shouldn't break things either," Andres countered. "She flies into fits if I'm there or not there. It is madness. And half of London believes I am a scoundrel."

"Or are trying to take your place," an old gent at the table chimed in. "It's the price of a too pretty face."

"Whose? Lady Dobbins or our friend the barón?" the marquis drawled, and the others laughed.

Andres wanted to cringe. They all thought he was Carla's cicisbeo. No one took him seriously. He had no money, no land, nothing . . . except for looks. The only reason they tolerated him was his friendship with Holburn.

"She said she won't stop until you come to her," Holburn said. "Banfield sent me. He wants to announce his daughter's betrothal, but everyone is preoccupied with calming Carla down."

"Who is she marrying?" the marquis asked.

"Bossley's son," Holburn said.

"Ah, that's one for me," the young captain of the guard sitting across the table from the marquis said in triumph. "I have a wager on the book at White's that she'd go with Sherwin. Lady Corinne and Sherwin. Thought they'd be a match. They've been paying particular attention to each other." The "book" he referred to was the Betting Book and a sacred document for placing wagers.

"Well, are you going to go calm Lady D?" the marquis asked Andres.

"Why? Do you have a wager on that as well?" Andres wondered.

"I might," the marquis said with a cynical smile.

At that moment, the duke of Banfield came charging into the room. "Barón, you must do something. She's like a wild woman."

"There is nothing I can do," Andres insisted. He would be expected to take Carla someplace more private, listen to her carry on about how he'd broken her heart and receive a list of demands of what he must do to make amends. He hadn't acted on the last list she'd given him, and he wouldn't act on this one either.

"Please, you must quiet her down," Banfield pleaded. "You *must.* She's sitting in the middle of the supper room hysterically crying."

A crying she'd stop once Andres came to her side.

He could almost hate the woman. She was manipulating enough to enjoy these scenes. Still, her behavior wasn't Banfield's fault. And she did serve a purpose. By now, everyone seemed to have forgotten Miss Montross.

"I shall come," Andres said. "But I don't know what I can do to help."

"Thank you, Barón. Thank you, thank you," Banfield said. "I must tell the wife. You'll go right now? This minute?"

"I am walking toward the door," Andres said, making good on his word. Holburn shot him a sympathetic glance.

"I don't know why Dobbins doesn't have more control on his wife," Banfield muttered.

"He's too old to care," the marquis called out.

"Nonsense," the older gent at the table said. "No man is too old to care. And you each owe me a fiver. I said Lady Dobbins would have her Latin cavalier, and so she has."

His words rankled. Andres started to stop, but Holburn had fallen into step behind him. "Don't pay attention to them. They are jealous. They know their wives would chase you, too."

"But it isn't because of my face," Andres replied under his breath to his friend. "It's because the men sit on their derrieres in card rooms instead of being with their wives." Still, he hated appeasing Carla. "It's blackmail," he told Holburn. "She blackmails me with her tantrums and her scenes. She goes too far."

"She does," Holburn agreed. "Do you need help?"

"No, the farther you are from this, the better. I disgust myself when I have to toady to her."

"Do you want the duchess and I to wait for you?" Holburn asked.

Andres shook his head. There was no telling how long Carla could take. Banfield had already chased off on another one of his duties as host.

"Very well, then. Good luck," Holburn replied and went in search of his duchess.

Walking across the ballroom toward the supper room, Andres could feel people stare. As he passed a group of women, one almost fell in front of him. He caught her in his arms. She was a young matron, comely and bosomy.

"I am so sorry," she said. "I must have tripped on the hem of my skirt."

But as he released his hold, she pressed a note in his palm, her eyes dancing with her intentions. Her female companions burst into conspiratorial giggles.

Andres stifled a sigh and kept moving.

But he wasn't moving alone.

Two men had started to shadow him. They were big men in new evening clothes. One of them had a nose that had been broken so many times it was almost flat.

They didn't fit with this crowd, but no one seemed to notice. Not after all the punch and champagne that had been served.

Andres had to cross the front hall to reach the supper room. He quickened his step, testing the "gentlemen."

They kept right up with him. Two huge bruisers.

Well, if they wanted a fight, Andres would send them to Carla.

As he anticipated, they made their move out in the hall. "Barón de Vasconia?"

"I am," Andres said. Two footmen were

stationed here. He wasn't in danger —

There was the click of a pistol being cocked.

Andres glanced down and noticed that the smaller of the men had his hand in his jacket, a place that could easily hide a gun.

"Will you come with us, Barón?" the large bruiser said.

"Do I have a choice?" Andres asked.

"No."

"Where are we going?"

"To the front drive," the bruiser said. "Lord Dobbins is waiting in one of the coaches to talk to you, my lord."

"And if I choose not to go?" Andres asked.

"His lordship has given us permission to blow a hole in you."

"Won't that create a scene?" Andres asked, intrigued.

"His lordship says considering the way his wife has been acting, he don't think anyone will be surprised by a little blood. Especially if it is yours."

From down the supper room came a loud crash followed by the sound of hysterical crying and the twittering and laughter of gossips.

Andres took his hat from the footman holding it and said, "Please, lead the way."

CHAPTER FOUR

Andres knew Carla had married a man much older than herself. He'd pictured her husband as a small, wizened figure without the will or ability to put a check on his wife's escapades.

The reality he discovered inside the heavy, ornate town coach was far different.

Lord Dobbins was of middle years. He had a paunch on him but appeared of robust health. His steel gray hair was clipped close to his head, and his eyes were clear and sharp. He wasn't tall, and the fur collar he wore around the collar of his coat reminded Andres of a lion's mane.

"Come in," he invited Andres, his tone civil. Cordial. And putting Andres on guard.

His lordship indicated the velvet tufted bench seat opposite his in the coach. "You will not mind if we take a ride."

Seeing as he had no choice, Andres smiled. "Of course not." He removed his hat and climbed in the coach.

Lord Dobbins nodded to his henchmen to close the door and they were off.

They rode in silence a moment. Andres sat, rubbing the brim of his hat with his thumb, waiting.

He didn't have to wait long.

"You've made quite a conquest of my wife."

Andres didn't respond. Response led to being called out. If he told the man his wife had been the aggressor, he'd be named a liar and called out. If he told the truth — that he'd slept with Carla once when he'd been too drunk and full of self-pity to realize what he'd been doing — he'd be called out. If he —

Enough. Andres was tired of it all. He'd hoped to make something of his life in England, and yet here he was, back in the same traps as before.

"Over the last four months, I've fought three duels with men whose wives chased me," he informed Lord Dobbins.

"I know."

"I didn't search their wives out and I didn't sleep with any of them. I'm not saying I am an angel, but I'm not a rutting pig either."

"I am also aware of that," Lord Dobbins agreed.

"You are?" Andres sat back against the seat.

"I am. I also know that you *did* sleep with my wife. Rogered her nicely. At least, that is what she's told me," Lord Dobbins said. "And the rest of the world."

In all the times Andres had confronted offended husbands, he'd never met one so calm. And he started to suspect that all wasn't what it seemed, that he might have found himself in something he'd rather not be involved with.

Lord Dobbins watched him with a look of benign amusement. "Do you understand?"

"I don't know if I wish to," Andres replied, and Lord Dobbins laughed.

"Well said. Too many people ask questions they shouldn't," his lordship replied. "However," he continued, his tone changing to one of mild concern, "you have created a problem for me. You see, I like my arrangement with my wife. We live separate lives, but she is *mine.* She's dallied with many men. However, she has some nonsense in her head that she might leave me . . . for you."

"I have not asked her to do any such thing."

"Of course you haven't. Carla is becoming a trial to you. She's becoming a trial to me as well. Her ability to be discreet appears to have been misplaced in matters involving you. These tantrums and hysterics are embarrassing. People are asking questions quite openly, and I am not comfortable with the situation."

"I have not encouraged your wife in these behaviors," Andres said, uncertain what the man wanted. He felt some comfort in knowing the bruisers sent to fetch him were not with them in the coach — or he didn't think they were. They could be with the driver for all he knew.

He wished he'd had his walking stick, the one that hid a sword. He might need it.

"Relax," Lord Dobbins said. "I didn't search you out to hurt you."

Andres doubted his words. "Then what do you want?"

"I want you to leave London."

"I would rather be called out," Andres said without hesitation.

"Unfortunately, that isn't going to happen, Barón," Lord Dobbins said. "I understand how you feel. Truly I do. And I'm not surprised. Before this meeting between us, I endeavored to learn everything I could about you. It was quite a task. You have an

78

elusive past."

"I've lived an adventurous life."

"Yes, and you've made the most with what you've had. For example," Lord Dobbins began, motioning with one dark gloved hand. He wore a huge golden ring on his index finger, right over the glove — just as Carla wore hers. The metal gleamed in the coach light. "You aren't truly a baron." He smiled as he said this.

"My father *was* the barón de Vasconia." Andres stuck with the truth.

"He was," Lord Dobbins agreed. "But your sister kindly pointed out to my man that you are the illegitimate son, the one who couldn't, or shouldn't, inherit."

"That was my sister's impression. She was jealous our father treated me well. I received the education of a nobleman's son," Andres said, a hardness forming in his chest.

"But you filled the role of a groom in his stables."

"Fathers give their sons many tasks."

"But it must have been hard watching your brother receive so much."

Andres had not been close to his half brother. Emilio had considered him inferior and had been more ruthless in his opinions than Delia. "Is that not the way of brothers?" He kept his tone light.

"He died, didn't he? How did it go?"

"He fought at Trafalgar, on the other side," Andres said, knowing he was being toyed with — and almost hating the man for it.

"Yes, that was it," Lord Dobbins said, as if suddenly remembering what he'd known all along. "Some would think him an enemy and perhaps consider you with suspicion if this was known. What is the saying, the chestnut never falls far from the tree?"

Andres shrugged. "I have enough trouble with English to have to remember your sayings."

"That is not true, Barón. Your English is very good. Or should I call you Ramigio? Most of Europe, Greece, and Turkey know you by that name. Barón is a title you saved for London. What? Did you think we were too removed from Spain for your subterfuge not to be discovered here?"

"I've always claimed the title. Otherwise how would you have traced me? And how is my sister? Or should I be clear and say half sister?"

"My man said the Contessa Delia Digassi has a gaggle of children and a husband who is a disappointment."

"There is a God," Andres answered. Delia had been so proud of her Italian nobleman, so anxious to leave the family compound.

"After your brother's death, your father elevated you. But you weren't enough. An illegitimate son never is. There is always a taint of something unsavory about him. A reminder that man is weak."

Andres forced himself to meet Dobbins's gaze. It was hard.

"But then, your father *was* weak. He died by his own hand."

"It is a cure for disappointment." Tight, he had to hold himself tight.

"He saw nothing worthy to live for after they took his properties."

"And his horses."

"Yes, the horses. You've tried to save them, haven't you? From what I've learned, you've done everything in your power to keep the horses, including many unsavory schemes."

"Some of my efforts have been perhaps a bit criminal, but not all of them," Andres said. "I won the silver mine in a game of cards."

"Ah, yes, that was in the Viceroyalty of Peru."

"Did you send a man there?" Andres knew he hadn't. There hadn't been enough time, and the mine was done. It had been tapped out before he'd arrived. He'd spent two years of his life searching for a rumored vein of ore and never found it. He'd given up, turned the mine over to the natives, and returned to Europe.

"Should I have?" Lord Dobbins asked.

Andres was tired of being baited. "It is true that I am the illegitimate son, but I've claimed the title. The blood flows in my veins. It is mine."

"But it came from the wrong side of the covers," Lord Dobbins argued. "That is something you must remember. You can't just label yourself or claim the title for yourself, knowing most of us would never question your right to it. It's a bold move, Barón, one I rather admire — but it is ultimately dishonest. All those people in Banfield's ballroom, even your friend Holburn, have standards. And *you* don't meet them."

"I wonder if your wife would say the same?"

That barb hit home.

The false smile vanished from Dobbins's face and Andres found his weakness. For all of the man's bravado, his wife *was* more than a possession. They both knew Carla's nature was such that if she wanted something, nothing would stand in her way, not even her powerful husband.

"Someday," Andres vowed, "I shall return

the name Ramigio to where it should be, title or not." He spoke with conviction. This was his goal in life. What *he* wanted. Dobbins was welcome to Carla.

His lordship's manner changed, the smugness replaced by a grudging respect. "I believe you, but you don't have two shillings to your name or any other. You're into the duns. You own a share of that horse Holburn is holding for you, but little else. It's a pity, really. I quite like you."

"So, it is my finances you wish to discuss?" Andres pressed, wanting to come to the heart of this interview.

"I actually wish to offer you an opportunity."

"To what? Disappear?"

"Exactly." The smile — angry, vindictive — returned to his lordship's face. "I want my wife back the way she was." He waved a dismissive hand, as if he could read Andres's mind. "Don't be excited. I'm not paying you off, not in the way your type expects."

"I wouldn't take a payment anyway," Andres returned.

"Ah, yes, your latent, misplaced pride. I wager five years ago I could have bought you off."

Five years ago, even as much as a year ago, Andres had been a different man. . . . Gillian's love, and her rejection, had changed him.

"I know your weakness, Ramigio," Dobbins said. "I know what you want. It's not my wife. In fact, you have been rather generous to her considering her behavior. And please understand, I am just attempting to prevent her from making more of a fool of herself than she already has. She has ignored the boundaries. There is a price to pay."

"So this is more about punishing her than dealing with me?" Andres asked.

"Oh, yes," his lordship assured him.

"I won't leave England." For the first time, Andres had friends. He could build something here.

"I suspected such. Also, I have money, but not enough to guard the whole of the British coastline to prevent your return. What I want to offer you is this." He picked up a leather portfolio from the seat beside him. He pulled out a piece of parchment covered with tight, cramped writing. A legal document. At the top was the word *Deed*.

"This is for a property I own," Lord Dobbins said, all business. "Its name is Stonemoor. It's in Northumberland. Do you know where that is?"

"North?"

"Exactly. As far north as a man can go

and still be in England. It's a house, stables, and two hundred acres of fields and forest. It's yours."

He held the deed out to Andres, who stared at the document in disbelief. *Stables. Land.*

Dobbins did know what he wanted. With two hundred acres, Andres could do anything.

He remembered how he'd felt when he'd won ownership of the mine. He'd been overwhelmed then, too. Land meant wealth. Permanence. Stability.

And no one just gave it away, either through gift or gambling.

"What is wrong with the property?" Andres asked.

Dobbins laughed. "You have every reason to be suspicious. Why trust me? Then again, you know I want you removed from my wife's life. This is a more pleasant way of going about it, considering *other* options."

"What is wrong with Stonemoor?" Andres repeated.

Lord Dobbins lowered his arm. "I haven't an idea what it even looks like. The property has been in my family for a generation or two. It means nothing to me other than an account on my ledgers. But it could mean everything to you. Especially since it would be *yours.* There is no entailment, no lien."

His.

Andres let himself believe. He couldn't stop himself from doing so. He was a dreamer. It was his nature to wish the impossible. Had it not served him well before?

He didn't care where Northumberland was. He'd already traveled to the ends of the earth in pursuit of his dream — and he did have the mare he shared with Holburn. Destinada was her name. The perfect name for the horse upon which he would build his reputation. And now here he was, being offered stables, land . . . a home.

Of course it was a trick. It had to be. Dobbins owed him no goodwill.

But did it matter? He was a man with nothing. Land could be molded into whatever he wished. If it was marshy, he'd drain it. Dry and arid? He'd build a canal to the sea if need be.

He reached for the document, but Lord Dobbins snatched it back. "One requirement."

Of course. "Yes?"

"You must depart London immediately."

"How soon?"

"Tomorrow?"

Andres laughed. "You are jesting."

"Very well then, three days and then you are gone. Out of London. And you will not return. If you do, if you step foot in this city again, and I most certainly can monitor that, then the deed reverts back to me. It's mine."

Never return to London again — in exchange for land, and stables? For a home?

"I will agree to that," Andres said.

"Good," Lord Dobbins answered. He slipped the deed back into the portfolio. "My man of business is Harold Deeter, Esquire. His offices are on Atherington Street. Meet me there tomorrow at half past eleven and we shall go over the formalities and sign papers." He laughed lightly. "I can see by your expression, Ramigio, you don't quite trust me. If I were a man like yourself, one who has worn many hats, I would feel the same. However, the offer is good. The property will be yours." He reached up and rapped on the roof of the coach, a signal to the driver to stop. "You don't mind if I drop you here, do you, Ramigio? I have another engagement."

Andres shrugged, still stunned by the turn of events. Two hundred acres. A house. *Stables.*

The coach rolled to a halt.

"Until tomorrow," Dobbins said.

"Yes, tomorrow." Andres searched his lordship's face in the coach light and did not read subterfuge. Either Dobbins was an unusually adept card player, or he meant exactly what he said.

Andres opened the door and climbed out. The coach rolled away. He watched it until it turned a corner and was out of sight.

Two hundred acres.

He then took stock of his surroundings. He was not in a bad section of town. There was a park across the street and the roads were wide and modern. He thought he might be in Mayfair. He couldn't see a street sign, but he knew that if he walked, he'd find one.

The night was cold and clouds were moving across the moon. He'd not worn a coat, and he now regretted it . . . except that he was going to own a piece of property — in Northumberland.

Stonemoor. He liked the sound of it. He began walking, not caring where he was going, his mind working feverishly enough for him to forget everything, even the cold, as he began accepting and planning for Stonemoor. He would be Andres Ramigio Peiró, lord of Stonemoor.

His mother, his father's lover, had always promised him that he was destined for great things. She'd whispered that a village crone with a gift for sight had told her so on the eve of his birth. She'd died when he was seven and that is when the barón had taken him into his house.

Andres had believed then that going to live with his father had been the fulfillment of the crone's prophecy. Yet the years had not proven it true.

But *this* must be what she'd meant. With Stonemoor and the mare Andres had at Holburn's country stables, he could rebuild a dynasty. The mare was already breeding. Holburn had covered her with his best stallion, a leggy Thoroughbred known for speed. If Andres had the money, he could purchase more mares and breed an even more spectacular stallion of his own. . . .

Money. Estates needed money, especially to build what he had in mind. He saw stables of the sort that his father had had. A cobbled stable yard. Grooms to see to the horses' every need.

He'd have to ask Dobbins if the house was furnished or if there were wagons and equipment. The list of what he needed expanded in the space of a few steps.

Andres stopped. Two gentlemen wrapped up in heavy greatcoats were approaching him from the opposite direction. They cast him curious glances as they walked past. He was just standing there, but little did they know that his mind was flying.

He needed money. He could borrow it, but then he'd be beholden to whoever lent it. Andres wanted Stonemoor for himself.

And then he remembered Miss Montross's conversation in the library.

She had money. Her own money. Money not connected with the dowry or any inheritance from her father.

Money that came to her upon marriage.

He knew she wasn't completely fond of him. In fact, she might be the only woman in the world who wasn't attracted to him.

But if he could win her over, he could have his every dream. He had to believe his path had crossed hers for a reason. Certainly, now, he understood that moment of connection in the library. Fate was trying to capture his attention.

Andres started walking. Abby Montross was not going to be one of his usual conquests. She was smarter, wiser . . . and truly in love with another man.

But he'd think of a way around her.

And he was looking forward to the challenge.

CHAPTER FIVE

Abby Montross was never, *ever* going to marry.

She made that vow silently over luncheon. Her father had invited Lord Villier to dine. It was supposed to have been a spontaneous idea brought on by the night before. However, Abby caught on quickly that this meal had been planned for at least a week.

First, there was Cook's menu. Luncheon was usually a light meal, some cold chicken, bread, perhaps a soup. This day, it was a Portuguese ham, a round of beef, *hot* chicken, seven different side dishes, and Cook's almond cake. Her father even ordered his finest wine to be uncorked, a wine he'd boasted he was saving for a special occasion.

Her father had also ordered up the full complement of servants — a footman behind every chair.

Abby wouldn't have minded all the fuss if

Lord Villier had turned out to be a different person from the one he was.

She didn't think she was picky. After all, if she couldn't marry the man she loved, what did it matter? At least that had been her attitude toward Mr. Lynsted. However, Mr. Lynsted had been a gentleman of refined tastes, quiet, dignified, and rather shy.

Lord Villier was as wide as he was tall and walked with vigorous arm movement, as if he pumped himself forward. He had a balding pate with tufts of graying brown hair over each ear and the most narrow-set, watery blue eyes Abby had ever seen. She hoped he hadn't passed on such an unfortunate trait to any of his thirteen offspring.

He also had a tendency to belch.

The first time he did it, he held a fist to his mouth and handled the matter rather politely . . . considering what it was.

But by the time Cook's cake was served, he was so mellowed by good food and good wine that he burped aloud.

Abby caught her mother's eye. She looked as offended, and worried, as Abby felt herself.

Her father seemed not to notice, signaling instead for the dessert wine to be poured.

Indeed, her father gave every impression of admiring Lord Villier.

Abby discovered why when the conversation turned to money. Lord Villier's interest, his life, revolved around investments. In his position at the Treasury, he received a great deal of information the common man would not know. A man such as her father could make good use of this knowledge.

That Lord Villier was interested in her was plain to see. The more he drank, the more he leered in her direction. By the time lunch was finished, he was talking to her bosom more than he was talking to her.

This her father did notice.

He hurried his lordship out the door.

Returning to the dining room, where Abby and her mother still stood, their heads together to share their grave reservations, he immediately burst out, "I know, I know. He's not ideal. However, he does have very good contacts. And he liked Abigail." He said the last in a rush of words as if in fear of their reaction.

"Heath, certainly we can do better," Abby's mother protested.

Her father looked pointedly at the servants, who were clearing the table while listening to every word. "That will be all for now," he told them.

The footmen dutifully left the room.

Once Abby was alone with her parents,

her father repeated, "He *likes* her. The man is powerful. Now that he has decided she would make a good Lady Villier, I don't know many who would challenge him for her."

"A good *third* Lady Villier," Abby pointed out. "I don't think I can do this, Father. I can't marry that man. If he belches in public, what does he do in private?"

Both her parents gave a shudder.

Her father wasn't ready to let it go, though. "Abigail, you would have a good life. I don't want you married to just any man. I want one who has a fortune and won't be reliant on yours. Do you want someone younger, more attractive —"

"Better personal habits," her mother interjected.

"Fewer children," Abby added in agreement.

"Stop that," her father said. "This is a serious subject."

"We are being serious," her mother answered.

"Catherine, we discussed this last night," her father said. "You agreed that if I could find a man willing to marry Abigail for her money, there was a risk he'd forget her as soon as he had it in hand." He looked to Abby. "Those sorts of men are philanderers, gamblers, scoundrels. I want much more for my only daughter. I want security for you."

"I want the same, Father. Can you not trust me to make my own choice?"

"No."

His answer stunned her.

"I've spent years watching you moon over Freddie Sherwin," he said. "And while you were thinking him so heroic and marvelous, I was thinking him a proper idiot. He can't make up his mind about anything. A real man sets his sights on a goal and goes after it with the intensity of a dog after a bone."

"Are you comparing me to a bone, Father?" Abby asked, knowing such a deliberate misunderstanding would annoy him, and it did.

"None of your games, Missy. I'm well aware that you've a shrewd mind . . . although why you dream of Sherwin is a mystery to me. I'm protecting you for your own sake — and your mother agrees."

Abby rounded on her, wanting the truth of it from her.

Her mother's lips parted, as if she'd been caught in surprise before she admitted, "I did agree. We want you well taken care of."

"And did you marry Father for security, Mother?"

"It was a different day and age," her mother hedged. "Everything now is so push, push, push. I know what the poets say, but the truth is, Abby, falling in love is a ticklish prospect. As we've said to you before, your father and I were most fortunate. And I do think Freddie loves you. But he's not courageous. Your father was, and perhaps *that* is the big difference between them. Love calls for courage."

"There must be someone else," Abby insisted. "I can't sleep in the same bed with Lord Villier. I *won't.*"

Both of her parents were rather reserved. Her words brought color to her mother's cheeks.

However, her father surprised her. He muttered something under his breath and then said with steely resolution, "You might not have to put up with him very often. He has enough children as it is. But if it comes to that, daughter, and it must, because a marriage has to be consummated to be valid, then I expect you to carry on smartly. Let him do his diddling while you think on other things. I can't imagine it will take a man like him more than a minute or two."

Now it was Abby's turn for her cheeks to burn.

Her father continued, pressing his case.

"Lynsted is a bastard for jilting you, but we can salvage this. Villier is considered a catch by many —"

"None of them under forty, I'd wager," Abby murmured.

Her frankness earned an amused light in her father's eye. "It's a wager I'd not take," he conceded. He looked to her mother. "This is what happens when I teach my daughter to speak her mind and value her intellect. And I'm not sorry for it, except for times like these, when I must act for your own best interests, Abigail."

Everything inside Abby wanted to rebel . . . but there was the small fear he might well be right.

Her father crossed over to her. "You may never understand this until you are much, much older, Abby, my girl, but I am acting in your best interests. I will accept Villier's offer if he makes one." He placed a kiss on her forehead and left the room.

A moment later, the front door shut. He was gone, back to his banks, to his investments, his other life.

Her mother broke the silence. "He really does want what is best for you."

"Thirteen children." That's all Abby had to say.

Her mother nodded, understanding.

From down the hall, someone rang the front bell. They had a caller, and Abby thought that both she and her mother were thankful for the intrusion. Abby had to believe things would be better. She wouldn't marry a man like Lord Villier. She *wouldn't.*

Harrison, their butler, rapped on the door her father had left half open when he'd left. "My lady," he said, speaking to Abby's mother, "you have a caller. It's Lady Barnes."

Both Abby and her mother smiled their delight. Lady Daphne Barnes, or Jonesy, as she expected family to call her based upon nothing more than her whim, was her mother's oldest sister. She'd been widowed for a decade and was dearly loved by both of them.

"She's waiting in the sitting room," Harrison informed them.

"Have the Madeira prepared," her mother said, knowing what Jonesy liked. "And tea," she added, following Abby, who was already on her way to throw herself on Jonesy's common sense and shrewd wit.

"Yes, my lady," Harrison said.

Jonesy had seated herself in the center of the settee before the fire and was busy unwrapping colorful Indian scarves from around her neck as she made herself comfortable.

The sitting room was one of Abby's favorite rooms in the house. It was designed for receiving visitors, with guests walking from the front hall through a paneled vestibule into the well-lit spaciousness that spoke louder than words of her father's wealth. Huge windows draped in gold brocade overlooked the back garden. Thick, patterned carpets in green, blue, and gold covered the floor. Upholstered chairs and settees were positioned in front of two elegantly carved marble fireplaces, one at each end of the room, that provided a friendly warmth against the cold.

"I'm so happy you are here," Abby said in greeting as she entered the room, her mother at her heels. If there was one person who could sort this all out, it was Jonesy. Always unconventional, always bold, always daring. Abby so wished she was like her.

"I'm happy I'm here as well," Jonesy said, pointing at a place on her cheek where Abby could place a kiss. She had a deep, almost manly voice. "I have so many questions for you. Of course, I've been driving around the block for the past half hour and more waiting for *himself* to leave." *"Himself"* was her favorite pet name for Abby's father. Jonesy swore that her father had more pride than Banfield, and that was saying quite a bit.

The doorbell rang again.

"You are going to be busy this afternoon," Jonesy predicted.

"I wonder why. We rarely have visitors. You know that," her mother said. A maid entered with a tray of wine, tea, and biscuits. Her mother nodded for the tray to be placed on a side table.

"Your daughter is a participant in the most spectacular goings-on at any ball of the last three years and you wonder why? Really, Catherine. I vow your banker has turned you quite provincial."

"What are you talking about?" her mother asked.

"Did not our Abigail give London's most eligible bachelor and Lady Dobbins's cicisbeo a set down at Banfield's ball last night, or did my ears hear wrong? I'm so sorry I had to miss it. Tortured, really. I would have adored the scene. And were you there when Lady Dobbins had a complete crisis over her Spanish lover's attraction to Abigail? They said she tore apart Banfield's supper room, sobbing hysterically and vowing to throw herself into the Thames if he did not come immediately to her. Of course, he didn't. The fellow has that much sense. He can glean more out of her and her odd husband by keeping her on pins and needles."

"Tore apart the supper room?" her mother echoed in disbelief, even as Harrison ushered in Lady Honoria Gilbertson and her daughters Miss Jane and Miss Nanette, who were eighteen and nineteen, respectively. The Montrosses knew them from church but had never received a call from them before.

"Yes," Lady Gilbertson answered, jumping into the conversation without preamble. "She was knocking over tables and throwing food."

"And supposedly drinking a barrel of wine at the same time," Jonesy quipped.

Lady Gilbertson opened her arms. "I had to run over here as soon as I heard. How horrible for you, Lady Catherine." She used Abby's mother's title, as many did. "How unfortunate! How extremely trying! How will you find a husband for your daughter? Oh, Miss Abigail. I didn't see you sitting there."

"Bulls balls," Jonesy replied, and Abby almost dropped the teapot she'd picked up to pour.

"Tea, Lady Gilbertson?" she managed to ask, choking back laughter.

"Of course," her ladyship answered without any sign of remorse or consternation over Jonesy's comment. "How are you, Lady Barnes?" she asked, perching herself on the edge of a chair and motioning her daughters to sit in the chairs next to hers, which they obediently did in the same perching manner.

"Do you care?" Jonesy wondered.

Lady Gilbertson trilled her laughter. "Original! Always so original!"

"Yes, I am, yes, I am," Jonesy mocked. She leaned toward Abby to confide, "She probably brought her daughters here for a look at you so they know what *not* to do in the future."

Abby knew Jonesy was being waggish, but the comment hit home because there was a good deal of truth in it. Jonesy didn't notice the impact of her words. She rarely did. She flung them out into the world and ignored how they were received.

More guests were flowing in the door, but Jonesy was too enlivened by so much entertainment to give a care to anyone other than herself.

But her mother had noticed.

From across the room, Abby could feel her mother's gaze, saw her sympathetic smile, and Abby knew her mother hurt when Abby hurt.

Forcing a smile on her face, Abby continued as hostess. More tea and biscuits were sent for. Amongst the next guests were friends of Abby's whom she hadn't seen since they'd married — Lady Edgars and Lady Mortimer. They came with tales of their husbands and their children and how they wished they'd been at Banfield's ball the night before because they'd heard the most remarkable things.

Polite society dictated that a call was no longer than fifteen minutes, but these women weren't here to be polite. They were on a mission. They wanted gossip and were using their tenuous connections with Abby to learn information. They'd probably dine on the tales they heard here for a week.

"Everything you heard is true," Jonesy assured them. "My niece had this Spaniard eating out of her hand and Lady Dobbins whirling like a jealous dervish."

"What a relief that someone managed to subdue Lady Dobbins long enough for Lady Corinne to announce her betrothal," Lady Edgars commented.

"Who'd she fix herself to?" Jonesy asked, surprised.

Abby's mother answered, "You know about this other but haven't heard the news of the night? Lady Corinne is now betrothed to Lord Freddie Sherwin."

Jonesy pulled a face over the name. "Don't know him. No doubt he is boring and wealthy. I can't imagine Banfield wanting anything less for his daughter."

"Lord Sherwin is very good looking," Lady Gilbertson said.

"Well, that is something," Jonesy said, holding her wineglass out to Abby to be refilled.

As Abby poured wine, she realized a part of her had been hoping the betrothal had not been announced. She shouldn't have been expecting anything . . . and yet, she had been.

It was done. Freddie would marry her cousin.

And she would . . . what? Become stepmother to thirteen children? The task seemed overwhelming no matter how much a marriage to such a powerful man would please her father and elevate her in society. *Lady Villier.* It had a European flavor, but the name felt to her old, crusty, stifling. . . .

"Miss Abigail, you appear so sad," Lady Gilbertson observed. "Is your sadness because of the scene last night? I must tell you I think it admirable that you put such a rakehell as this Spaniard in his place. It's a credit to you, Lady Catherine, that you have raised a young woman with high morals."

"Yes, high," Jonesy echoed. "Although every woman in this room has heard bits about him, and from what we've heard, we'd like to know what he said that caused you, the most sensible of all creatures, Abigail, to put him in his place."

And then she would duly report it to the rest of the family. Abby adored her aunt but was wise to her ways. Jonesy's loyalties often switched.

Her mother came to her rescue. "Please," she said, raising a hand and letting it waver in the air, as if she'd suddenly been overcome. "The evening was a trial for us all. We do not wish to remember it, do we, Abigail?"

"Um, no," Abby said, still uncertain what she did want to do.

"It was traumatic," her mother continued. "The whole evening. We are so glad it is over."

The women listened to her mother intently. They now turned to Abby, who felt a bit silly once again echoing her mother's words. "Over," she said. "It's over."

"But what was *he* like?" The question came from Lady Gilbertson.

"The barón? I don't know him," Abby

said. "Honest, I don't."

"Well, I've heard the most incredible things about him," Lady Edgars chimed in.

"Really, dear?" Jonesy said, drawing out the words. "Do tell."

Lady Edgars cast a look in the direction of Lady Gilbertson's daughters. "Posh, don't mind them," Lady Gilbertson said. "Tell us what you've heard." Her daughters nodded agreement, their eyes alive with anticipation.

Abby thought of the man she'd met in the library. Had sensed his privateness. "Really, this isn't the place," she protested, uncertain if she wanted to hear this gossip or not.

"Of course it's the place," Jonesy overrode her. From a distance, the doorbell rang again. More guests.

More gossip.

Abby decided the best tactic was to leave. She rose, holding the now empty teapot. "Excuse me, I'll ask the maid to fetch more."

She started toward the door, but she came to a stop when Lady Edgars said, "I've heard *why* Lady Dobbins was so angry with him last night."

Abby turned and faced the others. They weren't paying attention to her.

"I thought he was trying to untangle

himself from her," Jonesy said.

"Yes, he is, but she doesn't want to be untangled."

"I understand that," Jonesy replied. "What I want to know is why is she so upset? The woman has" — she made a loud *ahem* in place of a word — "with half the male population of London. What is so special about this one?"

Abby had to leave. She wasn't certain she wanted to hear this — except she did. A bit. Just a little.

"Lady Dobbins may have lovers, but she's only" — Lady Edgars made a loud *ahem* just as Jonesy had — "*once* with him," she ended triumphantly, knowing this was gossip few had heard. "She lets on as if it has been more often, but I was in a dressing room at Madame Giselle's being fitted for the dress I need to wear next month to my cousin's presentation and I overheard Lady Dobbins talking about him to someone in the next room."

"Who was she talking to?" Lady Gilbertson asked.

"I don't know," Lady Edgars said.

"Tell them the part that is so unbelievable," Lady Mortimer urged, excitement bubbling to the surface.

"Yes, tell us," both Jonesy and Lady Gilbertson encouraged, speaking the same thought aloud.

"Well," Lady Edgars started, obviously enjoying being the center of attention, "she said that he made — ahem — to her no less than *six* times that night. Six. One night." She held up her fingers to demonstrate the numbers so there could be no mistaking her.

Lady Gilbertson made a shrill, strangled noise — not because her daughters were listening but because she was impressed.

"Six times?" Jonesy said. "No man can — ahem — six times in one night."

"That's what her friend in the dressing room said," Lady Edgars reported, "and Lady Dobbins said he 'drove her to madness' *each* time."

"Well, that might be a short trip for someone like her," Lady Gilbertson declared dryly. "But I've heard rumors those Spaniards are bulls. And have you seen how handsome he is?" She started cackling and didn't stop, sounding very much like a crazed hen ready to lay eggs.

And she wasn't the only one. All the women joined in, giggling and casting looks and making that chuckling sound at each other as if sharing the grandest secret. Even Jonesy.

But not Abby and her mother.

Her mother looked like she wished she could disappear. She wasn't laughing.

Abby wasn't completely certain what they were going on about. She didn't think Miss Jane and Miss Nanette were either, although they snickered with the rest. Perhaps this was something only a married woman could understand. She did know what they meant by the "ahem." She wasn't naive. However, she didn't understand why the number six was so important —

Their cackling came to an abrupt halt.

Their eyes widened, then took on a look of appreciation as they stared at a point beyond where Abby stood in the doorway, the teapot still in her hand.

That's when hairs on the back of Abby's neck tingled.

Someone stood behind her. She caught a whiff of shaving soap. She remembered how warm the spicy scent had seemed the night before. How she'd liked that extra hint of sandalwood . . . only now it was mixed with the cold of the autumn wind, and she knew who had arrived.

Abby turned to face the barón. "Hello," she said, her voice faint. It was embarrassing to be caught gossiping, except he didn't appear to have noticed.

She sensed his tension. He'd come with a

purpose. His silver eyes didn't look around the room but focused on her, a small frown between his brows.

And she knew something was wrong. He still wore his greatcoat, although he had removed his hat and gloves.

He didn't even glance at the other women. "May we talk?"

"Right now?" she asked, ruffled by his intensity.

"Yes." He looked up then and noticed they were not alone. He seemed puzzled by it.

The women all watched him, their expressions a sight to behold. This was the first time Abby had ever seen Jonesy look impressed.

Well, the barón was a handsome man, and his accent was enough to make any woman swoon. It wasn't that Abby hadn't registered his attractiveness . . . but she noticed other things about him as well — such as this air of urgency about him. Whatever difficulty had brought him to her, it was of great import, and she felt a need to respond.

"Mother, everyone, will you excuse us a moment?" she asked, handing the teapot off to the footman who had escorted the barón into the sitting room.

Her mother said with no little confusion, "Where are you going? We have guests."

"Yes, we do," Abby replied. "But the barón needs to speak to me."

"I am so sorry," he apologized to the roomful of women as he took Abby's hand. The night before, she'd worn gloves. Now the touch of his skin on hers felt intimate.

"Where are you going?" her mother demanded.

"For a walk," he said. He glanced at the other women in the room. "If you will excuse us. It will be for only a moment."

"A walk?" Lady Gilbertson questioned. "It's brisk outside. It's not walking weather."

"We shall just take a turn around the garden," the barón answered, pulling on Abby's hand so that she would follow him.

And she went. Her curiosity was in full spin now.

Behind her, she overheard Jonesy say, "And she said she didn't know him, hmmmm?" Her poor mother would have to be the one to answer for her.

As for herself, she was following the barón. He led her out into the front hall, then she guided him toward the back door.

He grabbed a cloak hanging from a peg by the door and threw it over her shoulders. He opened the door.

She went outside and was conscious they were being watched. A glance at the win-

111

dows told her that all their guests, as well as her mother, stood peering out the windows.

However, the barón seemed undeterred by the audience. He took Abby's arm and guided her into the bare autumn garden, moving toward a bench beside a fountain. In the summer, the splash of the fountain's water was one of Abby's favorite things about the garden. Today, it was quiet. As they approached, a squirrel scurried for cover amongst fallen leaves, but even the hubbub of London seemed miles away.

"What is it?" she asked. "What has you so upset?"

He didn't answer until they'd reached the bench. He sat her down and knelt on the ground in front of her.

His expression was so serious that Abby didn't know what to make of him or his actions.

"Does this have anything to do with last night?" she pressed. Her breath came out as puffs of frigid air. The bench's wooden slats were cold even through the cloak.

"Will you marry me?" he answered.

CHAPTER SIX

Andres had not intended to be quite that blunt. He could see by her wide eyes and dropped jaw that she hadn't expected a marriage proposal. It was just that his mind was brimming with opportunities, challenges, things that must be done; he hadn't really developed his thoughts toward her completely . . . and yet she was instrumental to his reaching what he desired.

He wrapped his hands around hers, both for warmth and to keep her where she was until he could finish building his case.

"I've surprised you," he said, thinking rapidly. "I've surprised myself. I mean, I've thought about this . . . a little — well, a lot —"

"You can't have thought about it a lot. We've just met."

"In my life, twenty-four hours can be a long time," he confessed, and that was true. He'd never been afraid to make a quick decision and stick to it . . . although this was the first time his decision depended upon another person.

Lord Dobbins hadn't been jesting. He'd signed the deed to Stonemoor over to Andres. It was his now. *His.* He didn't know if she could understand what this meant to him.

And he prayed he had the right words to convince her. He'd never asked a woman for anything. He might have had a reputation for being a ladies' man, but that had more to do with them flocking to him than vice versa.

"Please, Miss Montross, hear me out before you make any decision."

She glanced at the house. "They are all watching us."

He didn't turn to look. He didn't care. His focus was on her. "I have property. Good property. It's a house, a huge house like what Holburn has," he assured her, knowing that if he confessed he'd never seen it, she'd wisely run. "And I have stables and land." In his mind's eye he could picture them. He'd spent the night plotting them out.

The stables looked like what his father had owned. He started describing them to her. "They are built around a shaded courtyard so when you go to relax or saddle the horses you are not burned by the sun —"

"Is this in Spain?" she asked.

"No, in Northumberland," he answered, the name still a bit alien on his tongue. Northumberland. It sounded very English.

"There is no sun in Northumberland," she said.

"You have been there?" he countered, her words interrupting his dream.

"No, but it's further north. I assumed less sun. People have said it is not as hot as London."

"There is still sun," he assured her. "And there is a bubbling spring nearby with the freshest water in the whole country. The tile roof is of the finest red clay and keeps everything cool —"

"A tile roof out of red clay? I thought they were slate."

Andres shook his head, realizing in his enthusiasm his mind was playing tricks on him. Of course it wouldn't be *red* clay. "It is clay," he said, uncertain and not wanting to be distracted with details.

He rose to sit on the bench beside her. "What it is, is *mine*. I am going to build something magnificent there. My horses —" He paused. It didn't sound right, not if he wished to win her over. "*Our* horses, the ones we shall breed, will be the most famous in all of the world."

She looked at him as if he'd turned into a troll. "Horses? Our horses? Barón, I don't like horses."

Andres had never heard of anyone not liking horses. He couldn't imagine such a thing. "How do you travel?" he wondered.

"In a coach or a carriage or on my two feet. I don't ride," she said emphatically. "I'm not good at it. They are dangerous animals. I fell once."

"And?" he prompted.

"And what?" she asked.

"So you fall. You climb back on the horse. I've fallen many times."

"I fell *once*," she informed him. "I broke my collarbone. I don't need to fall again," she assured him.

"How old were you?" he asked.

"Young," she said, her annoyance coming out. "Eight, maybe seven."

Andres shrugged her fear away. "Of course you fall when you are young —"

"I don't like horses," she reiterated. "They smell."

For a second, his confidence wavered, but a man who had nothing to lose and stood everything to gain could not be choosy. "I will deal with the horses," he said, smiling.

"You can see to the house and the gardens."

"*Your* house?" she confirmed.

"Yes," he said. "But it will be *our* house."

She studied him a moment. He waited, anxious for her answer.

"You want my money," she said at last.

"I'm being very honest about it," he answered.

"Perhaps too honest?" she suggested. "How did you come by this house?"

She was being prickly, and she really didn't need to know all. He lied. "I inherited it."

"Oh."

"I will be honest with you," he said, knowing that some of the truth must be told. "I have very little. I have my family name, Ramigio, which I hope to make once again important. That I value. I have the title. And I have a mare of my father's stock. She is in foal. With those two horses, I will make my mark. And, before you think I truly have nothing, I do own a silver mine."

"Where's the silver?"

Banker's daughters were not romantic. "It wasn't such a good investment. The silver ran out."

"Where is it?"

"In Peru."

"Where is that?"

"Far from here," he said and brought the subject back to where he wanted it. "Miss Montross, Abby, we can both help each other. You were angry last night — and I still don't understand why — but it is fine," he stressed, since she looked as if she was ready to jump in with a comment and he didn't want her once again distracted. "What is important is that we met. You do believe in Fate, do you not?"

"Fate?" She frowned, as if tasting the word and finding it not to her liking. "If you are asking if I believe our lives are preordained, I do not."

"Yes, but last night, there was something between us that is not usual," he pressed. "Would you not say that? In the library, when we met, did you not feel that —" He broke off, searching for the right word. "*Specialness?* It was as if we were supposed to find each other and at a time when we both needed someone."

"I don't need anyone," she said, her chin coming up.

"Yes, you do." Andres was not going to let her escape with that lie. "I can read it in your eyes. You were not comfortable in that room with those women. That's why you left so quickly."

"I left because you asked me to."

He shook his head. "You left because there is this bond between us. A bond that does not make sense. I think you like me, just a little. I like you. I believe we were supposed to meet, and I believe you are supposed to help me with Stonemoor."

Her certainty faded. Her chin lowered. "Stonemoor? Is that the name of your estate?"

Andres nodded. "If I had time, I would woo you — but I have no time. Sometimes life is like that. We must take risks. That's why I tell you everything so that you know all."

Well, he wasn't telling her everything. He couldn't. If he did, she'd run away screaming. Besides, it was never good to tell a woman all that one knew. They liked to hear what they thought they wanted to know.

But just for good measure, he confessed, "I have not always been the best of men. I have done things that were not always legal, but not in this country. I've been good in England. I did those things because I thought they were a way to restore my family name and I was desperate and young. I wanted to honor the name Ramigio. I was not wise. I've wanted this property all my life."

"Is that why you came to England?"

"Yes," he said, because it made sense. "But I had to wait for my inheritance. And now that I have it, there is no money." He leaned close to her. "Last night you asked a man to run away with you. He was a fool. He would not. But *I* am here. I will run away with you although I'd rather speak to your father first —"

"No." She pulled her hands from his, rose from the bench, sat down, rose again.

He understood her agitation. He came to his feet as well. "I have given you much to think on. This is not what you expected."

She glanced at the house. "Look at them," she said, her voice low, as if she spoke to herself. "They practically have their noses to the window."

Andres turned toward the house. Seeing him looking their way, the ladies in the sitting room practically jumped back for fear of being caught watching.

"Mother and I rarely receive visitors," she said, "not like we've received today. Usually, we're ignored. Most people feel my mother is no longer important because she had the audacity to marry a man who wasn't her social equal." She looked to him. "Mother married for love. And everyone acted as if it is a crime."

"If you marry me, you will be Lady Vasconia." Andres anglicized the title without a pang of conscience. Dobbins's discovery that he had no claim to the title aside, he'd used it for years to great advantage. If he did as Dobbins demanded and left London, there would be no problems. Abby could safely be titled in Northumberland.

And he *was* his father's son, he reminded himself. "Sometimes it is society who is wrong," he said, not realizing he'd spoken aloud until she answered.

"You're right. They can be so cruel. Jonesy is my favorite aunt, and yet she rarely visits . . . of course, she showed up today because she wants to know what happened last night with you. I've finally become interesting."

"Marrying me would make you even *more* interesting."

His promise sparked a laugh out of her. She shook her head and then replied thoughtfully, "You are right. You are the man they all want." She sat on the bench, her expression serious.

Andres could feel the wheels of her mind churning and knew the scales were tilting in his favor.

"I'm tired of being an afterthought," she murmured. "And I don't want to be the mother to thirteen children that are not mine."

"I beg your pardon?" What thirteen children?

She saw his confusion and started laughing. "Please, don't worry about it. My father thinks he has chosen a new husband for me. One with too many children."

"He's chosen a husband?" Andres didn't like this news.

"No, it's not anything firm yet, thank God," she said, hope rising to her face. "In fact, I *will* accept your proposal, Barón. I will be honored."

"You will?" He almost couldn't believe his ears. It was too easy, and he'd learned through experience that when things were too easy, something would go wrong.

"Yes, I will. I can't marry Freddie. He's promised to my cousin, and he won't give a care if I'm married to Lord Villier. But if I married *you* —" She laughed again, this time the sound taking on the warmth of anticipation. "Everyone will be jealous. Including Freddie." She looked toward the house. He could see movement in the windows. The women still lingered. "Everyone will be talking about me but in a good way. You are the catch of the Season." Her triumph gave way to concern.

"What are you thinking?" he asked, already leery of Abby when her mind started working this fast.

"We'll be married . . . but I don't think we should, well, you know — ahem."

Andres waited for her to finish what she was saying.

When after a few seconds she didn't go on, he asked, "Don't think we should what?"

She scrunched her nose as if annoyed and said, "Ahem."

"Do you have a tickle in your throat?" he wondered. "Should we go in?" It wouldn't be good if she caught a cold or the influenza before they left.

"I'm fine," she said with exasperation. She stepped closer, as if wanting to block the view of the ladies in the window. "I'm talking about marital relations."

Andres was charmed by her reticence. He'd forgotten a woman could be self-conscious, discreet, virginal.

Abby was a virgin. Her purity touched him. He'd not even considered it. But she would be his and his alone.

She gathered the cloak around her as if she would hide.

He reached over and pulled her toward him so he could look into her wide, blue eyes. He wanted to sleep with her. The heat flowing through his veins was hotter and stronger than it ever had been, even for Gillian.

"Yes," he said. "Yes, we must consummate the marriage or it doesn't exist."

"I-I don't know if I can."

Lust died a quick death.

Andres stepped back. God must be laughing. The only women he wanted were the ones who didn't want him.

"I'm sorry, but ours would be more of a business agreement, correct?" she said.

"Yes," he reluctantly admitted, every male fiber in his being rebelling at what she was suggesting . . . and then he thought of his purpose.

Nothing meant more to him than rebuilding the Ramigio reputation for horses. If he had to remain celibate to do so . . . ?

Well, Andres had been working his way around women since he was in short pants. He could win Abby, or at least convince her that sex was a good thing.

"Actually, it would be better to not, ah — how do you say it?" he asked.

"Ahem," she replied.

"*Ay,* that is what you meant." He rolled his eyes. The English.

"I was being delicate," she defended herself.

124

"It is not delicate that I do not know what you are talking about." He frowned, wanting this settled between them — to his advantage. "Is it you do not like my plans for Stonemoor?" he asked.

"I do like them. And save for the horses, it will be exciting to help you build your stables. Certainly it would be better than the tedium of town as a maiden aunt or the prospect of mothering thirteen young ones. But I think we should agree to only be friends. After all, you took Lady Dobbins to your bed and you are not friends with her any longer. I imagine the same is true for a number of women."

Andres shifted, uncomfortable. "If the marriage is not consummated, it can be set aside."

"*I* won't set it aside. We have a bargain."

"How badly does your father want you to marry this Lord Villier?"

Abby pressed her lips together in concern.

"He could see the marriage set aside," Andres suggested.

"He could," she conceded.

"We consummate the marriage. We must. One time, *palomita.* If you dislike, no more." But he'd make certain she liked it.

"Once only?" she questioned. "Not six?"

"Six?" Her choice of that number confused him. "If you want to consummate the marriage six times —"

"No." She took a step closer to him. "And no, I don't want you to talk to my father. We'll need to elope."

That was not a thought Andres had considered. "We could marry by special license," he replied. He wanted to do what was right for her.

She shook her head. "Father really likes Lord Villier. He has connections with the Treasury. *You* have *no* connections. That's why I don't think it is wise you speak to him. My parents eloped. We will elope."

Andres didn't like the idea of sneaking around. It was not honorable . . . and yet, what recourse did they have? If Abby said they must elope, he'd be a fool to argue with her, especially when it fit into his plans. "May we leave tomorrow?"

She stepped back from him, crossing her arms at her waist. But before she could answer, a woman's voice called her name. "Abigail, is everything fine?"

Abby looked to the house. "Yes, Mother, it is all good."

"Aren't you cold?"

"I have on a coat," Abby said, but she was shaking.

"Come in, please," her mother said. "You

have been out here a long time."

Abby nodded. "We're coming in now," she called and turned to him. "Do you know the circulating library on Duke Street? Meet me there tomorrow at one. I'll be prepared to leave." She began walking toward the house.

Andres caught up to walk beside her. "Wait," he whispered. "How much do you stand to inherit?"

She didn't take offense at the question, and he liked that. Abby had a practical mind. "A living of two thousand pounds annual."

If the heavens had opened and a host of angels had appeared singing "Alleluia," Andres could not have been more surprised and blessed.

Two thousand pounds a year. A fortune. An incredible fortune.

Abby smiled, a conspirator's smile. She knew she'd pleased him. "My grandmother left it to me to spite my father and the other family members. I barely knew her, but she didn't want Father to have the money. And she was furious with my uncle the duke when he welcomed Father into the family with open ams after my uncle died. Everyone was surprised by my inheritance. No one had thought her particularly wealthy, and I suppose she used that to her advantage. Father called her a miser, but then many have used that word to describe him as well. She also left me some of her personal jewelry. Come, you haven't met my mother properly."

At that point, Andres would have walked over burning coals if she'd asked him to do so.

Two thousand pounds. A house, stables, horses . . . and a wife.

Fate had finally blessed him.

He'd be at the circulating library on Duke Street with bells on. But before he eloped, there were a few purchases he needed to make. He could buy some equipment that he knew he would find here and didn't know if any of it would be in Northumberland. And the marquis of Salisbury had been talking the other night about a pair of prime fillies with impeccable bloodlines that could be had for a very good price. He wanted to take a look at them as well.

Andres stayed long enough for introductions. He let the ladies ogle him, and when it was polite, he excused himself and left.

After all, he had an elopement to plan.

Chapter Seven

The moment the barón left the room, Abby found herself confronted by some very curious women. Politeness dictated they keep their questions to themselves.

Politeness had never been Jonesy's strong suit.

"Didn't you mention you didn't really *know* the barón?" Jonesy asked, as if catching Abby in her lie.

"Well, of course we've met," Abby replied. "We danced."

"And do all the men you've 'met' whisk you away and fall down to one knee in front of you?" Jonesy queried.

"Aunt, were you eavesdropping?" Abby returned, helping herself to a glass of Madeira. She was going to need it to steady her nerves. *She was eloping.* She was acting upon her life. Making her own decisions. The prospect made her giddy.

She wondered if this was the way her

mother had felt when she and her father had planned their own elopement.

Abby dared not look at her mother. She didn't know what could be read on her face. And the truth was this wasn't terribly bold of Abby. She would have eloped with Freddie — if he'd been willing to go with her.

Wait until he heard what she'd done. The thought gave her great satisfaction. She sipped her wine, its raisiny taste to her liking.

"If I *had* been eavesdropping, I would have had my answer, wouldn't I, niece?" Jonesy countered, a touch of acid in her tone. "It's not eavesdropping to observe what is happening right outside a window. Now, what is going on?"

"Yes, what?" Lady Edgars echoed.

Abby lowered her glass. "He was apologizing," she said, startled and a bit proud at how easy this deviation of the truth rolled off her tongue. "For last night and creating a scene. He was very gracious."

"And?" Jonesy prompted.

"And nothing else," Abby said, raising the glass to her lips.

"The two of you had quite a conversation," observed Miss Jane, Lady Gilbertson's daughter. "It seemed very important."

Abby smiled at the girl. She was a debutante, one of those who had looked with pity upon Abby because of her unmarried state once word of Richard Lynsted's jilting had become public knowledge. The girl would choke on her pity come the morrow.

"He's an earnest man," Abby informed them. "I told him no apology was necessary, but he insisted, perhaps because he is Spanish. He looks so distant, so cold and so —"

"Handsome?" Lady Mortimer supplied.

"That too," Abby agreed. "He is very handsome." She was starting to see what other women did. Strange how it had taken her so long. . . .

"An Englishman would have laughed off the incident," Abby continued. "The barón was more serious, more contrite."

"*More* handsome," Lady Mortimer added.

"Alicia," Lady Edgars chided, her own cheeks blossoming with becoming color.

"I can't help it," Lady Mortimer answered. "Seeing him here and so close, he's perfection. Pure masculine beauty."

"No man is perfect," Jonesy declared. "Not if he is a true man and not one of those foppy fellows." She stood, gathering her scarves around her neck. "Something is afoot, Abby. You've a different look about you. And if that man was on one knee just to apologize, then I am the Queen of Sheba. But I am not going to worry about it. That is for Catherine to do." She nodded toward Abby's mother. "If you are wise, you'll keep an eye on her."

Abby's mother's brows rose in worry. The other women now considered Abby with suspicion, too. Abby could have boxed her aunt's ears, and her aunt knew it.

Jonesy gave her a smile of supreme satisfaction. She paused in front of Abby before leaving the room. Placing a hand beneath Abby's chin, she said, "I was the oldest of four girls, niece. I have a very good sense of the little games we women play."

"But I'm not playing a game," Abby said truthfully.

Her aunt smiled. "I shall go now, Catherine. This was a very entertaining and *enlightening*" — she directed that word toward Abby — "afternoon. It was a pleasure to make the acquaintance of the rest of you." She left the room with the air of royalty.

There was a moment of silence. Abby could feel the other women digesting Jonesy's words and her attitude. She finished her wine without tasting it.

"Well, we must be going as well," Lady Gilbertson said. Her daughters hopped up

132

from their chairs.

Lady Edgars and Lady Mortimer joined the exodus. Abby smiled her farewell, knowing they would probably put their heads together and have a thorough discussing of the afternoon.

Too soon, it was just she and her mother alone.

The maid took away the tray of empty glasses and cups. Abby was conscious that her mother watched her every move while the servant was in the room.

The silence between them grew oppressive.

Her mother broke it. "*Should* I be worried?"

"About what?" Abby asked.

Her mother's gaze narrowed on her. "Your father wants this marriage between you and Lord Villier."

"And I don't understand why you can't let me choose for myself."

"Your father has been very clear —"

"That he doesn't like Freddie Sherwin and he is afraid I'll end up on the shelf, a dried-up spinster of no good to anyone. Yes, yes, yes, I know what he thinks."

Her mother's expression softened. "Abigail, that is not true —"

"*It is,* Mother. You and Father had a grand

passion. You gave up so much for him."

"And I have no regrets," her mother agreed.

"I don't want regrets either," Abby answered.

"You would have regrets if you married Lord Villier?"

"Wouldn't you?"

Her mother grimaced. "You are right. I'll speak to your father."

"Thank you," Abby said, meaning the words.

"But as to that Spaniard," her mother continued. "I don't have a good feeling about him."

Of everything Abby had heard women say about the barón, suspicion was not part of it. "Why does he make you feel that way?"

Her mother gave a little shrug. "I was at the theater the night he declared his love for Lady Wright. It was not that long ago. And her rejection was very public."

Now she had Abby's interest. He had been in love before, and just recently?

Funny that with all her talk of Freddie, he'd not mentioned it. "Who is Lady Wright?"

"Another married woman. The barón seems to make a habit of chasing married women." Disapproval colored her voice.

"Or is it that they chase him?" Abby said in his defense.

"Does it matter? A woman married to another man is not fair game. I know there are those who ignore their vows —"

"Usually in arranged matches," Abby had to point out.

Her mother ignored her comment. "I would not want my daughter to be caught up with a fickle man. He's handsome, Abby, I'll give you that. Those dark looks and his silver eyes make even me a bit dizzy when I look at him. But handsome is as handsome does. There were those who said your father was not handsome, but he's been a wonderful husband, and when I look at him, even at the age we are, there is no man more attractive to me."

"I haven't met a man like Father," Abby confessed. "He would fight dragons for you."

Her mother smiled. "He would, wouldn't he? Just like St. George."

"Yes . . . but I doubt if Lord Villier would bother to show up by my bedside as I birthed his fourteenth child."

The smile vanished from her mother's face. "I said I'd speak to your father, and I will."

Abby crossed the room and gave her

mother a hug. It was an impulsive action, spurred by no small measure of guilt. "I know you will, Mother. Thank you."

She pulled away, but her mother grabbed hold and hugged her closer. "Please trust us," she whispered.

And Abby wanted to. In fact, her mother's plea sat heavy on her shoulders the rest of the day . . . until dinner.

Her father was in good spirits. "Abby, Lord Villier likes you. He likes you very much."

Abby sent a glance in her mother's direction.

Her mother didn't meet her eye. She knew then that her mother had talked to her father and his answer was to continue his support of Lord Villier. Consequently the dinner conversation contained many references to his lordship.

As Abby pushed her food around her plate, she realized that her father's stubbornness was a gift. She was free of any doubts she harbored about running away. She could make her own choices. Her grandmother's money had seen to that.

But she was deliberately flouting his authority and thwarting his plans, and he was not a man who took such insult lightly, even from his daughter. Still, carrying such a secret without telling anyone was unbearable — almost impossible. Sooner or later, her absence would be noticed. She needed someone in the household to help hide the fact that she was gone, for she had no doubt her father would chase her down. Abby didn't know how fast the barón planned to travel, but she assumed they could be a good three days on the road. The more time she could buy them, the better.

Her mother would not support her, and she didn't know if she dared trust a servant. They would be given the sack if their help was discovered.

Finally, after a fitful night during which she slept little, Abby decided she must carry out her plan all by herself. In the hour before dawn, not wanting to cause her parents unneeded anguish, she wrote a letter letting them know she had eloped with the barón and begging their forgiveness.

However, she stressed that she would not marry Lord Villier. She'd chosen instead to "seek her Fate." She liked the sound of the word the barón had used so often in persuading her. She finished by saying she loved and respected her parents and hoped they would accept the barón into their family. She then hid the letter in the top drawer of her dressing table to be discovered once they found her missing and started searching for her.

Midmorning, a message arrived from the barón. He regretted that he needed to change their meeting from one until two that afternoon. Abby studied his handwriting. Freddie's writing was indecipherable. The barón's was clear, strong, direct. Much like the man himself. A wave of apprehension tightened in her stomach. She didn't know this man, and yet she was entrusting him with her future. There would be no turning back once she left the library with him.

And of course, when they gathered an hour later for lunch, everything was good with her family. Almost too good.

Pleased that he'd done his best for his daughter, her father was in excellent spirits. Over the luncheon table he said, "Abigail, you haven't been shopping lately. You and your mother should go out and enjoy yourselves. Go to the Royal Academy, see what exhibitions are there, and do a spot of spending on yourselves."

"That sounds entertaining, doesn't it?" her mother said with an enthusiasm that touched Abby's heart. "The weather is lovely for shopping. It's been so damp."

And how to beg off?

Abby decided to do so with a good pout. "I'm sorry," she said, affecting a wounded sensibility. "I don't feel up to shopping." She made herself sound deliberately ill-tempered.

Her tone had the desired effect. Her parents immediately assumed her manner was because of Lord Villier. Her father became decidedly grumpy, and her mother's manner grew distressed.

Abby felt a terrible person to behave this way. And she knew her running away would not make them happier.

But what recourse did she have?

The air for the rest of the meal was chilly.

After lunch, Abby escaped to her room. Her maid Tabitha was not there, which gave Abby the freedom to prepare for her elopement. She couldn't very well dance out the front door with a valise.

Instead, she dressed herself in several layers. First, she hurriedly put on her night dress, then a day dress, and then her largest walking dress. She didn't bother with petticoats. With so many clothes on, they were unnecessary.

She tucked a change of small clothing and stockings into the bottom of an embroidered bag she often used to carry books when visiting the circulating library. As an afterthought, she scooped up her jewelry. She would return someday, but it was best to take what she could now.

Her father had been generous to her and had given her some very fine rings and necklaces, including a perfectly matched pearl necklace in its own pouch that he claimed had cost a king's ransom. One of Abby's favorite pieces was a garnet brooch that had belonged to her grandmother, the one who had bequeathed her the money. She was just pinning the brooch to her walking dress, deciding to wear it for luck, when Tabitha entered the room carrying folded, clean laundry.

"I'm sorry, Miss Abby. I didn't anticipate you being here."

"I won't be long," Abby said. Tabitha was relatively new to the household. Abby's previous maid, Mary, had been with her for six years until she'd left their service to marry a butcher. Many a time Mary had served as lookout when Abby had met Freddie at the circulating library. Mary had also carried notes between Abby and Freddie.

Tabitha was Mary's cousin, but Abby had not confided in her, and she didn't think it wise to start doing so now. In fact, the less Tabitha knew about the elopement, the safer her position in the household would be after Abby was gone.

Still, Abby needed an escort to go out this afternoon. To not ask for one would invite suspicion. "Tabitha, I'm going out in half an hour. Please be ready to accompany me."

"Yes, Miss Abby," she answered. She set the laundry on the dresser and tucked the clothes neatly in the drawers where they belonged. When she finished, she made things right on the dresser and, in the course of things, moved Abby's bag for carrying books.

While she pretended to be working at her desk on some correspondence, Abby watched Tabitha out of the corner of her eye. She wondered if the maid had noticed the bit of weight in the bag when there should not have been any.

And she was not pleased when Tabitha walked over to the dressing table and started to clear it by putting the hairbrush into the same drawer where the letter was —

"That will be all," Abby said, hoping to divert the maid's attention before she noticed the envelope.

Tabitha glanced up in surprise at the abrupt dismissal. "Yes, miss," she said, shutting the drawer and bobbing a curtsey. She hurried toward the door.

"I'll meet you in the front hall," Abby said, feeling guilty and wanting to soften her brusqueness.

"Yes, miss," Tabitha said dutifully, bobbing another curtsey and leaving the room.

Abby released her breath in exasperation. Her nerves would be on edge until she and the barón were on the road. After this elopement, she vowed to never again involve herself in anything scandalous — especially if it had an impact on those she loved.

She chose a book from the stack waiting to be read on her bedside table. Even now that she and Freddie didn't have clandestine meetings, she was a frequent visitor to the Duke Street Circulating Library. She slipped the book into her bag and donned her coat and its matching hat, a pretty confection made of green and cream velvet bands that should keep her ears warm for traveling. She also threw on a wool scarf and her heaviest gloves. She gave herself a good look over in the mirror.

Her body appeared bulky, but the coat could be used as an excuse if anyone noticed. Probably no one would, especially if she moved quickly and with purpose.

Abby looked around at her room and felt a pang of remorse that she was leaving — yet part of her was alive with excitement.

A footman knocked on the door to inform her the carriage she'd ordered earlier through Harrison was waiting outside the front door. As she came down the stairs, Abby looked about for her mother. She would have liked to have spoken to her one last time before she left, but Catherine was nowhere to be seen.

Tabitha was still a bit standoffish. Abby chalked it up to her own kindness. She rarely raised her voice with the servants and Tabitha had probably taken offense. Sometimes servants could be extremely sensitive.

The maid sat next to Abby in the coach, her hands folded in her lap, her eyes downcast.

Abby didn't care. She was deep in thought as well. Now that Freddie was promised to her cousin, there was no hope for them. Like a heroine in a tragic novel, she would go to Northumberland with the barón and put Freddie from her life forever. She was making a sacrifice for all concerned — Freddie, Corinne, her family, and herself.

The vision made her feel noble and less guilty about leaving her parents.

The coach rolled to a halt. A footman opened the door to help Abby out. She reached for her embroidered bag just as Tabitha took it.

Their eyes met. The maid's slid away. "I'm sorry, miss. Did you wish for me to carry it?"

"I wish for you to wait for me here," Abby said, suddenly distrustful, though she didn't know why. The maid was only being helpful, and yet something didn't seem quite right.

Or it could have been Abby's own fears and doubts. She forced a smile. "I'm just returning this book and should be out as soon as I choose another." She took hold of the bag and climbed out of the coach. After telling the coachman to return for her in a half hour, she went into the library, the bell over the door jangling to announce her entrance.

The Duke Street Circulating Library boasted not one but two bow front windows overlooking the street. Inside, counters were placed in front of the book-lined walls. Clerks bustled back and forth behind the counters, fetching books for patrons to peruse and possibly check out.

As a rich man's daughter, Abby could buy any book she wished, but her father's nature was frugal, as was her own, and books were expensive. She'd grown up taking trips with her mother to this circulating library, and it felt like a second home.

Of course, once she and Freddie had started meeting here, the circulating library had come to have a much deeper meaning.

She was well known to the clerks. Although they were busy with other patrons, they looked up and gave her a smile, nodding a greeting.

Abby placed the book she wished to return in its proper place, noticing that her coach had not left yet to circle the square until she was ready for it. Tabitha was boldly staring out the coach window at the library, and the footman still stood on the walk. They both appeared very concerned.

When Tabitha caught sight of Abby staring back at her through one of the bow front windows, she quickly ducked back into the coach's interior. The footman climbed up into the box beside the coachman, but the coach did not move.

Abby's sense that something was not right grew stronger.

The barón was standing toward the back of the library, reading a periodical he had open on the counter. He stood out. He was taller than most and, on top of his good looks, had a commanding presence.

He was dressed in a many-caped, gray greatcoat and wore a sporting man's spurs on his boots. It was the fashion, but Abby knew he was prepared for travel.

Raising his head in her direction, he gave a small nod toward the back door. That was how he wanted them to leave.

She smiled that she understood and started to make her way toward him, walking along the counter as she pretended to search for a particular book.

A clerk began following her. "Is there something I may take down for you, Miss Montross?" he asked eagerly.

The front doorbell jangled as she answered, "I'm just looking —"

"Why, Miss Montross," Freddie Sherwin's voice said.

Abby turned. Freddie was in the doorway, and he wasn't alone.

"Cousin!" Corinne said happily and started walking toward her. "We saw your coach pulling away and feared you were gone." She was a vision in blue velvet that played up her fair complexion and blonde hair. Freddie appeared positively dashing beside her.

But Abby had to concede that he was not as good-looking as the barón.

It was an odd notion. She'd never thought that way about Freddie before. He'd always been the most important man in the room to her . . . but now he belonged to someone else.

Perhaps her feelings were changing because soon *she* would belong to someone else.

"Freddie assured me that often you had the coach drive around the square rather than wait for you," Corinne continued happily. "I say, I like the green of your bonnet with your hair. Very fetching."

"Thank you," Abby murmured. "And congratulations on your betrothal."

"See? I told you there were no hard feelings," Freddie said to Corinne, not bothering to lower his voice. It carried through the library. "Abby's not that way. She wants what is best for us."

Abby felt her temper sizzle. Freddie talked about her to Corinne? What a complete bounder!

"Is that true, dear?" her cousin asked, but Abby couldn't answer — because she suddenly had a new worry.

Through the glass windows, she recognized the man about to walk in: *her father.*

And he was moving with a purpose she knew too well.

She'd been found out. She didn't know how . . . but this did explain Tabitha's unusual behavior. The maid must have noticed the note, and now Abby's father was about to grab her by the ear and take her home.

If she wanted her freedom, if she didn't want to be the next Lady Villier, or to spend the rest of her life at family functions pretending Freddie was nothing more than a distant relative, she had only one choice.

She turned to the barón and shouted, *"Run!"*

CHAPTER EIGHT

Andres was annoyed. Here he was, ready to elope, and *she* was dawdling, jabbering with the buffoon, her Freddie, the man who wouldn't speak for her.

But when she shouted for them to run and came at him as if the building had been on fire, Andres proved his annoyance didn't interfere with his reflexes. If Abby Montross said "Run," he already knew enough of her character to believe her.

He'd paid a clerk to let them use the building's back entrance. He now reached for the door leading to the back storage room and opened it. Abby didn't pause but charged right through it, tossing over her shoulder the chilling words, *"My father."*

That's all she had to say.

The bell over the front door jangled and Banker Montross marched into the circulating library like a fighter entering the ring. "Where's my daughter?" he shouted before catching sight of Andres, who was already shutting the door behind himself.

Andres looked for a lock. There was none, so he scanned the back storage room, with its row of desks and chairs, for something he could use to block the door. Abby had reached the back entrance. She held the door open, urging him to hurry.

A clerk making entries in a ledger was sitting at the desk closest to Andres. His desk was piled high with books. With one swift motion, Andres grabbed the heavy wooden desk and dragged it in front of the door, startling the poor clerk while papers, ledgers, and ink bottles went flying.

"I say," the man yelped, but Andres wasn't offering explanations. He ran to Abby even as a body rammed against the door. The desk rocked, but held.

However, it wouldn't hold for much longer, especially if the clerk helped from this side.

Out on the back step, Andres grabbed Abby's arm. "This way."

The alley was narrow with just enough space for a cart to pass. Andres had left his phaeton, a light sporting vehicle made for fast travel, at the alley's exit on Oxford Street. Men proved their mastery of the whip on such a vehicle. It lacked a coach's security, but the truth was, Andres could drive his phaeton heeled on two wheels if he had to. Negotiating London traffic would be a challenge but not a problem, and the time they would save making their escape would be a godsend.

Abby tripped on her skirts even as her father burst through the alley door shouting her name.

Andres could see the lad holding his horses. He swept Abby up in his arms, throwing her unceremoniously over his shoulder, and raced the last few steps to his vehicle, almost knocking over two women who had the misfortune of crossing the alley at that moment.

The ladies screamed. Andres muttered, "So sorry, so sorry," before barking for the lad with his horses to pay attention.

He swung Abby up into the perched seat of the phaeton. "What are you doing?" she demanded.

"Eloping," he said, thinking it should be obvious.

Banker Montross was fast. He raced down the alley toward them like a hussar on the attack. There was no time for Andres to run around to the other side of the vehicle. He jumped up into the box, climbing over Abby — even as she started to climb down.

Andres caught her arm. "What are *you* do-ing?"

"I can't ride in this," she said.

"Yes, you can," Andres answered, picking up the reins while still holding her arm. With a snap, they were off.

"Sir! You promised me a guinea," the lad shouted, chasing them.

Slipping his arm through Abby's, Andres reached in his pocket and pulled out a coin. "Here," he said to Abby, "give this to him." He had to watch his driving. The traffic was heavy on Oxford Street. A man had to have his wits about him.

But Abby didn't take the coin. She grabbed the far side of the seat with both hands. "I can't ride in this. This is danger-ous," she announced.

Andres frowned and tossed the coin back to the lad, not bothering to look to see if it was picked up or not, because he could hear Banker Montross bellowing like an enraged bear that they had escaped. He was shout-ing at everyone to stop them. Andres found a hole in the oncoming traffic, picked up his whip, and, with a flick toward his team of horses, drove them right into it, passing a town coach smartly.

He swung the phaeton in front of the

coach before the oncoming traffic ran them over.

Abby was making high-pitched noises. When they were out of danger, she whirled on him, her eyes alive without rage. "That was so dangerous —"

"Then prepare yourself, for we are doing it again."

And they did.

Abby gave out a shout and shut her eyes.

After seeing them in and out of the traffic, Andres had to say, "I don't understand your fear. I am an excellent whip. I've raced these things and won every time."

"Please don't," she returned. "This vehicle, it is nothing but a board on four very unsteady wheels. It's dangerous. Vehicles like this should be outlawed."

He laughed. The truth was, he enjoyed driving fast, and now he had a good excuse. "You don't need to worry, Abby. I will take care of you." Holburn's team of matching grays was a sweet pair of goers. "We will be in Scotland before you know it."

"We are going to take this flimsy cart all the way to Scotland?"

Andres pulled his attention away from the traffic to give her a frown. The ribbons of her bonnet had come loose and the hat was in danger of flying off. Her curls sprung out every which way and her eyes were wide in her pale face.

"Yes, I think we shall," he said, teasing because she looked so alarmed.

She groaned an answer.

But Andres was enjoying himself. He liked the challenge of the chase, and he liked to at last be doing something. He was taking action. The deed to Stonemoor was in his pocket and he had Abby by his side.

"You will not regret this, Abby," he said, skillfully darting the phaeton around a brewer's dray. He cut in front a bit too closely this time. The driver yelled and shook his fist. Andres laughed, knowing he had complete control.

"I already do regret it," Abby said, sounding weak. "Please, Barón —"

"You should call me Andres," he said. "We are to be man and wife, and that is what should be done."

"If you don't stop this vehicle, nothing will happen," she informed him.

He scowled, not liking her threat — until he looked at her. Abby appeared ready to pass out.

"Hold on," he said. "You are going to be sick, but you will feel better —"

"I can't be sick here," she worried. "Please, let me off this thing . . ."

Andres turned down a side road. The neighborhood was a bit seedy. It was just as well. The moment the vehicle stopped, Abby started to climb down, but she didn't make it. She was very ill for a moment, right on the street.

Andres rubbed her back. "You will feel better now."

She looked around at him with an offended expression. "I've never done such a thing in my life. Not ever."

"It's the motion. It has not set well with you."

She nodded, her eyes troubled.

"You will be better," he promised.

"I need to climb to the ground," she claimed. She would have done so, but he put his arm around her waist. She had a trim waist, but one couldn't always tell with the style of dresses, and she looked a bit heftier than he last remembered.

"We must go on," he said.

"I can't. The motion." She shook her head in distress.

"I hired a coach. It's waiting for us at the Rose and Lion, an inn outside Edgeware."

"Is that far?" she asked, misery in her eyes.

"Not too far," he hedged.

Abby sighed her relief. "I was so afraid you were going to drive me all the way to

Scotland like this."

"We could not do that," he assured her. "The drive is a good two days, traveling without stop. I can't stay awake that long."

Her eyes took on an arrested expression. "I'd wondered about how long it would take to reach the border, but I hadn't worried about it," she said half to herself.

"But I did," Andres hurried to say. "Trust me, Abby. What you are doing is a very good thing for me. I will not let you down. I will always take care of you."

She studied him a moment as if uncertain whether or not to believe him. The color was returning to her complexion, and he knew part of her concern was embarrassment.

"You have never been on your own, have you?" he asked.

"No."

"You will like it," he promised. "I know this isn't a good start, but you have an adventurous spirit."

"Why do you say that?" she wondered.

"It is your hair," he remarked, smiling. He reached out and touched one of her silky, springy curls. "A woman with hair like this cannot be shy about life. Here, let me help you with your bonnet."

In all the commotion, the ribbons on her

bonnet had come free, and the hat was about to fall to the ground. He secured the horses' reins, then turned back to her to find that she had set the wide-brimmed hat in place so it framed her face. Her hands were shaking, whether from being ill or just the tension of the situation itself. Gently, he moved her hands away from the ribbons and tied them into a bow himself, taking a second to fluff it up properly.

"Thank you," she murmured, watching him, as if surprised that he would do such a thing.

He smiled at her. She was going to be his *wife.*

"It is my role to take care of you," he said.

She lowered her head as if digesting this and then nodded. "We take care of each other," she murmured.

"Man and wife," he said — and those words made him feel good.

They imbued him with a sense of rightness, of power.

She must have felt something of the same, because slowly, her lips curved into a smile. He smiled back . . . and almost kissed her. It would be so easy to just lean down and place a kiss right there on the tip of her nose. A silly kiss.

A familiar one.

Andres hadn't thought of a kiss that way. There had always been the intent of seduction, and he wouldn't mind seducing Abby. In fact, he planned to — it was just that at that very moment, he discovered he was the one being seduced, and in a way he'd not experienced before —

Startled, he broke the moment, leaning back.

She noticed the gesture, looked away.

Feeling clumsy, another emotion not common to him, Andres picked up the reins. "We must be going."

Abby nodded.

"Your stomach? It will be fine?"

"I hope so," she answered with her usual candor, and Andres couldn't help but laugh.

The laughter broke the tension between them. Abby wasn't afraid to laugh at herself. He thought it good. Too many women were deadly serious about themselves, and he realized Abby pleased him.

He wasn't daffy in love with her the way he'd been with Gillian, but he felt comfortable around her.

Andres began the task of turning the phaeton around in the narrow street. He knew how to make the turn, and the horses were well trained enough to understand what needed to be done.

However, Abby stopped him by clamping her hand on his arm. "Barón, halt." She stared toward Oxford Street. "My father."

Andres whipped his head around just in time to see a town coach drive past the intersecting street. Banker Montross stood in the boot, frowning at the road ahead as he strained in search for them. He didn't look down the side street.

"That's my coach," she whispered. "The one I took to the circulating library. I told them to drive around the square, and they must have picked him up. What do we do now?"

"We take a different route," Andres said and drove the horses down the narrow street. He didn't know this area, but a few answers from passersby put him on a route that would lead to the Rose and Lion.

"He's going to hunt us down," Abby said quietly, one hand holding the rail by her seat, the other gripping the small cloth bag she'd brought with her. Though she was holding on so tightly that her knuckles were white, she seemed more settled now that he wasn't traveling so fast or weaving around the traffic.

"This will hurt both of my parents," she continued.

"You have challenged them," he corrected.

"Your father is not one to let matters go."

"He'll chase us all the way to Scotland," she agreed. "And when he catches me, he'll be furious. He's never been angry at me before. He wants me to marry Lord Villier. He thinks it is important."

"If you were a princess, I could see some urgency that you marry one sort of man over another. But your father is a banker."

"A *very important* banker." She frowned at him. "And Lord Villier has a leading position in the Treasury."

"So you want to marry him?" Andres said, annoyed at this conversation. It made him feel second best.

"No, I don't." She drew a breath and released it with a disgruntled sound. "I just wish everything had been different."

"And that you are marrying Freddie, the Fop?" Andres muttered, a bit surprised by the stab of jealousy.

She didn't answer, at least not right away.

The road was not crowded here. Andres was glad they had not taken the Post Road as he'd originally planned. Her father would be looking for them there.

"He's not a fop," she said at last.

"Took you a moment to defend him," Andres observed.

Her brows came together. He did like that

hat on her. She looked quite adorable in it.

"I don't believe that I should have to," she murmured. "He's not mine."

"Good of you to realize it," Andres muttered. But she had feelings for him . . . and Andres realized that once again he'd involved himself with a woman who loved another man.

But he wouldn't fall in love with this one.

The light traveling coach was waiting as he'd ordered in the Rose and Lion's yard. Andres paid a driver, who was also one of Holburn's grooms, to return the phaeton to the duke's stables. He had packed a full bag for the trip and had attempted to include items Abby might need as well, knowing she would not be able to leave her house with too much in tow.

He'd had the inn prepare a basket of food, which was tucked inside the coach, along with some small pillows and blankets for comfort. It would be their traveling home for the next few days.

Abby had taken herself into the inn to freshen up. Pleased that everything was ready for their trip, Andres went in search of her. He found her sitting alone at a table in the inn's common room. Her indecision irritated him.

"Do you want to stay?" Andres wondered.

His question appeared to surprise her. "You need me. You need my inheritance."

He sat at the table. "I do. I have to admit I have already spent a good portion of it."

"You have?"

"Yes. The stables need equipment, more horses. Some things we could buy here in London and not up there. I do not know what the north is like."

"I don't either," she confessed.

"I made the decision and ordered supplies," he said, conscious he was spending her money, wondering what she was thinking. "It is exciting, isn't it?" he said.

Her clear, honest eyes took his measure. "A little. A bit frightening as well."

"Are you coming with me, Miss Montross?" he asked, uncertain what her answer would be.

For a second, she appeared ready to say no . . . but then she slowly nodded her head. "I am my father's daughter," she said. "I think I will like taking charge of my own fate." She smiled. "Fate. That word. How many times did you use it yesterday to convince me, and now I'm the one to bring it up."

"Then let me give you a new word, Abby. *Courage.*"

Confidence returned to her smile. "I know

that word." She stood, holding her bag with both hands. "Let us go."

That was all he needed to hear. Andres was not going to give her a moment more to change her mind. He took her arm and guided her out of the inn. They settled themselves in the coach, and with a snap of their driver's whip, they were on their way.

This vehicle was not as well sprung as even the phaeton. It had been for hire, so the interior was cramped and the bench seat was practical but not comfortable.

Andres had a bit of trouble stretching his legs out. He tried to be respectful and leave Abby half of the coach, but it was not possible.

"You can put your legs across here," she said, resting her own feet next to the food basket.

"You will not be uncomfortable?" he murmured.

"I'll be fine."

He used her space.

She leaned against the coach's glass window, seemingly watching the passing scenery. "I shall have to become accustomed to people staring at you," she said.

"I beg your pardon?"

Abby turned to him. "I was watching you cross the commons toward me in the inn.

Even men look at you. Ladies most definitely do. All of them — young, old, middling years."

"So they look at me."

She frowned as if he didn't understand what she was saying. "It's your looks. You are tall and handsome, strikingly so. It's quite intimidating."

He laughed. "Intimidating? Do I scare people?"

"I believe you are so handsome, you catch them off guard. Your features are too regular, almost refined."

"You make me sound like a woman," he grumbled.

"When I first met you in my uncle's library, I knew you were of good looks, but I wouldn't have stared at you. I don't know why."

"I noticed you."

That caught her interest. "You did?"

"I like your hair." He reached over and playfully pulled the bow undone. "Take your hat off."

Knowing Abby as he did now, he was aware she could refuse him.

She didn't. She untied her bonnet ribbons and removed the hat. Her curls formed a halo around her head.

"In Italy, I saw paintings of the Madonna,

and her hair was much like yours. Vibrant, alive." He had to touch one of her curls.

"I know so little about you," she said. "Why were you in Italy?"

Andres wasn't certain he wanted her to know the truth. But a little of it would not be bad. "I have a sister there. She is married to some Italian count I do not like."

"That is sad."

"No, it is not," he said with a shake of his head. "My sister is a jealous woman. She and I are not close."

"I have two brothers," she said. "They serve with Wellington."

"Brave men."

"The bravest," she agreed. "I'm the youngest of the family and some say a bit of an afterthought. I did have a third brother, but Robert was with Nelson. He died at Trafalgar."

"I'm sorry." Andres meant the words and then heard himself say, "My brother died at Trafalgar, fighting on the other side."

She tilted her head, her expression grim.

He had to explain so she didn't misunderstand in the way Lord Dobbins had painted the story. "My father didn't support an alliance with the French. He did not trust Napoleon or the French, and he was right. Emilio was an officer. He had no choice in the matter. It made Father more angry that his son was not in the calvary. A man on the ground has more chances to survive than one on the water." Emilio had not shared their father's love of horses. That had been Andres's gift.

She nodded, as if hearing what he hadn't said. "My parents, all of us, were distraught when we received word of Robert's death. It wasn't right that he should die so young, even for a noble cause. To avenge him, my brothers bought their colors. Father wonders why none of his sons wish to take up his profession. Why they have to put their lives in danger."

As she spoke, memories of Emilio, a man he'd barely known, rose in his mind, memories he'd thought buried. He'd grown up in the village, had known all the family on sight. Everyone had known he'd been the old baron's son, even his tutors — but they hadn't spoken of it. Not even his *abuela,* his grandmother, who had raised him.

And then one day, his father had come for him. One son had been killed. He'd been left with the bastard.

Andres had dreamed of the day his father would claim him. In the end, he'd not been enough. It had been Emilio his father had wanted. Only Emilio.

"After my brother's death, my father was angry with grief and spoke out against the French and those who supported them," Andres said. "It's dangerous in Spain to speak your mind — especially since so many of the peasants agreed with him. A Spanish peasant can be prouder than any three of your dukes. Those in power could not let him continue, not unless they wanted a revolt."

"Did something happen to your father?" she asked.

"They broke him," Andres answered. "They took all he had left, his land and his horses." He looked away, not wanting to add more, not wanting to tell her his father had also taken his own life. "He gave up . . . but I won't. I will recover what is ours."

"That's why the stables at Stonemoor are so important to you," she said.

"Yes, and the mare Holburn is keeping for me. She's the return of a great line of horses."

"Tell me about Stonemoor," she said. "Describe it to me again."

He started talking without any hesitation. He saw the estate in his mind. The greenness of its pastures, the size and cleanliness of the stables, his vision of what the house would be.

She asked questions, staying on her side in the cramped confines of the coach.

Andres found himself embellishing his ideas — just for her. He pulled upon memories of homes he'd visited, English homes — sturdy, safe places — and she seemed eager for every word.

He liked himself around her.

The thought caught him unawares. It came unbidden on its own, yet the truth of it resonated through his being. He was fated to meet her.

Slowly, he began believing that himself.

Abby fell asleep listening to him talk. Or maybe he fell asleep first, she wasn't certain.

She liked the sound of his accented English. She couldn't wait to see Stonemoor. To see this place that so obviously filled him with pride. She started to picture herself there, dreaming of moving through its gardens. Rose gardens, that is what he'd said, and she dreamed of them, with their big, full roses full of petals velvet to the touch.

They both woke when the coach pulled into the first inn yard for a change of horses. They didn't stay long. Andres — yes, she could think of him as Andres now — was anxious to return to the road. He was certain her father would chase them.

Abby didn't know if her father was angry enough; he might write her off completely.

"I think it was my Tabitha that gave me away," she said as they dined over the cold chicken, cheese and bread sandwiches, and other good things in the basket.

"More wine?" Andres asked.

She shook her head. The wine tasted good, but she was amazed at how tiring travel could be. "If I drink more, I will sleep."

"Why do you think it was the maid?" Andres asked.

"Just a feeling I had. And it would make sense. It was my unfortunate luck that she opened that drawer before I left." She chewed a moment and then confessed, "I pray my parents will forgive me."

If Andres had been Freddie, he would have laughed away her concerns. *His* parents carried great weight with him, but he was always discouraging of hers.

Andres was more thoughtful. "They will be upset," he said. "We shall contact them after we reach Stonemoor and invite them for a visit."

"That would be good," Abby said. "Or we could return to London and see them."

"Possibly," he agreed, but there wasn't

much conviction in the word.

She looked at him sharply. It was dark outside, and he had lit the single oil lamp in the coach. "You don't sound as if you'd like to," she said.

A shadow crossed his face, a concern. He caught her watching him. "There will be many things to command my attention with the stables," he said.

It was a plausible reason.

She didn't know why she didn't believe it was completely the truth . . . or was that another outcome of having loved Freddie? He'd made so many claims to her. He'd said he'd loved her, but he'd always had a reason to not act upon that love.

Perhaps her suspicion of Andres was nothing more than her disappointment with Freddie.

Then again, the Spaniard could be a cold character when he wished.

"Every thought you possess crosses your face," Andres said to her.

"And what was I thinking?" she questioned.

"That you are not certain of me."

Abby sat back, rattled by his accuracy.

"I don't know if I like being close to someone who reads me so well," she whispered. "Especially when I have a hard time knowing what you are thinking."

He shrugged, pulled back — and she realized he always moved away.

Andres had secrets.

The random thought was disquieting. She knew so little about him, and what she knew was mostly rumor from women who were so batty-eyed over him that they'd lost all sensibility and decorum.

And here she'd put herself in his hands.

"You can trust me," he said. "I will never hurt you. I am your protector."

"And what does that mean?" she asked. Their faces were no more than a hand's width apart, and she found herself staring at his mouth, noticing how masculine, how sensual his lips were.

Those lips curved into a smile.

Oh, yes, he knew what she was thinking.

"It means this," he whispered — and leaned toward her for a kiss.

CHAPTER NINE

Andres hovered a second over her lips, savoring the *yearning* for a kiss and the sharp, sweet feeling of desire.

He was hard, had been for some time while watching her at the simplest of tasks — the way she held her glass or tasted the cheese before deciding whether or not she liked it.

She didn't think she was beautiful.

He did.

Even more amazing, the longer he knew her, the more he *liked* her.

He moved to take the kiss —

Suddenly she turned her head away, ducking.

Andres pulled back in time. Otherwise he would have foolishly kissed her hair or an ear. "What is the matter?"

"I don't think that wise," she said.

Andres had never had a woman refuse his kiss.

Beyond his immediate annoyance was confusion. "Why not?" he asked, his voice harsh with lust.

She reacted to that tone, her back stiffening. "I'm not ready yet." Her eyes were pleading as she looked up at him. "Can you understand? I know we must consummate the marriage . . . but everything has happened so fast. I need just a bit more time."

Andres leaned back into his corner of the coach. Their knees touched. The interior was so close that they couldn't help but be constantly aware of each other. *Time.* He'd never had a woman ask for patience.

He took in her high cheekbones, that mouth he'd wanted to kiss, her curves — and decided he could wait.

Abby was a woman of substance.

"Talk to me," she said.

"About what?"

"Tell me of your mother," she answered. "Was she a strong woman or quiet? Did she have a pet name for you?"

The question startled a laugh out of him. The only "mother" he'd truly remembered with pet names for him had been the contessa de Vasconia, a woman as spiteful as her daughter. And her names for him were not ones fit to share with Abby. His father had protected him from her only to a certain point. And his birth mother had been young and kept by a series of men.

But Abby didn't need that story.

He began telling of a mother who was actually probably very much like her own. A mother who cared for her children.

Abby fell asleep listening to him talk. Only then did he realize how long he'd gone on. She slept as if she was exhausted.

He put away what was left of their dinner.

The air was growing colder in the coach. They'd spread the blankets over their legs, and the small pillows softened the hardness of the leather seats for their backs, but Andres did not think she looked comfortable slumped in her corner the way she was.

He reached over and gently pulled her to him.

She gave a start, much like a sleeping babe does when startled, but then she settled back into sleep. She was slumbering so deeply that he wondered if she'd slept at all the night before. He'd been excited but had not anticipated she would be.

More certain of himself this time, he brought her over to rest her head on his chest. Her body molded to his with the languidness of a sleeping cat. He stretched his legs out, taking most of the floor space in the coach, and tossed the blankets and his coat over both their laps for warmth. His booted feet stuck out from the bottom of the blankets, but he made certain she was covered.

Her hair curled around his arms and his hands. He liked that she'd worn it pulled back in a simple manner. He liked it styled high on her head as well.

And he enjoyed the weight of Abby in his arms. *Palomita.* His little dove. She was bringing so much more than her inheritance and her person to this marriage. She was also offering a sense of peace.

Andres caught himself smiling, even as he fell asleep.

Abby didn't wake at all during the night. Her first conscious thought was in the thin light of morning.

She woke, stretching and arching her back as she always did, and found herself on top of the baron's hard body. She froze, uncertain.

He was still asleep.

A blanket had been pulled over them, as well as his warm, heavy greatcoat. His body heat had kept her warm throughout the night, and she wasn't ready to leave it.

Instead, she used this moment to look her fill at this man she'd agreed to marry. He didn't seem so distant and cold now — or as composed. The shadow of his beard made him appear less perfect. More human.

The barón had a small scar right above the left corner of his upper lip. She'd not noticed it before, but now it stood out against the stubble of his beard. She wondered how he'd received it.

And he was starting to wrinkle. There were laugh lines around his mouth, although he didn't laugh often. He also had lines at the corners of his eyes from being in the sun.

He might be a barón, but he'd not had an easy life. She'd noticed that his hands were not white and soft, like those of so many of the noblemen from the Continent. He'd worked hard at one time.

Perhaps they'd gained their strength and callouses from working with horses.

Or dueling. She knew the rumors. This man-who-was-to-be-her-husband was said to be a crack shot and a formidable swordsman.

But she was learning he could also be kind.

His arms rested easily around her waist. He'd joined his hands, and they formed a loose-fitting bond. She lowered her head to rest it against the hard muscles of his chest.

He'd untied his neck cloth, and his shirt collar was open. She listened to the steady rhythm of his heart. Within minutes, it seemed as if her heart beat in time with his.

He moved, a sound rumbling in his chest. "You are awake?" he said, his voice deep with sleep.

"I am." She pushed away from him and he let her go. She went from being warm and comfortable in his arms to feeling disheveled and brain-muddled.

He rubbed his eyes as he pulled a watch from his pocket and looked at it. The case was not a fancy one, nor ornate and solid gold, as was her father's. But then, Andres was impressing her with how practical he was.

Her father's vow that he wanted a man like himself for her came back to her. She wondered if perhaps she had found one.

The thought was so outrageous that it made her smile. Imagine her father being compared to the rake of the Season.

"What?" he asked, then ran a hand over his unshaven jaw. "Me? I know. I'm a sight."

"I am as well," she confessed.

He shook his head, his silver eyes appreciative. "No, *palomita,* you are beautiful."

"Palomita." She tasted the word. "You've called me that before. What does it mean?"

177

"Dove." He smiled, as if self-conscious. "It is not so bad, no?"

"You are calling me a bird and think I should be flattered?"

Laughter came to his eyes as he said, "I could call you *loraita*."

"What does that mean?"

"My little parrot. Another kind of bird —"

"I know what a parrot is. Jonesy, my aunt, has one. He's a mouthy, rude creature."

"Whereas a dove is soft and gentle," he observed, holding up his hands as a sign that he was teasing about the parrot. "She brings a sense of peace wherever she goes."

Abby melted. "And you think that of me? No one has ever compared me to something so lovely."

"It's the hair," he predicted. "Red hair makes people think you are spicy and stubborn."

"I can be," she allowed.

"Then I shall keep you happy so that you remain peaceful," he promised. "Besides, in some places in Spain, redheads are thought to be so wicked that if you pass one in the street you are to spit on the ground and turn around. One should never cross a redhead."

For a woman who was rather self-conscious and worried that her hair made her stand out, his admiration eased long-standing doubts. "I haven't seen you spit yet," she challenged.

"That is because I am not a superstitious man. And I like vibrant women."

Vibrant. The word made her feel beautiful. The shield of pride and doubt Abby wore began to disappear. In its place grew a tiny sprout of trust.

"You'll do," she said. "You might very well be an excellent husband."

"You'll do, as well," he echoed, reaching up to brush her unruly curls back from her face, letting them slide through his fingers.

If he'd tried to kiss her then, she would have let him.

To her disappointment, he didn't.

Instead, he said, "We changed horses in the middle of the night, but it is about time that we should change them again." He started to sit up, and she had no choice but to take her place on the seat beside him.

The world was a cold place without his body heat.

He opened the window and questioned the driver about where they were. The driver called down that they were coming up on the inn where the barón had scheduled the next stop and would arrive in a few minutes.

Andres closed the window and began

repairing his wardrobe. He retrieved his neck cloth from where he'd folded it and looped it around his neck, his fingers deftly tying it into the knot Freddie had admired so much.

"You hardly gave that any thought," she observed.

"Gave what any thought?" He combed his hair back with his fingers.

"Your famous knot in your neck cloth."

Her comment made him laugh. Some men chuckled, some giggled — a sound Abby thought silly — and some just smiled, never unbending to open themselves up to laughter. Abby had thought the barón would be one of the latter.

He now proved himself to be one of the rare men who enjoyed a good, hearty laugh. He shook his head. "I don't know what they are talking about when they say special knots. I tie it so it looks decent." He shrugged. "And I started a craze."

The coach was starting to slow down. Abby took a moment to put herself in order.

Looking out the window, the barón said, "I think we shall rest here a bit. Perhaps have our breakfast?"

"I would like that very much." The idea sounded like heaven to Abby, who reached for her embroidered bag with her small stash of personal items.

"I packed a few things you might need," he offered, and retrieved his bag from under the boot. He had tooth polish and soap and a good brush. Abby tucked them into her bag.

"Is it possible I could use a part of your valise?" she asked, then confessed she was wearing several layers of clothing.

He laughed. "I thought you looked plump. Of course we will share."

Because that was what a man and wife did, she realized, pleased.

Fortunately, the inn was not busy this early in the morning. When they arrived, they were met by a driver who had been hired to take over for the one they'd had. The barón told him to see to the horses while they enjoyed their morning meal.

Inside, Andres hired a room for their use. "You freshen up first," he told Abby.

"How much time do we have?" she asked.

He shrugged. "The weather seems as if it will hold out. We've traveled fast. An hour or two should not be bad. I'll have the innkeeper send up hot water."

Abby happily agreed. A half hour later, she felt like a new woman.

The barón then took advantage of the room while she sat in front of the fire in the common room, sipping strong black tea. The barón did not take as long as she had, but when he came down the stairs, he was freshly shaved and, to her eyes, more handsome than ever.

At the foot of the stairs, he paused and took a moment to look at the coins in his pocket.

She hadn't thought about money. She'd left all the arrangements to him, as she would have to her father. But now she felt a touch guilty. The man was marrying her for money because he admittedly didn't have much. She sensed he knew the value of a coin, as well as how to be frugal — something she'd not had to think on.

Well, as soon as they were married, he'd not have to worry again.

The barón spoke a few words to the innkeeper before crossing the room to join her.

"Is everything all right?" she asked.

He seemed taken aback, as if he sensed she'd caught him counting his shillings. "Yes, of course. I spoke for our breakfast. And I see you have tea?"

"Yes, let me pour you a cup," she offered, not wanting any awkwardness between them.

The barón had good looks, but the things

182

about him that stood out in her mind were his manners, his kindness, his earnestness.

Breakfast was a leisurely affair. They shared likes and dislikes about food. He was not fond of any green vegetable. She couldn't abide fish. Small pieces of information that people who were married knew about each other.

They were on the road again before she wished it. Andres had brought along a deck of cards, and they passed the time that way. In fact, Abby was having so much fun that she began wondering if she ever wanted the ride to come to an end.

They were scheduled to arrive in Scotland late the next morning. Their stops grew longer. They enjoyed a good dinner together when they changed horses and drivers for the evening.

This time, when they prepared to sleep, he reached for her to snuggle against him — and she didn't hesitate.

Andres. His name was romantic. It rolled off her tongue. She didn't think she'd ever tire of saying it.

And she liked the way he said her name — his accent harder on the first syllable. His *palomita.*

The next morning was much colder than the first. They'd reached Yorkshire. The

Scottish border was only hours away. Over breakfast, Andres asked the innkeeper if he had ever heard of Stonemoor, adding, "It's close to Newcastle."

"No, can't say I have," the innkeeper answered, his broad North English accent almost harder for Abby to understand than Andres's Spanish one. "Newcastle is a right far distance from here." He hurried on with his duties of serving the other party of patrons at the table across the small room from them.

Andres leaned across the table toward Abby. "What did he say?"

She laughed and interpreted. "They say some Scots have accents so thick, their English is unintelligible."

"Just so we understand the priest," Andres commented.

The word "priest" caught her. "Are you Catholic?"

He shrugged. "There is only one religion in Spain."

"Are you religious?" Abby had not thought about these things. She did know some Catholics. They seemed no different from herself.

"I believe in *el buen Dios* — the good Lord," he said.

"As do I," Abby agreed.

Their eyes met, their gazes held. He understood what she was thinking when he said, "We are not so different, are we?"

"I think not."

"And we shall look at what is common between us instead of the differences."

Abby nodded . . . and that was when she started to fall in love.

Her attraction to Andres, her growing feelings for him, were different from what she'd had for Freddie. Her love for him had been intense, frantic, uncertain.

What she felt for Andres was trust and a belief he meant the words he said to her.

A great weight seemed to lift from her shoulders. She'd had doubts. She knew she'd jumped rashly into this agreement between them . . . but it was a gamble that she was beginning to believe was the wisest of her life.

And she thought he felt the same. There was more warmth in his eyes when he looked at her. He'd started a habit of placing his hand not only on her arm but also resting it lightly on her waist, even in front of strangers.

"How much longer do we have until we reach Scotland?" she asked.

"The driver told me three, maybe four hours."

"I suggest we should be going then," she said.

His lips curved into a grin. "Yes, we must," he agreed, rising from the table and offering his arm.

They put on their coats and hats and started for the door, but Abby stopped, hearing a gruff, demanding voice that sounded all too familiar.

"I say, innkeeper! Where are you?"

She pulled back, grabbing hold of Andres's coat. *"My father."*

Her warning came in enough time for them both to step back out of his view.

"Innkeeper!" her father called again. "I need a change of horses." He muttered something to someone with him.

"Who is he with?" Andres wondered.

"Probably Mr. Vaughn, his secretary," Abby whispered. "He often travels with him."

The other patrons of the inn were looking up from their breakfasts with interest.

"I'm going to talk to him," Andres decided.

Abby grabbed his arm. "No. He's here to stop us." And she didn't want that.

Her life was now interesting. She understood that. Two days ago, she'd had nothing to look forward to, nothing that had piqued her curiosity or challenged her intellect.

Andres and his dreams had changed her. "If you talk to him, he will take me back to London," she promised, speaking in a whisper because she didn't want the other guests to overhear.

"Do you not want his blessing?" Andres asked.

"If I thought I could have it, I wouldn't have eloped," Abby answered. "Do you want Stonemoor or not?"

His response was to grab her hand and race over to the window near the fireplace. He threw it open. "Come along."

Abby sat on the sill. Munching their sausages and toasted bread, the other guests watched with open curiosity as Abby ducked out the window and slipped out. The ground was cold and hard here, the window guarded by a holly bush. She stepped out of the way, seeing her father's lightest traveling coach in front of the inn's door.

Andres put his leg over the sill, his hat in one hand. But before he could pull his body through, there was a shout.

"Stop that man."

Her father had discovered them.

CHAPTER TEN

Andres didn't waste time looking over his shoulder. He heard Banker Montross's voice and he jumped through the window, landing on a damned difficult bush. His hat fell out of his hands. He didn't care. He grabbed Abby's arm and went running for their coach.

She was right in step beside him.

Their new driver had been leaning against the coach, talking to several other men in the inn yard. With a fresh team of horses, Andres believed they could make it to the border before her father could stop them.

He shouted to the driver. "Climb into the box. Drive out of here with haste, man."

The driver had given a start when he saw them coming. When one of the men he was talking to said something to him, a look of confusion passed across his face.

Andres reached the coach. He threw open the door, letting Abby climb in as he shot out a hand and grabbed his driver by the throat. "If he told you to ignore my order, you'd best not listen to him."

The driver nodded, his eyes wide and his face red. Andres let go of his hold. "And I'll double your price if we beat him to the Scottish border," he added.

Those words performed magic. The driver swung up into the box even as the inn's front door opened and Banker Montross came running out into the yard.

"Hold, I say," the banker yelled. *"Hold."*

But the driver obeyed Andres's orders. Two fellows tried to grab hold of the horses, but with a hard crack of the whip, the animals jumped into action.

Fortunately, Andres still had hold of the door, or he would have been thrown to the ground and left behind. He swung inside the coach, slamming the door shut behind him.

The horses picked up speed. Both Andres and Abby were rocked and tossed by the racing coach. He put his arms around her, trying as much as he could to shield her from being thrown around. She responded by putting her arms around him.

The driver called down to them. "He's following us, sir."

"Outrun him," Andres ordered.

"This mustn't go on," Abby said. She was extremely pale. "I didn't think he'd follow this quickly. He had to have traveled harder and faster than we did."

"He wants you back."

She nodded, then tightened her hold. "I'm afraid," she whispered. "If something happens to him because of my actions —"

"Don't think on it," Andres warned. "Our horses are fresh. His aren't."

"How can you be certain?"

"If he is this close to us, he didn't take the time to change teams. We'll outdistance him."

"He won't give up," she predicted.

"Then we shall stay ahead of him," Andres answered.

And they did. The road was good here and the traffic light at this time of year and this time of day. Their driver also had a skilled hand. It would cost Andres almost everything he owned to pay the man off, but he was worth it.

What pleased Andres most was that Abby had not wavered in her loyalty to him. Many women had wanted him in their lives, but at little sacrifice to themselves.

Abby was offering all. Her trust, her belief in him, was humbling.

As they rode, heading madly for the

border, he silently vowed she would not regret her decision. He would protect and keep her. It was his duty, a sacred obligation —

The coach slowed down.

Andres released Abby and threw down the window. "What is the matter?" he called to the driver.

"There is no need to race," the man answered. "The lads following us had an accident."

Abby heard his words and gave out a sharp cry. "*Stop.* We must stop."

The driver was already coming to a halt by the side of the road. "Give me a second, my lady," he said. "Have to let the horses walk."

But Abby wasn't having any of that. She crawled over Andres's lap and was attempting to open the door even before the coach came to a halt. Andres put his arm around her waist, holding her back lest she fall out of the coach.

"Please," she begged.

"A moment, a moment," he whispered. Once it was safe, he opened the door.

She didn't wait for him to help her out but tumbled forward. The coach was on a high knoll that overlooked a valley. They could see the road behind them to where her father's coach lay on its side almost a mile behind them. His horses' frightened screams carried through the air to them.

Abby started to charge down the road, but Andres placed his hands on her shoulder, holding her in place.

"*Let go.* I must help him," she cried, trying to throw his hands free of her.

"He's all right," Andres said. "He's fine."

And he was. So were the horses. The coachman cut their traces and freed them. The frightened animals ran off into a wide circle, each urging the other on. Andres knew they would stop once they sensed they were safe.

Banker Montross and his associate had both climbed out of the coach. They dropped to the ground and took tentative steps, as if testing for injuries.

"*Papa,*" Abby cried, the sound echoing throughout the valley in the morning air.

Her father looked in her direction. He began walking up the road toward them. Abby shook off Andres's hands and started down the hill, but she stopped after a few steps.

Her body stiffened; her chest heaved with anxiety.

She turned to Andres, her expression anguished, tears streaming down her cheeks.

"He could have been killed," she said. "Because of me."

"But he is alive —" Andres pointed out. She cut him off with a sharp gesture of her hand, her attention already returned to the man moving up the hill toward them.

"If I go to him," she said, her voice tense with indecision, "he will take me back. I'll return to everything the way it was."

Andres needed her. He needed her money, but he was also beginning to need her trust in him. He wanted to say something to call her back . . . but he couldn't. She had to choose him on her own. He didn't know why he felt this, when he would be completely ruined without her . . . and yet he stood silent, waiting, wanting —

"I can't," she whispered, as if horrified with herself. "I can't return. I don't want to. I've hurt them." She looked to Andres for understanding. "I've hurt my parents and I didn't want to. That was never my intent."

She glanced back at her father. He'd obviously banged his leg up a bit, because he'd started to limp as he made his way toward them. His associate, Mr. Vaughn, had started to follow him. The coachman stayed with the horses, which had come to a halt as Andres had predicted.

"But I can't return," she said. "I've come too far."

She walked toward Andres, her head down. He gathered her in his arms, leading her to the coach and helping her in. "Take us to Gretna," he ordered the driver, who nodded his obedience. Gretna Green was the village located right across the Scottish border known for the number of quick marriages performed there.

The minute Andres seated himself and closed the door, Abby fell into his arms, sobbing.

He hadn't comforted many people in his life. He hadn't been the sort others had looked to for advice or support. He'd been the outsider, the loner.

But not now.

Her conflict, her *pain* in making her choice, tore at his heart.

Especially since she had chosen him. No one had ever done that.

He tightened his hold on her.

Her crying was soon spent. She brought it to a close, sniffing and trying to put herself back together. She moved, as if needing her freedom, and he released his hold. Abby tilted her face toward him. Their lips were inches from each other. He wanted to kiss her but sensed now was not the time. Not when she was so fragile.

"I love them," she said.

His throat tightened. "They know that," he murmured.

"I hope they do."

"The child *must* leave the parent."

She lifted her shoulders as if not wanting to believe him, but then let them relax with a resigned nod of her head. "I wish it was less painful."

"I think you are blessed to have a father who cares so much."

Abby had heard what he hadn't said, what he hadn't completely realized he'd admitted — and he realized he was the fragile one. She was strong compared to him.

Brave. Courageous.

He'd asked so much of her.

"I promise you will see them soon," he said. "And this is not a bad choice, Abby. I feel it is the right one."

Those clear blue eyes of hers studied him a moment as if they could see all the way to his mind, his heart, his soul. Slowly, she nodded her head. "That's what makes this so painful. I *am* doing what I choose to do. But I hate hurting those who love me so well and whom I love deeply in return."

Andres tasted panic. How could he measure up to what she'd just said? He'd never had anyone love him. Not the way her parents cared for her.

And then she smiled. There was nothing in the world more loving, more beautiful, than Abby's smile. It carried such trust, such belief. It swelled his chest with pride . . . because she was now including him in her life.

His arm still rested around her waist. He pulled her closer to her. "You will not be sorry," he promised. "You will *not* be sorry."

She nodded, his jacket held in her fists.

In this manner, holding each other tight, they pulled into the village of Gretna Green.

The coach came to a halt. A moment later, their driver opened the door. "We're here, my lord." He all but held out his hand for the promised double payment.

Andres climbed out. Abby busied herself putting on her bonnet, giving him a moment to settle with the driver.

Andres's coin purse was growing lighter. He didn't have much left and prayed he had enough money to pay the clergy.

"The anvil priest I'd recommend is over in that guesthouse there," the driver said. "They can do the ceremony in a blink, and for an extra guinea they'll give you a room to finish the job, if'n you know what I mean." He winked in case Andres had any doubts. "David Laing's his name. His wife keeps the room. Nice and clean. You can have a good breakfast in the morning, too. Man needs that, doesn't he?"

"Anvil priest?" Andres repeated, not understanding.

"Up here, the blacksmiths are the best at marriages. Anyone can tell you so."

Abby had come to the coach door. She had her bonnet and coat on and carried the bag she'd had since she'd met Andres at the circulating library. Andres helped her down. Her face was still too pale, but she seemed at peace.

"In Scotland, you don't need clergy," Abby explained. "All that is asked for is a witness."

Seeing Andres's surprise at her knowledge, she smiled. "I learned this from the stories my parents told of when they eloped. The old duke was not about to give the hand of his favorite daughter in marriage to a poor banker."

"And so they ran away," Andres said, taking her hand and placing it on his arm.

"Yes, and had no regrets," she answered. "I plan to feel the same."

The house that the driver had directed them to was a white cottage. The overcast day had grown darker. It was afternoon, but one would think it evening. This was what Andres had assumed Scotland would be. Dreary and dull. Not exactly his choice for a wedding.

The driver fell into step behind them. Andres learned why when they reached the cottage gate and the woman who greeted them called to the driver by name. "Hey, there now, John Whitacre. Who have you brought to us?"

Whitacre mugged a face at Andres's raised eyebrows. "A man has to make a living, my lord. Besides, you need more than one witness, don't you?" Whitacre said.

"Aye, John's a good witness," the woman said. "And he won't cost you much."

Andres could have told her he'd already cost him plenty, but he held his tongue in front of Abby.

David Laing turned out to be a former soldier who worked as a blacksmith and performed marriages. Andres thought it an odd combination, but apparently it was the way things were done here.

Laing was happy to marry them for what he assured them was a very good price. "To be honest," he said in his roguish brogue, "business has been a wee bit slow since the days have been shorter. After Christmas they will start marrying again. You know, once they can smell spring."

"I'll ready the chamber," the woman Andres assumed to be Mrs. Laing said. Her words brought color to Abby's cheeks, which was not such a bad thing.

Within the half hour, Andres found himself standing with Abby before Laing in the front room of Laing's low-ceilinged cottage. Both Andres and Abby had removed their coats and freshened up the best they could. A fire burned in the grate, and lanterns had been lit against the gloom.

Abby placed her gloved hand in Andres's. Mr. Laing began the ceremony. He started by asking for their names and addresses and if they were both single.

"Are you here of your own free will, miss?" Laing asked Abby.

"I am."

"Go ahead now and pay me then," Laing said. "Have her make the payment," he instructed Andres. Seeing Andres's frown at the suggestion, he explained, "If she pays, no one can come back later and claim she was married against her will."

It embarrassed Andres to have to pour out his meager hoard of coins and pass two guineas to Abby — one for Laing and the other for their witness, Whitacre.

She seemed as dazed about the whole affair as he. She paid and the ceremony continued. It was nothing fancy — certainly not as thorough and inspiring as the clergy would have given.

There was one awkward moment when Laing asked if there was a ring.

Andres felt like a fool. He had no ring. "I don't have one," he murmured.

The mood in the room changed. Laing and the witnesses didn't speak; this was an important detail, one that a man of means like the barón should have anticipated.

And he could feel himself drop in their esteem, sensed himself the bastard again.

"I have one." Abby let go of his hand and reached for the bag she'd been carrying.

Sitting in a side chair, she pulled off the kid gloves she still wore and reached into its depths, pulling out a velvet pouch. She shook the contents out in her lap. Gold gleamed in the room's lamplight.

She picked up a simple band and offered it to him. "It was my great-grandmother's, the mother of the one who left me my inheritance. The pin I'm wearing had been hers as well."

Andres took the ring while she put her jewelry back in her bag. The band was heavy in his hand.

Abby took her place next to him and gave

him a smile. "It is not the quality I would want you to have," he said quietly.

"This ring is solid. It has lasted one marriage, and God willing it will last another," she answered.

She humbled him. She was giving. From the moment they'd met, she'd thought the best of him.

He took her hand. He didn't wait for the blacksmith's words. He had words of his own. "With this ring, I promise that you shall never regret this day. I shall cherish you with all that I am and all that I own."

Her eyes grew watery, her smile inviting. Andres leaned down and took that kiss he'd so wanted.

He'd kissed many women. He'd done so gallantly, and frivolously, and without conviction or hope, and sometimes desire.

That was not the way this kiss was.

This kiss was a promise. But the moment their lips touched, the moment he felt her soften and mold to him, in that moment magic happened.

Andres brought his arms around *his wife.* He held her close as he opened himself to her. Her kiss turned eager, hopeful, trusting, and his grew hard, demanding, needy —

"I pronounce you man and wife," Laing

said, as if attempting to take control of the situation. "What God hath joined, let no man put asunder."

The kiss broke, but Andres was not going to let her go. Not now. Not ever.

Abby Montross *Ramigio* knew how to kiss. Her reaction had been instinctive. And he was wondering what other instinctive things she knew how to do, too.

He swung her up in his arms. Looking to Mrs. Laing, he said, "Our room."

"This way," she said, her eyes wide and merry with delight. She gave a little giggle as she led him down the hall to where the room had been prepared.

It was not a particularly well-appointed room, but it had a welcoming fire burning in the hearth, not of peat but of wood. A four-poster bed covered in a white counter-pane begged them to explore it. There were colorful rag rugs on the floor, and the blue curtains were closed against the approaching night.

"I'll have the girl bring your dinner to you —" Mrs. Laing said from the doorway, but Andres cut her off.

"Thank you," he said, his gaze on the lovely woman in his arms.

"She'll bring the tray in an hour —"

He kicked the door shut.

"That wasn't nice," Abby chastised him, but there was no heat in her words. If anything, she seemed as ready for this moment as he was.

He slowly lowered her feet to the ground. She leaned against his chest. Her nipples were hard.

Andres was hard all over . . . but he wanted to take his time. He was married. Yes, it had been a marriage of convenience, but he'd come to respect and admire this woman. In fact, she was far better than he deserved.

"Kiss me," she whispered. "Kiss me as you did in the other room."

He was happy to comply. Only this time, he kissed her the way he really wished to do so. This time he showed her his passion.

Her lips opened to his and she let him kiss her deeply and fully. Her hands came up to his shoulders. They hovered there a moment, and then she slid her arms around his neck and pulled him close.

Andres was seduced, his whole body alive with desire.

He began undressing her.

Abby showed no false modesty, and the thought came to him that just as he'd learned to admire her, perhaps she had come to admire him?

And as much as he didn't want to fall under love's spell, he certainly was a captive of lust.

His fingers knew how to unlace the back of her dress. He kissed her neck and the line of her jaw, delighting in discovering those special spots that made a woman forget herself.

Abby had many of them.

When his lips brushed her ear, she gasped and her hands began pulling at his coat as if to rip it off of him.

He was happy to help. He shrugged off the coat and began yanking at the knot in his neck cloth, not once letting his lips leave hers.

Her dress fell to the ground at their feet. She'd told him about the layers she'd worn, but he hadn't believed her until he saw her nightdress serving as a petticoat. It was a heavy cotton that hid all of her curves. He was anxious to see what lay beneath.

Tossing his neck cloth to the floor, he said, "Here, let me."

She dropped her hands to her sides. Her skin trembled as he slid first one arm and then the other down her shoulders. He pressed his lips against her skin, tasting his way along her shoulder.

Her head fell back with a shiver of pleasure. She was so responsive. So willing.

The nightdress slid down to her waist, exposing a camisole made of the finest lace and lawn. It was spread over firm breasts.

Andres had to touch them. *"Beya,"* he whispered. *"Beya, beya, beya."*

"What is that you said?" she asked, her voice breathless as he circled a tight nipple with the edge of his thumb.

"Beautiful."

She shook her head, her curls falling around her shoulders. He combed with his fingers, tilting her head up to him. "Yes, you are."

"You meant your words that night to Lady Dobbins?"

Andres laughed at the impossibility that she couldn't see the truth. "Yes," he said. "I've thought you lovely from the moment I met you, from when you attacked me in the library —"

"I *saved* you," she argued with a smile.

"Yes, you saved me," he agreed with complete seriousness. "You've saved me from so much, Abby. And I've wanted you."

Those serious eyes of hers said she wasn't sure she could believe him. He took her hand and brought it to the front of his pants, where his hardness was clear for her to feel. "I've *wanted* you."

She pressed her hand against him, then caressed him, sampling his shape and hardness.

Andres almost went to his knees with desire. She was innocent but a quick learner.

"Unfasten my breeches," he whispered in her ear as he brushed her wild curls back and kissed her neck. He began undressing her, this time with earnest haste.

Abby did as he asked. Their tasks came to cross purposes when he pulled her skirts down her legs as she tried to stand on tiptoe to kiss him, but they laughed and took turns.

And when they were both naked, he lay her on the bed. She was ready for him, her body tense and moist. He hesitated. "I do not want to hurt you," he said.

"You won't," she promised and reached up and kissed him hard, her tongue finding his — and Andres was undone.

He entered her. She stiffened. He stopped, holding himself tight, letting her adjust to him. He whispered to her in Spanish, telling her she was beautiful, wondrous, magic.

Her legs opened wider. He went deeper. She arched and he wrapped his arms around her.

She felt so good. He'd never known a woman could feel like this. He'd been born to join with her. He'd been unconsciously searching for her all his life, and now this was their moment. Their blessed, precious moment.

Andres began moving. He knew how to make love. He'd done it enough, but he realized he had no control when it came to Abby. What he'd thought of as routine became something beyond his imagination.

She was his wife. And he had become a man of substance because of this wonderful, giving creature in his arms.

Andres went deeper, wanting all of her. He heard her cry his name. She liked this. She gave herself completely to him — and it made him want to please her more.

Abby gasped. Deep muscles tightened. They took hold of Andres, pulled him, claimed him — and his own release was like nothing he'd felt before.

Life flowed between them. For one brilliant, blinding moment, he was lost in her. They became one.

It had never been this way before. He'd not experienced such completion.

And when he was done, he was spent. He collapsed, so stunned by what he'd just experienced that he could barely breathe, let alone think.

They lay together, legs and arms intertwined, until the world intruded in the form of a ticklish chill. He moved, reaching for the bedspread and flipping it over the two of them even as he rolled to his side.

Her eyes were closed. Her hair fanned out behind her.

She was so lovely. So perfect. Her nose, her complexion, her freckles, the stubbornness in her mouth —

A tear escaped from her eye.

Alarmed, Andres brushed it away with the pad of his thumb. "What is it, *palomita?* Did I hurt you?"

Her eyes opened. She reached for his hand, pulling it across her body. "No, you did not hurt me."

"Then what is it?"

"That was astonishing," she responded. "I didn't know anything could be so completely —" She paused, as if words failed her.

"I understand," he said.

She snuggled to him, as supple and seductive as a cat, and began to trace the line of his chest with one finger. "Could we do it again?" she purred, moving her body against his.

Pride filled him. Male pride in all its glory. "We can do it all you wish, *palomita,*" he assured her, and proceeded to show her the truth of his words.

Later, Andres pulled on his breeches and opened the door to find a tray with covered dishes waiting for them. He brought it inside and set it on the bed for Abby to enjoy while he went about finding out if they could have a bath prepared.

Mrs. Laing assured him that the hour was late but one could be prepared. Andres told her to do so.

The thought struck him that now he really didn't need to worry about funds so much. What did it matter that his purse was all but empty? He'd married an heiress, one who was quickly fulfilling all his dreams of what a woman could and should be.

He hurried back to the room, where he found his wife sitting naked on the bed nibbling a chicken leg.

Later, it was his pleasure to bathe her. And wherever he washed, he placed a kiss . . . until it all led to the inevitable conclusion and he climbed into the deep but narrow hip bath with her.

For a bath, it was disastrous.

For lovemaking, it was full of laughter and a very satisfying completion.

What truly bemused Andres was that this laughter wasn't how he'd pictured marriage. And yet right now, his life was better than he'd ever dreamed.

Abby was embarrassed by the proof of her virginity on the counterpane.

"Don't worry on it," he whispered to her as they snuggled in bed together, their naked bodies so close as to be almost on top of each other. "I am certain Mrs. Laing has seen the likes before. Besides, I think it a gift. You are so precious to me."

She smiled up at him. "You are precious to me," she murmured. "And just think, we have three more times to make love to reach six."

"Six?"

Her eyes closing, Abby laughed. "You wouldn't understand . . . but I think even at six you were underestimated." She drifted to sleep.

Even though Andres was beyond tired, he didn't sleep immediately. Instead, he watched her. He would cherish, protect, and honor her.

He thought he was falling in love with her.

This love felt different than it had with Gillian. She'd been like a holy grail . . . but Abby? She was companion and confidante, lover and friend. Love with her was easier and more carefree.

She'd given him so much. And he was going to make her proud of him. He was now a man with an income of two thousand pounds a year. He had an incredible wife, and someday, his horses would be the best in England.

He slept with a smile on his face.

Andres woke the next morning thinking there wasn't anything he couldn't do. Since he'd met Abby, his life had taken on meaning, and today he was putting the first of many plans into action.

He wanted to make love to her. He held off, because she was walking a little stiffer and he feared they might have already overdone it for her.

But she was game to make love again.

It was a gift to a man to know he'd married a woman who shared his needs. However, he had to think of her well-being. "Not yet, *palomita*," he said. "Let your body become accustomed to this."

She pouted. "I thought we would do it three more times."

He laughed. "Wait until we reach Stonemoor," he said. "I'll make love to you in every room."

"And how many rooms are there?"

"At least twenty," he guessed. He hoped. If not, he'd build on the extra rooms he needed.

"I shall hold you to that promise, my

lord," she informed him in a voice so husky with lust that he was tempted to set good intentions aside and take her right there.

The truth was, he adored looking at his wife. He liked her untamed curls and regal bearing. His Abby was a study in contrasts, and he thought her perfect.

She let him know she liked him as well. As they dressed, he could feel her gaze shift shyly in his direction as if she, too, couldn't believe her good fortune.

But he should have known better than to underestimate his *palomita.*

As he started to open the door for her, she paused. "I have one question, my lord."

"Yes?" He took his hand off the door latch.

"That night in the library, when I came upon you . . . you truly were thinking of taking your life, weren't you?"

There was a question in her voice, but he heard a statement of fact.

"I would not have taken the coward's way," he said carefully, uncertain why she brought this up now. Had he done something wrong?

"It would have been a pity if you had," she said. "I would have lost so much. Please, don't ever lose faith in life again." There was no condemnation in her attitude.

And he realized this woman saw through

him. She didn't look at the features that God had blessed, or cursed, him with; she saw *him.*

For the briefest moment, he could tell her all, every bloody detail of it. He had a longing to confess the ruses and tricks and the lies he still lived.

But he didn't. Because right now, she saw the best of him, and he never wanted to disappoint her.

He'd received a gift. Along with the two thousand came a generous woman who was making him believe life was good. And he would see that it was for her, he silently vowed. Today was a new era of his life. He would leave the past behind and truly become the man he wanted her to see.

Andres sealed that pledge to God by kissing Abby. It was both her answer and his promise.

She lifted her hand to rest on the side of a newly shaven jaw. Their kiss ended, and all was well.

So it was in a good frame of mind that they left the bedroom that had brought them so much delight.

The smells of fresh baked bread and frying sausages wafted through the air toward them as they walked down the narrow hallway to the main room. Abby's stomach rumbled, and they both laughed when his followed suit, a laughter that came to an abrupt end when they reached the dining room.

For there, waiting for them at the table set for their breakfast, was Banker Montross.

CHAPTER ELEVEN

Abby was shocked to see her father. Guilt, as well as shame, stabbed through her. She'd been so involved with her husband that she'd forgotten all about the man who had raised her. Her first reaction was to go to him, to see that he was truly fine after the accident, but Andres rested his hands on her shoulders, holding her in place.

"Good morning, sir," he said.

"Barón," her father said, his tone unwelcoming. "Sit."

Abby started to obey, but Andres's hands held her in place. "I sense you are angry," Andres said to the banker. "Before we talk, understand your daughter is my wife and I will protect her."

Few spoke their minds to Abby's father, and no one openly challenged him. His brows came together in a hawkish expression she knew so well. His jaw tightened, but then he lifted his chin. "I have never taken my temper out on my daughter. Now, please, sit down."

Andres took her hand and led her over to the table. There was a tankard of ale in front of Abby's father. "Our plates will be out in a moment," he said to Andres. "I didn't know what you wished to drink." To Abby he said, "I ordered the chocolate you like, but they don't have it. You'll have to settle for tea."

She nodded. What was offered to drink was the least of her worries.

"Abby has been preferring tea," Andres countered.

Tension lit the air over the challenge concerning Abby's beverage preference.

Understanding she was caught between two men who cared for her, Abby sought to diffuse the situation. "Chocolate is good. So is tea."

The men acted as if she hadn't spoken.

Thankfully, Mrs. Laing came into the room carrying a tray with their plates. Her cheery presence was a respite from the two glowering gentlemen Abby found herself with. The older woman fussed around the table as if everything was exactly as it should have been. She even declared Andres and Abby "lovebirds" on several occasions. Each time she said it, her father's knuckles whitened.

At last she left and they were alone.

Abby didn't touch her food, but her father and Andres ate as if they hadn't had a care in the world.

"Eat, daughter," her father ordered.

"If you do not feel hungry, *palomita,* you must not force yourself," her husband said.

"Oh, no, waste away to nothing. That will make your mother happy. Speaking of your mother, I left her in tears."

Those words tore at Abby's conscience.

"A good mother always finds it difficult to release her daughter to the care of another," Andres observed. "It is the way of the world."

Abby rested her elbows on the table, burying her head in her hands.

"I want what is best for my daughter," her father said.

"As do I," Andres answered. He leaned over to Abby. "We have agreed, Abby. See? It is not so bad."

"Depending on what you want," her father responded. "Do you care for my daughter, Barón?"

"I do."

Her father put down his cutlery. He leaned back in the chair, and his fingers drummed the table in that manner he had when he was not happy.

Abby attempted to intervene. "Father, please. I meant no disrespect. But I could not marry Lord Villier. I wish I could have pleased you, but I couldn't."

"All you had to do is say you didn't want to marry him," her father answered. "You didn't need to elope."

That's not how Abby remembered her father's opinion of the Villier match, but before she could respond, he said to Andres, "And don't think I don't know what you want. You stole my daughter for her dowry. Well, I have news for you, Spaniard" — he practically spit the word out — "there is no dowry. It was mine to give or keep. I'm keeping it."

Abby was stunned by his words. "Are you *disowning* me? You are doing what my grandfather did to Mother?"

Her father acted ruffled at the accusation. The line of his mouth grew more set, as if he wished he could reconsider but was too stubborn to do so.

Andres placed his hand over hers. "I don't need her dowry," he informed the banker.

"That's what you think," her father answered. His gaze focused on Andres's hand holding Abby's. He picked up his fork to savagely stab a sausage, but he placed the fork down instead of raising the food to his mouth. "There is something else you should know, Barón. Something my daughter didn't know because I never told her. However, this information will change your attitude toward her."

"Abby is my wife. Nothing can change what I feel for her."

Her father pushed away from the table and stood. For a second he appeared ready to flee.

He doesn't like someone else having more control over me than he has, Abby realized. She didn't think it was out of malice, but for so long she'd done as he'd expected — and now here she was defying his authority, listening to another man.

"You and Mother eloped," she said, speaking as gently as she could. "Your marriage turned out well."

"Yes, but I don't know this man. He has no connections —"

"The same argument Mother's father used against you," Abby pointed out.

"At least I was English. Ah, Abigail, Abigail, *Abigail* . . . I want what is best for you. This man is a lothario. A rakehell, a scoundrel. A *gambler.*"

There was no worse accusation in her

father's vocabulary than that of gamester. He never gambled.

But she did. She was gambling on Andres.

Andres spoke. "I understand your feeling," he said. There was tension in his voice. He was offended, but he was holding his temper at bay. "I don't want us at odds. Abby cares for her family —"

"Or so I thought!" her father barked.

"Or so I *do*," Abby stressed. "Father, you and I are much alike. As are my brothers. We've all sought our own fortunes."

The harsh lines of her father's face crumpled into sad ones. "You are a woman, Abby. It is my role to see you safe."

"Now it is my role," Andres said.

His claim seemed to suck the bluster from her father. He sat heavily on Mrs. Laing's wooden chair. "Yes, it is your role now." He reached into the pocket of his coat and pulled out some papers. "Mrs. Laing," he called.

She appeared immediately at the doorway, leaving no doubt she'd been eavesdropping. "Yes, sir?" she said, sympathy in the look she gave Abby.

"I need pen and ink. Do you have it?" her father asked.

"Aye, sir, I do."

"Bring it here."

Her father shoved his plate of uneaten food to one side. "This paperwork concerns the trust Abigail's maternal grandmother left to her." He glanced at Andres. "She didn't like me and wanted to ensure that I never put my hands on the monies that would have come to me through my wife. That was fine. I knew how to make my own money."

He said this last in a tone that could be understood to mean he didn't think Andres could.

Abby laced her fingers through Andres's as a silent request for patience. They had each other.

The gesture was not lost on her father. "Ah, yes, miss, we shall see how supportive the two of you are to each other. I tried to spare you from this, Abby. But it is your choice. Remember that. This is *your* choice."

"I accept responsibility for my actions," she said.

"Good," he answered and opened the folded pages of parchment. It was a legal document. She knew her father. He'd meant what he'd said about there not being a dowry. This must have had something to do with her inheritance from her maternal grandmother.

"I have before me the paperwork for a

trust that I set up." Her father took his spectacles from their case and perched them on his nose. "As I said, your grandmother thought to circumvent me by leaving these monies to you, daughter. Her wish was that I should never place my hands on them. However, I am more clever than she could ever have thought."

"What do you mean?" Abby asked.

"I placed everything in trust." Her father looked to Andres. "Do you understand what a trust is?"

"Is it like an entailment?" Andres answered, his brows gathering in concern.

Her father frowned. "Somewhat. Very good, Barón, I didn't expect you to understand the process."

The lines tightened around Andres's mouth at the insult but he kept quiet, which Abby appreciated. Her father would have liked Andres to lash out.

Mrs. Laing entered the room with ink and a sharpened quill. "Thank you, Mrs. Laing," her father said and unstopped the ink bottle. He dipped the quill in it.

"According to the trust, Abigail may not have access to her inheritance until her twenty-seventh birthday — July 17, 1813 — almost three years from now."

"I thought it was to come to me upon

marriage," Abby protested.

"Yes, those are the terms of your grand-mother's will. However, I set up the trust. Even though you may be married, this trust will hold your inheritance until the stated date. Nor can any changes be made to it without the permission of the trustees, who include myself, my assistant Archibald Vaughn, and your two brothers, until you reach the age of twenty-seven."

Andres pulled the papers to him. Abby leaned over so that she could read them, too. She didn't understand all the legalese, but her father was a smart man. If he said he had seen this done, so it was.

"Why didn't you tell me this?" she asked.

"There was no reason to do so," her father answered. "I had anticipated giving you a dowry, and this trust fund would have been superfluous — to the proper man."

He pushed another paper toward them. "This must be signed and dated to show that I have given you the papers of the trust and that you acknowledge receipt. When you turn twenty-seven, Abigail, you can bring the documents to my bank and have access to the money, which is currently sitting in the funds gathering interest for you."

Abby couldn't move. She couldn't believe her father was doing this. She pulled her gaze from the paperwork to meet his eyes and found him a stranger. He was truly that angry that she had defied him.

And he wished to teach her a lesson. She knew it.

Well, she'd not let him have the best of her.

Abby took the quill he offered, dipped it in more ink, and signed her name.

"Very good," her father murmured. "But the name that matters is your husband's. You are a married woman now, Abby. You have few rights. As you both pointed out to me, you are in his hands."

Andres would like nothing better than to slam his fist into the banker's smug face.

But that would have confirmed the man's low opinion of him. Banker Montross assumed that in spite of being titled, his Spanish birth made him inferior.

Andres might have been a bastard, but his father's aristocratic blood flowed through his veins, as did his pride.

Andres took the pen and signed his name.

"Leave us," he ordered her father.

The banker did not appreciate the command. He sat back, blinking at Andres's audacity. Andres stood. He'd not spend a moment more in this man's company. "We are done," he said. "You have insulted my wife. I wish not to see you again." He offered his arm to Abby.

She'd gone very pale. But she stood, her hand shaking as she placed it on his arm.

Andres didn't hesitate; he left the room quickly, taking Abby back to the bedroom they'd shared. "Prepare to leave," he said as he dropped her off at the threshold, then went in search of David Laing or his wife.

He found Mrs. Laing in her kitchen. "I need a vehicle to take me to a place called Corbridge in Northumberland. I was told it isn't far from Newcastle."

"I don't know," Mrs. Laing said. "Johnny Whitacre left this morning with some passengers and there isn't much else in town unless you go to Carlisle. Everything leaves out of Carlisle."

"Are there horses I can hire to travel to Corbridge?"

"Oh, that, yes there are."

"And how much would they be?" Andres didn't want to sound anxious, but he was concerned.

She rolled her eyes as if trying to guess and then shrugged. "A good amount. Perhaps, if you are going any distance at all and wish to save funds, my lord, you'd best consider the mail. It comes through here but never stops. You'll need to board it in Carlisle. How far will you be traveling?"

"I'm not certain," Andres had to admit.

And he was just now realizing the enormity of what it meant to have Abby's funds in trust.

He was done up. He had supplies coming, horses, and tack — and he had no way to pay for them. He had a wife, property, expenses . . . and no money.

"The reason he can't tell you where he wants to go," Montross's voice said from the door of the kitchen, "is because he doesn't know. He has no idea where Corbridge is."

Abby's father had donned hat, gloves, and coat and was ready to leave. He walked into the kitchen. "You thought to steal my daughter. Now what?"

"Now what?" Andres echoed, offended by the man's manner because he was right. "Now I take *my wife* and leave."

The words "my wife" wiped the smug expression off the banker's face. "You don't truly care for her," her father said. "You look at her and you see pound sterling. But I have nurtured and protected her from the moment she drew her first breath. Let her come home with me, Barón. We'll strike a bargain, you and I. I pay you five hundred pounds and you disappear. Vanish. Just as Dobbins bribed you to vanish."

So, Montross knew Andres had accepted payment to leave London . . . but he didn't think the banker knew more, for he would have used it to his own advantage.

"You think she is only worth five hundred pounds?" Andres challenged.

"She's worth far more," her father said, hands doubling into fists at his sides. "Of course, now you've ruined her —"

"I've done nothing of the sort," Andres flashed back. If Montross wanted a fight, he'd picked the right man. Andres wouldn't mind releasing the tension he was feeling with a few throws, especially at a man who mocked him. . . .

"Stop it! *Please.*" Abby rushed into the room and placed herself between the two of them. Her back to Andres, she faced her father. *"Go,"* she told him. "You've had your say, now go. Let me live my life."

"This isn't what I want for you," her father said.

"It's what I have chosen for myself," Abby countered.

"A life in the poorhouse?" Her father stepped back, as if amazed. "He's no good, Abigail. I can smell with my nose that something is not right here. And if you leave with him, if you don't come home with me now, don't think you can turn to your mother and me later when you discover the mistake you've made."

"She has made no mistake," Andres said. He would have lunged at the man if Abby hadn't been standing between them. As it was, he raised a fist.

"Do you see? He's hotheaded and a fool," her father predicted. "Look at him. Some nobleman."

Abby's back straightened. "He is my husband," she said. "Please tell Mother I love her. I love both of you, but I have chosen my own course."

Her father stepped back, his lips pressed together so tightly that he had to force himself to answer her. "Very well. Have it your way. Enjoy your ride on the Mail," he said to Abby and walked out of the room.

Abby started to collapse, as if struck by the finality of what had happened.

Andres caught her, wrapping his arms around her. "You've made the right choice, *palomita.* The right choice."

She shook her head and pushed away. "Let's go," she pleaded with him. "Let us go to Stonemoor."

"We shall." He looked to Mrs. Laing, who had been watching this whole scene with a dazed expression, her hands gripping her apron. Andres decided then what he would do — it was the only thing he could do. "I need to hire a horse to take us to Carlisle."

"I'll go ask Mr. Laing," Mrs. Laing said and hurried out.

Andres and Abby were alone.

Andres had never ridden on the Mail, but he had an idea that it would be like many public vehicles he'd taken in other countries. He was certain, however, that Abby had never experienced such a ride.

"I'm sorry," Abby said.

Andres shook his head, his mind pre-occupied with all sorts of "what if's?" He had to reason it all out. He had to think. "I'll bring us through this," he promised, but he knew he sounded curt. "Come, let's gather our things. The sooner we leave, the sooner we reach Stonemoor."

She nodded and hurried through the door in front of him. They didn't speak much as they prepared to depart. Andres wanted to tell her what a bastard her father was, but he knew it would be the wrong thing to say.

And he wondered if her own silence meant she was wishing that she'd left with her father. Wondered if she didn't regret coming with him.

His saving grace was that he had been

honest with her. There had been no false promises of love in his proposal to her. He'd remind her of that if she expressed recriminations.

As it was, she held her tongue, so he held his.

The trip to Carlisle did nothing to clear the air between them. Andres tried to act as if all was well . . . but Abby answered him with monosyllables. Nor did she look at him.

The horses were very tame. She had been telling him the truth when she'd said she wasn't a good rider. Her balance on the back of her beast was too stiff for enjoyment. Andres offered to take her reins, but she rebuffed him with a shake of her head.

And so they went . . . taking twice as long to reach Carlisle than it would have if Abby had unbent and let him help.

CHAPTER TWELVE

Abby knew she'd made a mistake in her marriage.

Her father's final words burned in her mind. She shouldn't have run away. She'd hurt her parents deeply, especially after they'd lost Robert not more than four years ago.

She couldn't imagine what her mother was feeling . . . and she wished everything was different.

And the guilt of what she'd done to Andres weighed heavily on her.

He'd married her expecting a fortune. She'd *told* him she'd had a fortune. He'd built his dreams on that belief, and now they were in a terrible situation.

Abby had never experienced fear — or doubt, its uncomfortable companion — about her future. Her life had been cushioned by doting parents and no cares about money. Overnight, all had changed.

It didn't help that she was on a horse, never her favorite place to be. She was all too aware that her husband, who had an excellent seat, was riding slowly to accommodate her.

He couldn't hide his annoyance either. She saw it in the tight lines of his mouth and in his silvery eyes, now dark with frustration. She'd learned to tell his moods by the color of his eyes. When he was upset or concerned, they darkened. When he was pleased, they were brighter than the stars.

And as if to add insult to injury, riding sidesaddle was even more difficult when a certain part of her anatomy was very sensitive from making love. Who would have thought it? Not herself — and yet, she was now more aware of her private areas than she could ever have believed possible.

They reached Carlisle late in the afternoon. It was growing dark. They turned the horses over to the stable Laing had told them about, and Andres, for the first time since they'd left Gretna, took Abby's arm. He made some inquiries and found a respectable house where they could spend the night.

The owner, Mrs. Rivers, was a bosomy widow in a lace mobcap who had at least five cats that Abby could see, although her watering eyes warned her there were more.

Abby ducked her head, not wanting to let Andres see how his choice of establishment was affecting her . . . yet she did not know how she could stay here.

These shabby accommodations were not the sort Abby had been accustomed to patronizing when traveling with her father. She tried to be receptive to Andres's choice. Their financial situation was critical, and taking lodging in a private house was a sensible idea.

Still . . . so many cats?

Abby smiled and held her eyes wide, hoping no one noticed how distressed she was. Then again, she wished she could close her eyes, because closer inspection revealed a layer of dust and cat hair coating every table and cushion. It also didn't help that apparently there would be fish for dinner. The smell filled the air.

She could feel Andres watching her, judging her. She refused to meet his eyes. He already had enough on his mind without thinking she was being critical.

Even if she was.

He took her arm, and they followed Mrs. Rivers to a small room with two separate beds. "Will this do?" she asked.

"It will be fine," Andres said.

And it would be, Abby silently vowed. She'd muddle through . . . but it would have been nice if he had asked her opinion.

"We'll be taking the morning Mail to Newcastle," Andres said to Mrs. Rivers. "I believe it leaves early?"

"Oh, yes, earliest," Mrs. Rivers said brightly. She had picked up one of her cats from a hall chair. It was a fat tabby with a disgruntled expression. She shifted the kitty's weight from one arm to another. The cat growled its displeasure. "I'll leave you alone, sir, while I set the table. I can see you are Quality. Who would have thought I'd have the likes of you here under my roof? Such an honor to have you here. Such an honor," she repeated, backing out of the room. Abby and Andres were alone.

She was exhausted.

Her first action was to sit on the edge of the bed furthest away from the window. There was a *meow,* and a calico kitten dashed out from under the bed. It raced to the door but turned and froze, as if uncertain what to do, when it saw that the door was closed.

"He acts as if Mrs. Rivers doesn't receive many lodgers," Abby observed.

She'd meant the comment to be a lighthearted remark, but it didn't come out that way. Her nose was starting to run and she sounded more pinched and annoyed than she actually was.

With an angry sound, her husband opened the door for the cat, who scrambled in his rush to leave them. "I need to see to something," Andres said, not looking at her. He still wore his coat, but he'd lost his hat in the inn in Carlisle when they'd jumped out the window. "I'll be back."

Abby did not want to be left alone. "Must you leave?"

He stopped. From where she sat, she could see his jaw tighten. She wanted him to look at her. He didn't.

"I must," he said, his voice quiet — and she let him go.

The door shut. She sat still for a long time. She was tired. Defeated, actually. Yesterday she'd been so happy.

Today, she didn't think she'd ever felt worse, and she sensed that Andres was experiencing the same.

Abby stood. She had to do something. She couldn't just sit there. What she needed was to wash her face and brush her hair and feel civilized.

As she'd done since the beginning of the trip, she'd layered her clothes; even now she was wearing the day dress with the nightgown beneath it. Abby stripped down, thinking to take a quick sponge bath, and was not pleased to discover there was no water in the pitcher by the wash basin. She dressed again, leaving off her nightclothes, then picked up the pitcher and left the room.

Mrs. Rivers was singing at the top of her lungs from some point in the house. Abby followed the sound, which grew louder as the smell of fish grew stronger. Abby was not surprised to find her hostess in the kitchen cooking their supper. She was surrounded by very hungry, very demanding cats.

Ten of them.

They looked to Abby for support in commanding their dinner. Several jumped down from the chairs or turned from pestering Mrs. Rivers to rub Abby's legs and yowl mightily.

"Ah, good of you to come," Mrs. Rivers said. "Supper is almost ready." She tossed a piece of fish from the pan onto the stone floor. The cats fell on it.

Abby's stomach churned.

"I was going to wash my face," Abby said. She held up the pitcher. "And I don't know how hungry I am —"

"Nonsense, you must eat. You are paying

236

for it. Ah, water! I don't know why I didn't think of it." Mrs. Rivers took the pitcher from Abby and carried it to a bucket by a door leading to a small garden. She began ladling water as she chattered, "As to food, in these trying times, what with winter upon us, a wise traveler eats when the opportunity presents itself. I'm preparing my special buttered beans."

Abby didn't know if she'd like buttered beans. And while the advice was that nourishment was needed, she didn't know that she could manage one bite surrounded by cats. She took the pitcher from Mrs. Rivers, saying, "I'll see how I feel later."

"Very good, missus," Mrs. Rivers said.

Walking back to the room, Abby reflected that Andres had not used their titles. She was glad he hadn't. Right now she wanted to be unknown. She needed time to adjust to this new station in life: poor nobility. As she washed with cold water, she decided it was humbling.

She'd just re-donned her day dress when Mrs. Rivers knocked. "I have food," she said cheerily, speaking through the door. "I thought since you weren't up to coming to my table, I'd bring a tray to you."

Abby was tempted to pretend she wasn't there.

Mrs. Rivers knocked again, and Abby knew pretense would be to no avail. She opened the door. Mrs. Rivers held a huge tray with a dishcloth over the food.

"May I come in?" Mrs. Rivers sang in her happy voice.

"Please," Abby murmured, but the woman was already walking in. Fortunately no cats followed her.

Mrs. Rivers set the tray on the bed by the window. "Here now, you can enjoy your dinner and not worry for one moment that your husband has gone out without you."

"He had an errand to run," Abby said, startled by the woman's words and her familiarity.

"Oh, you needn't pretend with me. I was married a good long time, and, like you, to a man who made women look twice, if'n you know what I mean. Much as your own circumstances, there were many who wondered what such a strappin' good-lookin' man was doing with the likes of me. My George could have had any woman he wanted . . . and sometimes he did."

Abby wasn't certain she'd heard her correctly. She must have shown her confusion, because Mrs. Rivers nodded. "That's right," she said. "My George liked the ladies and they liked him. I know exactly how you feel."

"I don't believe you do," Abby answered, not liking this conversation.

"But I do," Mrs. Rivers pressed. "Women would stop in their tracks and watch my George walk by. Sometimes I overheard them whispering about how he could have done much better for a wife than myself. You know, someone who was pretty."

This was not a conversation Abby wanted. It hit her insecurities.

"And George told me he was fond of me just the way I was. Of course it helped that my father owned this house." She looked around the room with satisfaction. "And as time went by, George calmed down. He thought I didn't know when he'd snuck out to sample a bit of the neighbors. I could always tell." The smile left her face. "He'd say he was going to a public house and I would smell the whiskey on his breath . . . but I knew different. Those women were always after him and he didn't hesitate to dip his wick whenever he had a chance —"

She broke off as if coming to her senses. "I don't know what I'm going on about. George has been dead these past ten years and more, God rest his soul. I'd give all I own to have him back, although I sleep better at night now than I did when I had to worry over whose bed my husband was visiting. A man that is so good-lookin' can be a curse."

Abby didn't want to be keeping tabs on her husband all the time . . . but she also didn't know what to do with the sudden rush of jealousy and fear she was feeling.

What if Andres had left her? If he'd thought he could manage better alone? He'd expected her inheritance. If she didn't have that, what good was she to him?

Her stomach twisted painfully.

Mrs. Rivers didn't seem to notice anything amiss. "Enjoy your meal," she chirped and left the room.

Abby collapsed on the edge of her bed. Darkness had fallen. This small haven against the turbulent events of the day was growing cold. There was no fire in the grate here, no warmth at all save for the light of a single smoking candle on her bedside table.

She didn't move toward the food or to prepare for bed. She waited for Andres, praying he hadn't abandoned her.

Or left her for another.

Funny how the night before she'd been mesmerized by what he'd been able to make her feel. She liked being with him. Loved him.

There must have been something about her that was *un*lovable. After all, Freddie had professed to love her and had chosen another.

She should never have let Andres make love to her. She knew they'd had to consummate the marriage to make it binding, but her feeling right now might have been more independent and less jealous if she'd kept herself separate from him. As it was, she could close her eyes and feel him deep within her.

Abby didn't know how long she sat there. She didn't eat. She couldn't. Her mind conjured one disastrous, terrible scenario after another — all of them including women as beautiful as Lady Dobbins seducing Andres away from her.

And it didn't feel good. It hurt to be so vulnerable.

It hurt more than when Freddie had left her —

A step sounded outside the door.

"Abby?" Andres knocked lightly on the door, as if he'd been a stranger. The door started to open.

Uncertain, she stood abruptly.

He came into the room. "You are awake," he said, as if surprised. He took off his coat and tossed it on the bed by the untouched tray of food.

"Shouldn't I be?" Her voice sounded

strained.

He looked very tired, and his hair was disheveled, as if he'd run his fingers through it — or someone else had. He shrugged at her comment. "I had thought after the day we'd had, you would be asleep."

"I waited for you."

He nodded as if distracted. "Have you eaten?"

"No . . . I'm not hungry."

Andres picked up the towel covering the food and frowned. "I don't think I am either. Is there water?"

"Yes, in the washbasin."

He nodded and picked the tray off the bed opposite hers, carrying it over to the bedside table between them. As he passed, she caught a scent of whiskey.

"Have you been to a public house?" she wondered.

His brows came together, as if he was irritated that she should ask. "I have." He crossed over to the washstand and began undressing.

Abby watched him remove his shirt and fold it. He began washing his face, using the bar of homemade soap on the stand.

She waited for more information or explanation as to where he'd been all this time.

He didn't offer it.

Turning from him, she started to ready herself for bed, but Abby was not good at holding back questions. They'd been building inside her all evening, making her crazed with curiosity.

Finally, she could take it no longer. She faced him as he sat on the edge of his bed, tugging off his boots. *"Where have you been?"*

The words burst out of her, carried by overwrought emotions. She sounded shrewish, and she wished that she could have called them back or that she had tempered her tone — but she didn't like the way she'd felt keeping them caged inside her.

He set his boots aside. "I checked on the Mail times."

"You were gone quite a while."

"I had another errand to perform," he said evenly.

"What sort of errand? One that took you to a pub?"

He muttered something in Spanish under his breath, then answered, "Yes, it did. Now, we are both tired. This has been a hard day. Go to sleep, Abby. We will talk tomorrow."

"I may not feel like talking tomorrow."

It was a challenge. She wanted him to talk to her.

His eyes were as brooding as storm clouds.

She didn't waver. She held herself steady.

"I don't feel like talking *now*," he said. "Good night." He then proceeded to climb under the covers, turn his back on her, and fall asleep.

Abby could have shouted in frustration. She wanted to grab the pillow off her bed and pound him soundly with it.

But she didn't, because that would have told him she was jealous.

And told herself she was weak.

Instead, she climbed into her own bed, so agitated that she didn't think she could sleep. But she did. The moment her head rested on the pillow, her eyes shut. Her last thought was that she hated the smell of Mrs. Rivers's cooking.

Abby woke the next morning to Andres shaking her arm.

"*Palomita,*" he said gently. "Wake up. We must hurry to board the Mail."

She moaned her protest. Her eyes felt as if they'd been sealed shut.

"You must wake now," he insisted. He pulled the covers off her. She rubbed her eyes and stretched. He was already dressed and had taken time to shave.

"Come, Abby," he coaxed.

She climbed out of bed, and he helped

her dress in her layers of clothes, as if she'd been a child and needed the help. Her arms and legs felt as if they had turned to lead. She polished her teeth, tied back her hair, and they set off.

The streets were still dark when they reached the inn yard. The Mail had not yet arrived. Andres purchased a jug of cider and two hot rolls for their breakfast. Abby yawned as she ate.

Of course, with food and awareness came memory.

She was angry at him. She'd almost forgotten.

The Mail arrived. They heard the horn announcing its arrival first. The inn's ostlers scurried forward with fresh horses. Time would not be wasted changing teams.

Other travelers came to their feet, ready to jump in and take the best seats. Andres grabbed her arm. "It's going to be a clear day, although a bit cold. We should ride on top. I paid for the seats."

Here was her chance to let him know she was not pleased with him. "I don't want to ride on top."

"But, Abby, you don't —"

"I don't want to ride out in the cold," she said, not looking at him.

"The air will be fresh," he argued.

"*Fine.* You have made up your mind. Why ask me?"

Andres took a step away from her. She could feel him looking at her. She offered him her shoulder. He wasn't the only one who wanted matters his way.

The maroon-and-black Mail coach came thundering into the yard. The driver pulled up and jumped down, seemingly in one movement, then went into the inn while the ostlers changed teams.

"Do you want to sit on top?" she overheard Andres say to some gentlemen.

They weren't as picky as Abby and gratefully accepted the opportunity.

"I paid extra for those seats," Andres grumbled.

Abby pretended not to hear him. Maybe next time he would consider her opinion.

Two passengers had been traveling with the Mail and already had their seats. The other passengers at the inn quickly jockeyed for the seats that were left.

Andres took her arm and more or less muscled his way to a corner seat for her. He sat next to her, taking the middle seat — a very uncomfortable position, considering the fact that the other passengers were also good-sized gentlemen. One was a ruddy-faced man, who introduced himself to them as Deacon Daniel. The other gentleman, a thin, nervous type, offered his name as Mr. Barnesworth. He was a clerk and carried papers that were obviously very important to him, since he kept his rather large leather portfolio in his lap at all times.

The rest of the passengers, including Abby and Andres, kept their names to themselves.

In all there were eight of them crowded into a space that could have comfortably sat six small people.

Abby found herself crushed against Andres's side. She realized now that he'd created a bit of a haven for her, and she was grateful.

The driver came out of the inn still chewing his food and wiping his mouth. The guard-in-charge jumped down from the boot and hurried into the inn, passing his weapon to the driver.

"Hey there, lads, ready now?" the driver demanded of the ostlers.

They mumbled something that he didn't like. He walked around the coach, peering in the windows at his passengers. He paused in front of where Abby sat and doffed his hat with a toothy smile — until he saw Andres's frown. Then he moved on.

"I'm sorry," Andres muttered. "You should not have to be part of this."

Abby didn't answer. She didn't think she should have been part of this either. "What time is it?"

Andres shrugged. "Around seven o'clock."

"What does your watch say?" she wondered. Before, he'd always checked his watch when she'd asked what time it was. Now she realized how he'd paid for the tickets. "You don't have your watch. You sold it."

He proved her accusation by ignoring her.

Abby hunkered down into her corner, thankful she had the brim of her hat to hide the shame she felt.

The guard came out of the inn. The horses were in their traces. With a snap of the coachman's whip and a blow on the horn to warn everyone out of the way, the coach took off with a heaving jerk.

Movement didn't make those inside the coach any more comfortable. Abby leaned her head against the coach's glass window and pretended to watch the passing scenery. What she was really doing was feeling very guilty.

Andres noticed her withdrawal. "It wasn't a very good watch," he said. It was too early in the morning for conversation; he kept his voice very low, speaking in her ear.

She looked up at him. "Did you sell it in

the pub last night?"

"It is the best place to go. There is always someone willing to buy something there."

"Why didn't you tell me?"

A shadow crossed his eyes. He shrugged. "And how would you have felt?"

"After behaving in such a crotchety manner?" She frowned. "Spoiled." She couldn't believe the way she'd spoken to him last night, or this morning. "We should be sitting on top of the coach. I should have listened to you."

"You should have."

In spite of being apologetic, Abby didn't know if she liked his agreeing with her. "You could say something nice," she prodded. "Forgiving?"

At that moment, Deacon Daniel had a case of flatulence. Abby had never heard anything so loud in her life.

Andres didn't miss a beat. He lowered the window.

"Sorry, sorry," Deacon Daniel said. He was reading a prayer book, his glasses low on his nose. He had another bad round.

The other passengers groaned.

But Abby started laughing. She couldn't help herself. Andres joined her. They laughed so hard that they were holding each other. All the tension, all the fear that Abby had been nursing disappeared.

She looked up at her husband. "I'm sorry you had to sell your watch."

"I told you, it is nothing."

Abby could have confessed that she'd thought he'd been dallying with other women, prettier women who had money . . . but she realized now how silly she'd been to be jealous. So foolish.

And she couldn't say anything, because if she did, he'd know how much she cared. How she'd fallen in love.

"Tell me about Stonemoor," she urged. "Describe it to me again."

There was a question in his eye. Andres seemed attuned to her every mood. He'd noticed how she'd stopped laughing, how she'd turned introspective. She tried to smile.

He smiled back, unconvinced . . . but then he began telling her about Stonemoor.

His voice walked her through the stables. He described the gardens that every spring were full of irises and roses.

"Why did you plant irises?" she asked.

"Because they are named after the Greek goddess of rainbows," he said. "And their shape is that of the fleur-de-lis of the king of France. I always fill a garden with hundreds of irises."

Hundreds of rainbows. Her husband had a poet's soul. He was a believer. She hadn't realized that. Her mother was that way. There had been many times when Abby and her brothers had been thankful that their mother had seen the world differently from their pragmatic father. Her brother Christopher even had the opinion that their father wouldn't have been as successful as he had been if it hadn't been for their mother.

Andres described the house again. It was a huge Georgian manor made out of yellow brick. He walked her mind's eye through every room, every piece of furniture. None of it was elaborate. He made it sound as if it had his Spanish taste, and that was fine with her.

This was going to be their home. She'd become so engrossed in her husband's talk that she hadn't even noticed if Deacon Daniel had continued to have digestive trouble or not.

Before she realized the passage of time, the driver was blowing his horn and shouting, "Corbridge."

She and Andres were both happy to be free of the crowded coach and on firm ground.

Andres took her into the inn that served as the Mail's way station. He purchased a meat pie and black tea and left her to this repast while he made travel arrangements for them to reach Stonemoor.

Refreshed, she was pleased to see that he'd hired a pony cart for their trip, so it was in good spirits that they set off. Abby even drove a bit — as long as Andres let her have the reins. She discovered her husband was not the easiest passenger. He definitely liked being in charge.

The path to Stonemoor was a wandering one, through several back roads. They crossed the South Tyne River and came across the Roman ruins known as Hadrian's Wall. Abby was very impressed . . . and starting to wonder if Andres knew where he was going.

A few times, they had to turn around and take a different road. She became very confused. Once, as they passed some crofters' huts, she suggested that they ask directions, but her husband pretended to not hear her. That seemed to be a pattern of his. He just didn't answer what he chose to ignore. She wondered if it was true of all men or just Spanish ones. Her father and brothers always had plenty to say.

As it was, a weathered sign, shaped like an arrow and nailed to a tree, with the word *Stonemoor* in faded script, told them which way they should take. At first, Abby didn't think the two ruts on the ground were really a road.

She was proven wrong when they followed it down to a rickety bridge over a lazy stream and around a copse of trees. She saw a roof. Andres did, too. The pony cart picked up speed, bouncing along the poorly constructed drive. They would need to do something about this if they wanted visitors.

They clopped over a small bridge and turned into a smaller path — and there was Stonemoor.

But it wasn't a glorious Georgian manor or a charming country house.

No — it was a dumpy, gloomy Tudor abode with a mossy roof, broken windows, and a yard full of dry, gray grass and weeds.

Chapter Thirteen

Andres was stunned, especially at his own naivete.

This was not the house he had imagined he owned. He'd pictured it in his dreams and *this was not it.*

Dobbins had made no promises. Andres had gulled himself. He'd wrapped himself up in his dreams to the point where he'd ignored common sense and reality. This wasn't the first time it had happened to him. He'd been this way when his father had taken him in and when he'd won the silver mine.

But this was worse because Abby was involved as well. He'd made promises, told stories he'd begun to believe.

He tied off the reins and jumped out of the cart. He had to see all of this for himself, to know how completely he had duped himself. He bypassed the house and went around back, stumbling on stones and broken glass in his rush to see the stables. A low stone wall separated the house's garden from the pastures beyond. The moors.

A long, low outbuilding was off to his left. It leaned precariously. There were openings like stables . . . but they couldn't be stalls. . . .

They were. This row of beaten-down wood with a roof that appeared ready to crash to the ground at any second was the stables. A lean-to against the side was for hay. There were even remnants of old, molding hay in the hayrack.

There was no stable yard where he could proudly show his horses to buyers. There were only weeds.

Several paddocks had been built, but like so much else at Stonemoor, they were in sad disrepair. Most of the fencing was little more than stone posts, the wood for the railings having been carted away for some other purpose.

"This isn't what you were expecting," Abby's voice said from behind him.

Andres couldn't speak. He'd been such a bloody fool.

Of course Lord Dobbins wouldn't have given him a worthwhile property — why would he have? He'd thought Andres nothing more than his wife's cicisbeo. A man who lived off women by using his looks.

And here was Abby. He faced her, so shamed by Stonemoor that he couldn't speak.

Then again, he had been played the fool in his marriage, too. She now became a convenient target. "I married you for your money," he said, bitterness in his heart and voice. "Do you see why I needed it?"

His words were sharp. He knew that. They could have cut a stone in half.

But then, so could disappointment, and at this moment Andres wasn't thinking clearly.

All his life he'd trusted that things would be better. He'd been the son who had not been able to save his father from suicide. He'd stolen, begged, gambled, and finally sold himself in marriage, all to chase the dream of restoring his family's name. He'd wanted to prove to his father's family that he was one of them.

And he wasn't.

"Go away, Abby," he said. "Take the cart. Go back to your father."

She took a step back in surprise. "I can't."

He didn't want argument. That was another thing she did too much of — she argued. He cut the air with his hand, a sign he wanted her gone. *"Go."*

But she didn't leave. One thing about

Abby; she was stubborn. If anyone was going to leave, it would have to be him.

Andres started walking off, stumbling over his feet in his desire to run away.

Lord Dobbins must have had a hearty laugh over his eagerness to take possession of Stonemoor.

In his sour mood, Andres wouldn't have been surprised if Montross hadn't wanted to dump his daughter on him as well.

But the truth was, he didn't deserve her. He didn't deserve good property either, or a silver mine that actually held silver. He wasn't a barón. Or a gentleman.

And the taunts he'd heard in school, that he'd heard all his life, echoed in his ears. He was a bastard, his mother nothing more than some senseless, but lovely, woman who had spread her legs for Don Ramigio and other wealthy men.

Walking soon wasn't enough. Andres started running. He ran from his past. He ran from his present. And he didn't care where he went.

He ran until he thought his lungs would explode, and when he stopped, he had to bend over, drawing great gulps of air.

Slowly, the chaos in his mind — the confusion, the anger, the shame — came under control.

He had few options. He could sell the property, but who would want it?

He could walk away now and never return. But then he thought of Holburn, a man Andres had once betrayed and who had forgiven him. A man who'd trusted Andres enough to invest in a horse on his advice. The duke had eight hundred pounds in that mare, and he expected Andres to train her foal.

And then there was Abby, who had bravely tied her life to his. She'd trusted him to be what he'd said he was, and he had lied.

Walking away would be the best thing he could do for her. She needed to think of herself. He was no good . . . and yet leaving her would ruin her, especially since even now there was the possibility that she could be carrying his child.

He looked in the direction from which he'd come. If he had any honor, he'd tell her the truth so that she'd know she'd made a terrible mistake in marrying him.

The sun was starting to set. A dismal dreariness settled over the late autumn landscape. Wisps of fog rose from the land like ghosts of his past.

And he knew he had to return, because in the end, he had no choice. He had no money and nowhere else to go. As he walked, he decided that he should leave England. He would sell Stonemoor for what he could and use the money to repay Holburn.

He'd also confess the truth about himself to Abby. Then she wouldn't walk away; she'd run. She'd be glad to be rid of him.

Andres tried not to think of what would happen then. Of how his life would be without her. He was startled to realize how empty the thought made him feel —

The cart was gone.

As he'd walked up the hill toward the house, his eye hadn't taken in the stables or the house's walls. He'd looked directly at the drive — and the pony cart was gone.

His feet felt rooted to the ground. For a long time, he stared at empty space.

Why should he have been surprised she'd left? He'd told her to do so.

In fact, he was glad she'd left. She was being wise —

The sound of someone sweeping came from inside the house.

Andres walked up to the front door. It was made of solid oak and had held up over the years in spite of rusty hinges. He gave the door a shove. It didn't budge. He put his shoulder to it. The door opened with a lurch.

He found himself in a narrow front hall. The plaster on the wall to his left had crumbled. Water had come through the roof and down from the floor above.

The good news was that the ground floor was paved with stones that had been set together so well that they were still in place. He followed the sound of the sweeping.

Abby was in a room one would call a main hall. Its window overlooked the stone-walled garden and a small courtyard.

She still wore her bonnet and her gloves. Her embroidered bag was on her arm, and she was sweeping the floor with a broom that appeared to be as ancient as the house, the ends of it worn to a nub. As he watched, she lifted her broom and started swiping at cobwebs, fussing when one seemed to drift in front of her face.

Abby. Wonderful Abby. His *palomita.*

"Where did you find a broom?" he asked, speaking past a growing tightness in his throat. No one had ever stayed beside him before. Not when his fortune had been bad.

"On the floor amongst some broken furniture." She didn't look at him.

"Don't you do anything I tell you?" he asked.

She turned to him, her broom still poised to attack the dust and gloom. "Only when you are right."

Her eyes were red, as if she'd been crying, or the way they'd been with the cats. Perhaps the dust bothered her.

She frowned at him, knew he'd noticed her eyes . . . and let him know the answer by saying, "I was afraid you weren't returning."

Her fear went straight to his heart.

"I put the pony away," she said, as if determined to fill the silence between them. "The stable is a terrible mess." She returned to her cleaning, sweeping the floor with new vigor. "I gave him hay, but I don't know that I did the right thing. I suppose it will be something I'll have to learn if we are going to build a renowned stables here. And you were wrong about the furniture —" She stopped her sweeping and looked at him, placing an indignant hand on her hip. "This is definitely not Georgian style."

Andres's answer was to cross the room in three long steps, lift her into his arms, and kiss her bloody hard.

Abby hadn't left him. He wasn't alone.

But he had to think of her.

Andres broke off the kiss. Her bonnet had fallen back and now hung by the ribbon tied under her chin. Freed, her hair was a glorious mass. "I want you to return to your

261

father," he said, his earlier anger gone. "You can't live in this. The house is ready to fall down."

A frown formed between her eyes. She raised her chin. "I'm not leaving you."

He hugged her to him, savoring the beauty of those words.

She struggled her way out of his hold. "Stop this. You act as if this is the worst place in the world. Well, you are right. It is . . . unexpected. But it is also our home. I'm not returning to my parents, Andres. I decided that yesterday morning when I thought I'd made a mistake in my marriage. But you sold your watch for me. For this!"

"It was a waste of a watch," he told her.

"No, it wasn't." Her hand tightened on the broom handle. "You've sacrificed everything you have for this dream. In London, when you asked me to marry you and enter this venture with you, I gave my word I'd be here, and so I will. This is where we are supposed to be, Andres. This is where you must build your stables."

He laughed, the sound cruel. "*This* is going to fall down around our ears." He indicated the building with an angry sweep of his hand.

"Then we shall have to build it up."

Andres studied his wife. Conviction shone

from her eyes. "How can you be so certain?" he asked.

Setting the broom aside, she held out her hand. Curious, Andres placed his hand in hers. She led him to a steep, spiral wooden staircase. Upstairs, she entered the first room on the left. It had a massive arched door, and the good-sized room was paneled.

"This is the master's bedroom," she said. "There are three other bedrooms up here."

"You've done some exploring," he murmured. The room had a bank of mullioned windows with what appeared to be the original glass overlooking the yard below. He could see the pony standing in his stall, looking as if he was afraid to move lest it all cave in on him. The cart stood where Abby had left it by the lean-to.

"I have," she said. "Come here. I saw this silhouette when I was putting the pony away. I thought my eyes were playing tricks, so I climbed the stairs for a closer look and was absolutely astounded."

"By what?" Andres said, scanning the room.

In the day's waning light, he could see the plaster walls were in good shape and the wood floor was solid. There was no smell of mold.

"This glass in the window," Abby said and pointed to a small square in the corner of the window. There, painted on to the glass, was a dove.

Andres moved forward to have a closer look. It was no larger than his palm.

"This is a sign," she said. "That Fate you are always talking about is giving us a sign. But as I looked out the window, I noticed something else. Look down, Andres."

He did as instructed and was surprised to see this same dove inlaid in the stone courtyard below.

"This is our home," Abby said with a voice that brooked no disagreement. "I know it needs work, and the stables aren't the magnificent ones you described to me . . . but that doesn't mean those stables can't be built. We have — how many stalls? Seven?"

Andres glanced at the stables. "Eight."

"Eight," she said, as if he'd said something clever. "We don't even have eight horses yet. We can build on this. I know we can."

Her enthusiasm was infectious.

And yet, for once in his life, he had to be sensible. "Abby, I want to believe in signs. But not when I'm playing with your life. Look at this place. It needs so much work. Even if you and I pounded nails and cleaned ⁊d oiled and repaired every broken window

— well, we couldn't. I'm done up, Abby. I have no money. I've nothing."

She reached up to the brooch she'd worn since they'd first left London. She unfastened it and placed it in his hand. "Here. This was my grandmother's. The one who didn't like Father. I don't think she'd be happy with him now either. I know she would want you to sell this brooch so we can use the money for the house."

Andres was surprised by how heavy the brooch was. There was a good amount of gold here.

"Those are garnets in the petals," she explained. "Her father had ordered it made when he worked for the East India Company. Funny how *her* father being in trade made her look down on *my* father."

For a moment, Andres was tempted to do as she asked. And then he shook his head, trying to give the brooch back to her. "I have taken so much from you, Abby. My conscience will not let me take more —"

She shoved him in the chest with both hands. *"Stop this."* Her eyes burned bright in her face. "Don't tell me to go home again. *This* is my home. And my place is not with my parents but with the man I married. You swore to cherish and protect me, Andres Ramigio. You made a vow in front of witnesses. I meant the words I said. The promises I made to you. Are you saying you didn't mean any of the words *you* said?"

"I did. And I don't suggest you leave because I don't want you, Abby. I want you to leave because I am a failure. I am nothing as you think I am, Abby. I'm a fraud."

He took a step back, almost afraid of himself now . . . and knew he had to go on.

"I'm not a barón, Abby. I'm the barón de Vasconia's bastard son. He took his own life, Abby. Shot himself." He knew this news would not surprise her. "He had nothing and couldn't live with the idea. I didn't have anything either. I left Spain and started using the title. Who would care? And it opened many doors." He realized he was ahead of himself . . . and so he began at the beginning.

He told all. Once he'd taken a breath, once he'd admitted to being an impostor, the story poured out of him.

Abby listened. She didn't ask questions or interrupt him. He found himself telling far more than he should have, and it felt good.

At one point, they adjourned to the room that had been the scullery. There was a huge fireplace. Andres used the flint box from the kit in his valise and started a fire, using the broken pieces of wood, presumably from what had once been furniture. Abby helped him build that fire, then said, "Please continue."

Still wearing their coats, they sat on the floor in front of the fire, where he finished his story, ending with what she already knew. "I was bought off. But what you don't know is that I'm not to return to London. Ever. Or I forfeit this property." He looked around the cavernous room. "Dobbins must be laughing. He's rid himself of me and will receive the property back if I go to him to complain."

She was silent a moment. She'd been so serious all the way through that he'd not dared to look at her. He studied the fire instead, ashamed of this story that was his life.

He felt her move and he turned, not knowing what to expect. If she was smart, she'd double her fists and beat him bloody. It would be what he deserved.

Instead, she'd reached for the bag and pulled out the jeweler's pouch, which she now pressed into his hands. It was heavy with the weight of good, solid gold. "I know the brooch is not enough. Here. Take all of this to Newcastle. There is a pearl necklace my father gave me in there. It's in its own pouch. Be careful with it. I'm certain it will bring more than a pittance."

"Abby —"

"I wish to keep my ring, if that is fine with you."

She still hadn't looked at him.

"Of course," he said.

"Fetch the best price you can. We only need three years, and then my money will be turned over to us."

"I don't deserve your support," he whispered. "Did you not hear anything I said, of the schemes I've attempted, the lies I've told, the people I've betrayed?"

Her gaze met his. "I thought you wished to change?"

"I have."

"Do you wish me to leave?"

Here it was. If he said yes . . . she would go.

A true nobleman would think of his lady first. Of what was best for her.

But Andres was done with lies and half-truths. "No."

"Then I am not leaving," she answered.

He looked down at the jewelry in the bag. Her trust didn't make sense. Abby was not a woman whose head was turned by a man's looks. She didn't hesitate to let him know when she saw right through him. And here he was, confessing everything, and in return, she was giving all that she owned.

"Why?" he asked.

Abby heard the confusion in his voice.

He didn't understand. Andres, a man who had women throwing themselves at him, couldn't see her love.

It broke her heart. Made her fear that perhaps she was wrong.

Perhaps there would never be anything between them save — what?

Not friendship. They were already more than friends. More than just lovers. He'd proven that by confiding in her.

Then again, a cynical voice inside her whispered, had he a choice? They were married, bound by the laws of man and God. Just how vulnerable did she want to be to him?

"You've stayed beside me," she said, braving the simple truth. "My father disowned me, but you stayed. No one has ever done that before . . . not my friends, not Freddie —"

Freddie. He seemed nothing more than a distant memory.

Andres was her present, and her future. Even if he never loved her, she believed she had love enough for both of them.

"You will not regret this," he vowed, taking her hand. "Stonemoor will be what we both want."

She could have told him he was wrong. She didn't care about this shabby, run-down property. She was doing this for *him,* and it twisted her heart that he couldn't see that.

"I'm tired," she answered. The moment she spoke the words, her muscles went lax. She felt beyond exhaustion.

He jumped to his feet. "Of course. Here, let me prepare a bed for us." He surveyed the room, as if considering what he wanted to do.

Abby watched him, struck by how handsome he was, even in these circumstances. Funny, whereas most women immediately noticed his looks, it had taken her time to appreciate them. He'd become more attractive to her as he'd grown more dear to her.

The lines of his mouth flattened with determination. "This will be a hard night for us, *palomita.* However, tomorrow will make a new beginning. Wait here while I see what we have in the stables."

He took off before she could comment. Abby sat pensive before the fire, too tired to move. Her stomach rumbled, reminding her that it had been hours since she'd eaten, but she wasn't really hungry.

Andres was gone for almost half an hour.

Abby grew anxious and stationed herself at the window to watch for him.

She had to admit she liked that so many rooms looked out over the back courtyard, and she liked a view of the stables as well. For a moment, her imagination could conjure a vision of this house whole and well cared for. Whether she wished it or not, a spark of what was possible took hold of her.

After all, if she had not come with him, what would she have been doing now? Mooning over Freddie? Lamenting an upcoming marriage and immediate motherhood?

Oh no, this was a thousand times better.

She heard Andres then. He was in the house. He came into the scullery carrying an old chair with three legs, a small stool, and other pieces of broken furniture, along with a bucket of water.

"I found a pump," he said happily. "It's off the kitchen door. I gave the pony water."

"Good," she said. "I didn't know what to do."

"You did very well," he said encouragingly. He was smiling and full of energy as if the work — and the confession — had renewed him.

"The water is cold," he continued, "but tastes very good. Sweet."

Abby had never thought of water having taste.

"I can't find a pan to heat it up," Andres continued, "but I shall find one on the morrow. There are all sorts of things tossed aside behind the stable."

"Tossed aside?" Abby crossed her arms against her stomach. She'd been a rich man's daughter. She had never used anything that had been "tossed aside" or, at least, not as far as she knew.

He seemed to catch wind of her concerns. "It will seem hard at first, Abby. But I will succeed. You do believe in me, don't you?"

"Yes, Andres, I do." Certainly she had many doubts, but more about herself and less about him.

Andres would succeed because he'd spent a lifetime fighting for everything he had. In fact, his background and his experience made him very well suited for this sort of endeavor.

The question was, how would she fare? And she realized that perhaps Stonemoor and building its reputation for horses was not a dream she could grasp . . . but supporting him, loving him, was.

He smiled at her, a smile that reached those amazing eyes of his, a smile that told her she'd made him happy. "Thank you,

Abby." He took her hand and kissed it. "You will not have any regrets."

"I will if I don't sleep shortly," she said.

"I know, I know," he answered, already out the door. "I'll return in a moment. Stay right there. One moment."

She watched him sprint across the court-yard with the energy of a man on a mission. He went to the hayrack and returned with his arms full of old hay. He made a bed on the floor for them, using the broken chairs as a makeshift frame and her coat and his jacket as a cover for the hay mattress.

"Tomorrow I will find you a better bed," he promised, pulling off his boots.

Abby ran a distracted hand through her hair. "You've made many promises for to-morrow."

"And I will keep them," he said.

Believe in me. That was all he asked.

"You are tired, Abby. We both are. Let's go to sleep."

She nodded and all but dropped on the hay bed, not bothering to undress. The "mattress" was not that uncomfortable. She lay on her side, making a place for herself, her face toward the fire. She slipped off her shoes, kicking off one, then the other —

Her husband started undressing. She was so aware of his every move that she could hear him pull his shirt over his head, then fold it and set it aside. He sat beside her and pulled off his boots. One hit the ground, then the other. He picked them up and placed them by the shirt.

Abby closed her eyes, feigning sleep. Conjugal rights aside, it was one thing to promise to trust him, and another to open herself completely to him.

She didn't know what she felt or what she wanted.

And yet she was attuned to his unfastening each button of his breeches. He slid them down his legs. Long legs.

He must have shucked off his socks at the same time because she did not hear a separate movement.

Andres stretched out beside her, pulling his heavy greatcoat over them.

Their bodies did not touch; they didn't need to. His body heat and the spicy hint of his shaving soap proclaimed his presence.

Her heart pounded in her ears so hard that she almost didn't hear him whisper her name.

She didn't respond. She was tired. She was "asleep."

And making love to her husband might ask her to risk more than she could afford —

He curled his body around hers.

Even through all the layers of her clothes, his arousal was very real and present. She braced herself, even as a part of her longed for what he offered.

However, Andres didn't move. He sighed as if content . . . and all went quiet.

Had he gone to sleep? Had he drifted off as content as a baby while she lay here almost overwrought with a hundred different emotions? Here she was, armored against him with all her layers of clothing and he hadn't even tried to kiss her, let alone make love to her?

Abby was tempted to pull her arm forward and shove her elbow into his chest. How dare he ignore her? And the worst was that he'd gone to sleep when she needed him to hold her in his arms to reassure her. She wanted to feel him inside her, needed the heat of him —

"Do you really believe I would go to sleep on you, my *palomita?*" his voice whispered in her ear.

Abby turned, surprised. His face was inches from hers.

Too late, she remembered she'd been pretending to sleep. He'd caught her. His lips curved into a devilish grin and then came down to claim hers.

CHAPTER FOURTEEN

No one had ever sacrificed so much for Andres. And it made him love her more.

He couldn't tell her that. Words were a poor substitute for what he truly felt. Besides, he'd used words before and had discovered they meant little. But Abby was *his.* No husband, no lover, no one lurked in the shadows waiting to claim her. In a short amount of time, he had come to know her in a way he'd never known another — and she'd freed him. The guilt he'd carried with him was gone. It had vanished the moment she'd put her trust in him. She was his dove, his madonna.

He knew she had doubts. She should. But he would never fail her. That was his vow, a vow he pledged with his kiss.

Abby was ready for him. He'd known she would be. Her heart had been confused and uncertain. He'd lain beside her, waiting for the moment when she'd give up this pretense of sleeping and open to him the way a wife should. Even an uncertain one.

Because here was a way he could prove what she meant to him.

Andres began undressing her. All these clothes had been her armor against what she feared was foolishness.

It wasn't. She was strong when he was weak; he was strong when she had fear. This had become the pattern between them from the moment they'd met, and he realized it was a blessing —

He became aware that Abby was attempting to break the kiss. He looked down at her in his arms. Feeling a tenderness he'd never known, he whispered, "What is it?"

He had her clothes down over her shoulders, her breast still covered.

She stared up to him, her eyes reflecting the flames in the fire. A small frown line had formed between her eyes. She didn't speak, but he understood.

"It is hopeless," he answered her unspoken question. "It has been from the moment our paths crossed." He placed a kiss on that frown line, laying his hand over her heart, feeling her nipple harden against his palm.

His lips sought and found hers. Slowly, intently, he undressed her. And then he made love to her.

He took her in his arms and buried himself deep, savoring the way she always smelled like fresh flowers and reveling in the texture of her.

Some women controlled their emotions. Abby was not one of them. As she did in all aspects of her life, she gave herself completely to passion. Andres had never experienced a woman who so satisfied him. It was as if they were parts of the same soul.

And this night, as his seed found her heat, as he released himself in the most satisfying, shattering moment of fulfillment, he knew she had been what he'd been searching for in his life.

She was his treasure.

Abby cried out his name. Her legs encircled him, drawing him closer, deeper.

They held each other and he never wanted to let her go.

He felt the tension leave her. Her solemn eyes opened, studying him. Even in the firelight, he could see the deep circles beneath them.

"Sleep," he ordered softly. "Tomorrow you may worry." He slid off her and gathered her close. He was exhausted, but he'd not close his eyes until she closed hers.

Her back rested against his chest, her body nestled in his.

It was a long time before he finally felt her find peace.

Abby waited at a small inn in Corbridge while Andres took her jewelry to Newcastle.

She used her morning to visit several local shops and introduce herself. To her surprise, many knew that a Spanish barón now owned Stonemoor. She didn't correct their impression of Andres's title, though she didn't claim it either. The truth was, she didn't know where to go with it. Continuing with the ruse seemed productive for now. After all, what worth was there to a Spanish title in England? Her "Ladyship" was really more a courtesy than anything else. And now that revolutions and wars had flooded Britain with émigrés, who knew how many others also pretended?

Her innate practicality decided it would be best to not waste time explaining but to allow people to believe what they wished.

She managed to meet a local crofter whose wife was reputed to be a good housekeeper. The cook at the inn where she waited for Andres approached her about going into service at Stonemoor, and a number of young men took a moment to politely inquire if they were hiring.

All in all, it was a productive day.

But Andres's was more successful. He received three hundred and forty-five pounds for her jewelry. The pearls had fetched the highest price.

And he'd returned not on the Mail but driving a wagon loaded with furniture. He pulled to a stop in front of the inn and hopped down to give her a bow. "I have a bed. And a table and chairs."

Abby walked to the back of the wagon to inspect the furniture. It was old-fashioned but well constructed and would match the style of their house. "How did you find this?"

"The jeweler knew a man who wished to rid himself of this furniture. I bought it for a very good price."

"You have a shopkeeper's soul," she said and didn't mean it as an insult.

He didn't take it as one but grinned his pleasure at her compliment.

Three hundred and forty-five pounds. Abby sat next to him on the wagon, and they discussed how they would manage this small fortune. The amount would be a pittance to live on for three years in London, but they thought they could manage quite well in the north.

That night, they made love in the bed. The mattress turned out to be *very* comfortable.

For the first time in her life, Abby was truly busy. Nothing she'd ever experienced compared to life at Stonemoor — and she relished every single moment.

Within two weeks, she'd hired maids and made the house relatively inhabitable. There was still much for the workmen to do, but once the windows were repaired, the house became livable.

Andres spent his time working on his beloved stables. The horses, tools, and equipment he'd ordered from London arrived at the end of their first week. Abby had been anxious about how they would pay for it all. Growing up, she'd been protected from the bills and daily chores of a household.

Andres didn't protect her. He answered her questions and she admired the way he skillfully dealt with their creditors. Her husband had the gift of a golden tongue. He convinced the stable owner who had delivered the two horses to accept partial payment with the promise of full payment in six months' time.

Over the course of that first week, her husband's dream became hers as well. She started to picture the gardens at Stonemoor as vibrant with roses and irises, even though they were full of brown, straggly weeds. She hired some boys to clear out those weeds and turn over the soil. A group of men repaired the drive, and Abby herself repainted the sign.

Two important events lifted Abby's spirits. The first was when trunks of her clothes arrived from London. Her mother had sent them to her along with a note praying that Abby was well. She'd also packed linens, fine milled soaps, sachets, and a journal of housekeeping hints that she had thoughtfully written out.

This told Abby that although her parents might not be pleased with her decision, they hadn't truly cut her off.

She sat down and wrote her mother a long letter about the goings-on at Stonemoor. When she was done, she surprised herself with how much she'd had to share. In fact, her life before Stonemoor seemed shallow and empty when compared with how she now spent her hours.

The other important event was the day Destinada arrived. This was the Andalusian mare Andres had convinced the duke of Holburn to buy and cover with his prized Thoroughbred.

Abby had never seen a more beautiful

horse — or met a kinder one. The mare was snowy white, and her mane and tail were like silk. The mare was in foal but appeared pleased with her state and with the stall Andres and his grooms had labored to prepare.

For the first time, Abby bonded with an animal. Because they'd lived in town, her parents had not wanted animals. Abby was charmed by how this horse knew her. Every morning after her tea and before the start of her day, Abby would pay Destinada a visit. Once, she was late going to the stables and Destinada waited by her paddock gate, flicking her tail with impatience for Abby to appear.

The other horses liked Abby, too. Andres did not believe in treats, but Abby always had a little something to share with them — and with the barn cat.

The cat had shown up one day during their second week. Abby had caught Andres sneaking food to him. The cat was not like one of Mrs. Rivers's fat tabbies; he was a scrappy-looking thing that was all skin and bone.

Andres had immediately apologized for keeping the cat when he'd known she hadn't been able to tolerate them, but Abby hadn't had the heart to send the kitty away. And the truth be told, the cat hadn't made her eyes water . . . perhaps because she'd only seen him out in the barn.

Whatever the reason, within his first three days of taking up residence at Stonemoor, he killed a huge, fat rat, and not another was ever found there again. Andres named him Pedro. The name made Abby laugh, especially since Pedro followed Andres around the stables like a faithful dog.

Abby's favorite time was in the evening, when she and Andres would make their plans for the next day. Usually this was after they'd made love. She'd lie in his arms and they'd talk about anything and everything.

Andres teased about the flock of ducks and geese they would purchase once the weather was warmer. And there would be a cow, he promised, and they would make their own cheese instead of purchasing it from the neighbors.

Abby had plans for the gardens. She'd lived all her life in town and had not watched anything but flowers grow. However, Cook's insistence on an herb and vegetable garden had sparked Abby's curiosity.

Her husband predicted she was becoming a farmer's wife, and the thought filled her with a deep satisfaction. He was happy, too. And in that way, with the sharing of dreams and plans, they'd fall asleep.

The days grew shorter. There was talk of Christmas. It was not far away, and it was a time of family and friends.

Abby and Andres started attending services at St. Andrew's Anglican church in Corbridge. Faith was important to her. The first time he took her, Abby worried a bit about how Andres would feel inside such a church, but he acted completely relaxed and seemed to enjoy the services.

Afterward, the warden, a Mr. Gardner, introduced them to all the local gentry. They were soon flooded with invitations for dinner. A good number of locals were also interested in Destinada's foal when it was born. Andres told Abby he was surprised. He had not thought there would be such enthusiasm this far north for the Andalusian breed, but he and Abby soon discovered the gentry were a well-heeled lot. Newcastle-Upon-Tyne was a bustling harbor town. Its residents seemed more aware of the world beyond England's shores than the Londoners had been.

Furthermore, country women didn't hesitate to call on each other. Their calls had more to do with the need for company than an interest in social status. Yes, there were a few who preened and carried on, but most of the women were open and honest. Abby began making friends. She soon started driving the pony cart Andres had purchased for her, paying return calls. She was finding her neighbors to have a wealth of knowledge about gardening and housekeeping.

Many of the local homes had very rich furnishings. From Celeste Higgins, Lady Landsdowne, Abby learned where to buy thick India carpets to cover Stonemoor's floors at a quarter of the price such goods would cost in London. However, Abby turned her nose up at china and porcelains and set her table with local pottery. To her surprise, her neighbors followed suit.

Around the middle of December, Andres and Abby hosted a dinner party to thank their new friends for so generously including them in the local society. They didn't have the rooms for the guests to spend the night so they held the party in the middle of the day.

Following a Christmas tradition from Spain, Andres built a fire — a *Hogueras,* he called it. Their guests were from all levels of Corbridge society, from the church warden and priest to the squire and Lord and Lady Landsdowne. They gathered around the *Hogueras,* drinking wassail, made from the recipe in the journal Abby's mother had sent, and enjoying themselves — until Andres informed them of the rest of the tradition. As a guard against illness, the men were called upon to jump the *Hogueras.*

No Englishman with a bit of punch in him could resist such a challenge. Andres went first, demonstrating his Spanish prowess and almost burning his breeches — but he did gain good health for him and Abby for the new year, or so he claimed. Many attempted to follow suit, to great hilarity. The affair was an enormous success.

The following Sunday, when Abby and Andres walked into St. Andrew's church, she felt part of a large, welcoming community and there by her own right.

Abby had never been popular. She'd always lived under the shadow of her uncle, the duke of Banfield, and her much prettier cousins. At Stonemoor, she was the mistress. There was no one else to compare her to. Nor did the friendly, good-hearted people of Corbridge seem to wonder why a man as handsome as her husband was with her — until a few days later, when she caught a glimpse of herself in the mirror and noticed she was changing.

They were to be guests of Jonathan and Celeste, Lord and Lady Landsdowne, for dinner that evening. Celeste had begged

them to come. Their house would be over-
flowing with her relatives, and she'd sworn
it was always deadly dull. She wanted Andres to build a *Hogueras* for them and teach
her guests how to jump over it. She claimed
their relatives were all dreary and boring
and needed some enlivening.

Abby was taking a moment to decide what
she wished to wear and what needed to be
packed, when her reflection caught her by
surprise. In truth, her days were so busy
that there was little time to primp. She
rarely even glanced at herself.

Now she leaned close to the mirror,
uncertain if her eyes deceived her. But it
was true. Her marriage had given her
confidence. New maturity and happiness
showed in her face. She'd grown softer. Her
eyes were alive with purpose, and she'd lost
the petulant lines around her mouth.

She even carried herself differently, as if
her less rigid attitude had relaxed her entire
body and given her grace.

For that evening, she decided to wear her
hair down with a velvet cap on her head.
Her gown had some of that same blue velvet.

Andres liked the look and showed his appreciation with kisses that Abby couldn't
refuse. They were newly married, after all,

and enjoying every moment of it. Consequently, they were late arriving at Lord and Lady Landsdowne's house. The butler greeted them with the information that all the other guests were assembled and dinner would soon be served. Abby gave Andres a covert pinch, a reminder that their being late was his fault.

He appeared unrepentant.

The Landsdownes' ancestral home was the Georgian manse Andres had once described Stonemoor as being. It had enough rooms to store an army, but Abby discovered she liked her Tudor hovel. It was a fraction of the size of the Landsdowne property, but she felt it had personality and charm.

The sitting room was crowded with guests when Andres and Abby came down from the bedroom they'd been given. Most of the guests were from London.

Abby was surprised. Celeste had told her there would be family, but Abby had not expected such a large, extensive family.

Jonathan claimed Andres's attention while Celeste took Abby's arm and started leading her around the room, introducing her as an honored guest.

There were so many people. Abby knew she couldn't remember all their names. She'd just met Celeste's three maiden aunts and was being brought over to a new group more of their age — when she stopped, stunned.

Freddie Sherwin stood by the fireplace.

Abby hadn't even realized he was here until she'd almost come upon him. And when she did recognize him, she felt him a stranger.

He didn't share that reaction. He'd obviously been anticipating the meeting. Abby knew Freddie's ways. His pleasure at surprising her was in his eyes and the smug set of his mouth.

Celeste introduced him. "This is my second cousin, Lord Frederick Sherwin, here for the holiday. We so rarely have him with us," she confided. "He's heir to the earl of Bossley."

Freddie interceded. "Lady Vasconia and I are old *friends*."

He bowed, but as his gaze came up, it scanned her body, undressing her with his eyes. He'd never done that before — at least, not that she'd been able to tell. Of course, now that Andres had introduced her to the sensual side of life, she understood a great deal more about men.

Both confused by his presence and offended by his presumption, Abby took a step back — and bumped into the commanding figure of her husband.

CHAPTER FIFTEEN

Andres was outraged Sherwin was here. He'd barely noticed the man in London. At the time, he'd had a host of his own concerns to worry about.

However, the moment he heard his name and saw Abby's reaction to him, his memory of Sherwin took on the intensity of an arrow in flight.

This was Abby's "Freddie," the man she'd loved enough to beg him to run away with her. The man who, not that long ago in Banfield's library, had suggested she marry someone else and then they could be lovers.

Jealousy was an alien emotion for Andres. He'd yearned for things, wanted them . . . but he'd never experienced jealousy's power to burn a hole in the heart.

He did so now.

Common sense reminded him that *he* had been the one to suggest marriage to Abby. This had not been a ruse on her part.

However, it took all of his self-control to not grab her and carry her out of the house *now.* This minute.

He placed his hands on her shoulders, a husbandly gesture. "Sherwin?" he heard himself say, his voice almost pleasant. "Have we ever met? Ah, yes, in London —" Andres shook his head, as if memory returned. "You commented on the knot in my neck cloth. Begged to know my secret. Did you ever master the knot?"

The knot jibe was a deliberate poke. Everyone around them could see that Sherwin had indeed attempted a poor execution of Andres's famed knot. For a dandy like Sherwin, such attention could be intimidating.

The man's face flushed. Andres smiled, enjoying his rival's discomfort.

The butler's "Dinner is served" interrupted them before Sherwin had to respond.

Andres wasted no time in offering his wife his arm. He and Abby started to follow the others to the dining room, but Celeste chastised them all, "Please, please, I find parties where everyone stays with their own little twosomes so tedious. I have names at place settings around the table, but let us start now. I want every gentleman to escort a woman he doesn't know into dinner. That includes you, my love," she said to Jonathan.

There was a shuffling around. Andres did not want to give Abby up. Sherwin went right for her, but Andres blocked him with the reminder, "Our hostess says someone we don't know."

"I know everyone here," Sherwin countered, but Abby had taken matters in her own hands. While the two men had been squaring off, she'd placed her hand on the arm of a much older gent who needed a cane to walk.

Pleased at his wife's choice, Andres felt a tug on his own arm as a woman slid her hand around it. He turned and found himself chosen by the local squire's oldest daughter, a very bosomy woman of some eighteen to twenty years of age. Her dress was extremely low cut so that what she had was right there for him to see.

Andres had to look away, wishing the toothsome girl had had the good sense to cover up — and his gaze met his wife's.

She'd caught him eyeing the girl's overabundant cleavage, and she let him know with a lift of her eyebrow that she expected his vision not to stray again — but there was a smile on her face, too.

He winked at her. There was only one

woman to his tastes — and that was his *palomita.*

Abby's shy, pleased, answering smile as she leaned over to listen better to what her escort had to say told him she'd understood.

And Andres was humbled by love. His life had been empty before her. What a gift it was to be so close to someone that you could communicate with using no more than a look or a nod.

If "Freddie" thought he was going to come between that, he was wrong. Andres would rip him in two.

However, doubt raised its ugly head during dinner.

Celeste had been true to her word. Couples did not sit together but were interspersed all around the table. Andres found himself surrounded by some of Jonathan's matronly aunts *and* the squire's flirtatious daughter.

Abby sat close to Sherwin.

It seemed to Andres the conversation from that end of the table was livelier than where he was. Sherwin's voice could be heard over the laughter. He was witty, clever, and English.

Whereas Andres was definitely the outsider.

Over the soup course, Jonathan's oldest

aunt, an outspoken, wizened woman called Dame Edith, demanded to know why he talked strangely.

"I have an accent, my lady," he said politely, in deference to her aged years.

"What sort?" she barked.

"Spanish. I am from Spain."

Dame Edith contorted her face as if trying to remember where Spain was.

The gentleman on her right, Robert Ramey, a local barrister, thought he'd be helpful by telling her, "That country is one of our enemies. The Spanish allied themselves with Bonaparte."

"My family did not," Andres quickly assured her and everyone else listening. "If we had, I'd be in Spain at this moment." The moment his words hit the air, he realized they were not particularly reassuring. "I mean to say, my family did not support Napoleon and lost all for it."

Too late he realized how unsettling he sounded.

His attempt to remove doubts failed. He smiled at Dame Edith, but she didn't smile back and continued to watch him with suspicion throughout the rest of the dinner. She was so concerned, she barely touched her food, spending her time tearing her bread into pieces and downing repeated glasses of wine.

The others around him thought it great fun, especially Ramey, who did apologize after the women had withdrawn. "I didn't know the biddy was going to think you some French spy," he said to Andres, chuckling over the joke.

"What is this about?" Sherwin piped up with interest, and of course Ramey told him. Andres didn't think he'd escape the story for the rest of the time he was there — and he was right.

When the men joined the ladies, Sherwin made sure that everyone knew the story. Dame Edith had fallen asleep in a chair by the fire, presumably from overindulgence, which added even more to the telling.

Those who thought they were sophisticated twittered away. Another group laughed but eyed Andres with Dame Edith's same suspicion.

The squire's daughter shyly touched his hand and whispered to him, "I don't think you are a traitor."

Andres murmured some bit of nonsense about gratitude, but he caught sight of the squire, who scowled at Andres in a manner that would have made Banker Montross proud. Andres moved across the room and found that most of the men had broken into small groups that didn't seem open to him.

This wasn't the first time he'd sensed that his foreignness kept him on the fringes. Sometimes it added to his celebrity, and other times it made him an outsider. Usually the latter.

Only this time was different. He planned on establishing a life for himself here. In the past, when he'd found things not to his liking, he'd moved on. He'd left, to try his luck somewhere else.

But the time had come for him to set down roots. He wanted to breed his horses and watch them grow. He wanted to train and gain a reputation for something other than his looks. He wanted to be a man like his sire, one who was well respected in his community.

Abby seemed not to notice there was an issue. She and Celeste had their heads together in a corner, and Abby appeared to be enjoying herself. She'd been readily embraced by those around them.

She caught Andres's eye and gave him a brilliant smile, but then Sherwin walked right over to her and whispered something in her ear. She pulled back and started to shake her head no, laughing.

Sherwin turned to the others. "Lady Vasconia is too shy, but I know she has a lovely voice. She sings like a bird. And we want her to entertain us. Please."

"Oh, yes," Celeste said. "You must sing. You'll play, won't you, Freddie?"

Andres frowned. What did she want Freddie to play? His wife?

His earlier good humor with his new friends went flat with distrust. Did Celeste know of Sherwin's interest in Abby? How close were Celeste and Freddie?

And it didn't help that Abby *could* sing — something Andres had not known.

She'd finally given in to the calls for entertainment and graciously taken her place by the pianoforte. Sherwin sat at the instrument. Without consulting Abby, he launched into music she knew and obviously enjoyed.

Her voice was radiant. It wasn't one of those warbling sopranos that always left Andres scratching his head as to why anyone feted them.

No, she had a lush, warm voice, much like her personality. Andres didn't know the tune or the melody, but like most songs, it dealt with love lost, not his favorite topic at the moment.

When she was done, the room sat silent, then burst into applause.

Celeste approached Andres. "Did you

know your wife had such a marvelous voice? Or do you sing as well?"

Andres ignored her first question and confessed, "I sing, but my voice is more that of an owl than a dove."

He smiled at Abby as he said it, to let her know how proud he was of her. He'd meant for the comment to be taken lightly by the other guests and was impressed with himself for doing so. His modest humor was met with more laughter, then calls for Sherwin to sing.

Apparently he had a fine voice as well.

And he was not modest about it.

"Abby — I mean Lady Vasconia —" Sherwin said, correcting himself with a rueful glance at Andres, "and I sang a duet years ago that was popular in every London drawing room. Do you remember, Abby?"

Sherwin didn't correct the familiar use of her given name the second time.

Abby scrunched her nose, her red curls bouncing as she shook her head. "Which one do you mean?"

Which one? Was she saying there were several of them?

Andres shifted his weight from one foot to the other. His jaw was starting to hurt from gritting his teeth while he smiled.

" 'The Knight and His Lady,' " Sherwin

prompted, and she nodded with sudden memory.

"That was fun," she said.

"Let's sing it now," Sherwin suggested, and the other guests clapped and called out for the song.

Sherwin put his arm around Abby to whisper in her ear. She nodded at whatever he said.

Andres crossed his arms. He felt exposed where he was standing. He was jealous and didn't like Sherwin being in the same house with Abby, let alone preening and prancing around in front of the company.

And he couldn't stave off the knowledge that Abby had loved this man. He was Andres's only rival.

Their duet was spectacular. Abby was a different woman when she sang. She had a bit of the theater in her. Her eyes were lively and her manner saucy as she sang the part of the "lady." When they finished, the other guests called for more, a request Sherwin was happy to accommodate.

In fairness, Abby did try to beg off. The squire's daughter offered to sing, and Abby generously encouraged her to do so. Abby looked over to Andres and gave him a smile.

He smiled back, hoping the Spanish words

going through his mind didn't show on his face.

But they must have, because Abby's smile died. She became more serious, though she didn't return to his side. He got the impression that for some reason, he'd done something wrong.

After the squire's daughter finished her song, Sherwin led the demand for Celeste and Abby to sing — and so it went for the longest, worst evening of Andres's life.

It didn't help when Dame Edith woke with a start during one of the lulls between musical pieces and asked in the loud voice only the aged possessed, "Is that foreign man still here?"

She was shushed but not until once again everyone looked at Andres with those damnable raised eyebrows.

He was tired. He'd risen early to work the horses, and this sort of dinner party had never been enjoyable to him.

But tonight was worse. And the only thing that would make it better would be shoving Sherwin's face in his pianoforte.

Unfortunately, women thought Sherwin attractive.

Even the squire's daughter was eyeing Sherwin with favor.

Celeste stood, a signal that the evening

was coming to an end. "Everyone, this has been so enjoyable. Such a good way to honor the Christmas season. Tomorrow we have a special treat. Landsdowne, do you wish to tell them?"

"I will be happy to do so," Jonathan said. His ruddy cheeks were ruddier from the amount of brandy he'd been drinking. This was true of most of the men in the room, save for Andres . . . and Sherwin.

"Our new neighbor, the barón de Vasconia, will be honoring us with a Spanish Christmas tradition — a bonfire. I'll have the wassail ready, and we shall enjoy ourselves tomorrow afternoon." He raised a hand in Andres's direction, but Dame Edith interrupted.

"What is so special about a bonfire?" Dame Edith pulled a face of distaste. "We have them all the time. I don't think foreigners invented a bonfire," she grumbled to those around her.

"I didn't say the Spanish invented bonfires," Jonathan clarified with an apologetic look to Andres. "I said it is a Spanish *tradition* to light a bonfire at Christmas."

"Yes, Dame Edith," Andres said, wanting to speak for himself and his country. "We light the bonfire; we call it *Hogueras* and jump over it as protection against illness in the next year to come."

"It's great fun," Celeste said. "Landsdowne jumped one at the baron's estate and almost burnt his breeches." She laughed and her husband laughed, but the other guests appeared puzzled.

Andres attempted to explain again. "You know the fire is a symbol of light. A good thing for Christmas."

"Well," Dame Edith said, "if it is dark, fire is always good. But here, we have enough good sense not to jump into a fire."

There was a smattering of giggles at her English common sense.

"You shall see how it is on the morrow, Aunt," Jonathan said.

"I doubt it," Dame Edith replied. "I'm not going out there to stand in the cold and watch you gents set your breeches on fire."

Her stance was seconded by a good majority of those around her. She then announced, "I for one am ready for my bed. Come, everyone."

People moved from the chairs, heading toward the door. Andres started toward Abby, but Sherwin was beside her. Whispering in her ear. *Again.*

Andres forced himself to walk forward at a sedate pace. He ignored Sherwin and took his wife's hand, raising it to his lips. "You were excellent this evening, *palomita*."

She gave him a distracted smile that didn't reach her eyes and pulled her hand back. "You will tell me if you hear anything else, won't you?" she said to Sherwin. There was a line of worry across her forehead.

"Of course I will," he said. He nodded to Andres. "Barón." He left.

Abby took hold of Andres's arm. "He said my mother has taken ill. My father is very concerned for her."

Andres didn't know what to say. "I'm certain your father will do everything he must for her."

She nodded, her expression troubled.

"Why did Sherwin wait until now to tell you?" Andres asked, anxious to add another reason to his dislike.

Abby flinched at his tone. "He said he'd been waiting for the right moment. There really hasn't been a private one until now."

Andres attempted to rein in his jealousy, to focus on her. "Come, it's been a long day. We will think better on this in the morning."

She let him lead her away, but her step was slow and he knew her mind wasn't with him.

Meanwhile, on the stairs ahead of them, Dame Edith was telling anyone and everyone that she thought it foolish to jump over a perfectly good fire to make "Frenchie lovers" happy.

Andres offered no argument. In fact, he was heartily tired of the whole group.

At the top of the stairs, Celeste waited for them. She glanced down the hall to be certain they weren't going to be overheard, then said, "I am so embarrassed. Please, Andres, do not take our older relatives' stubbornness to heart. It's the war. Newcastle is always certain the French will come sailing up the Tyne."

"It is not a problem," Andres said, more concerned with Abby than he was with the *viejos.*

"Well, there is a problem," Celeste continued. "Perhaps we should wait on having the bonfire. It was a wonderful experience at your house last week . . . but that was with a group of friends who are rather sophisticated, even though we live out in the country. Jonathan and I do not want you to be insulted by a lack of interest."

"It is fine," Andres said with a shrug. He would rather not be subjected to more of Dame Edith's opinions as it was.

"Thank you for your understanding," Celeste said with relief. "Sleep well." She walked to her room.

Abby hadn't said anything. Andres doubted if she'd even registered the conversation. He waited until he and Abby were alone in their room to say, "Your mother will feel better."

"I hate this. What if my being away, her unhappiness with me, has added to her illness?" Abby said, and Andres felt his temper flare. She was worried about disappointing her mother while her husband had just been all but flayed alive downstairs?

As he undressed for bed, he told himself that was fine. But then there was that element of newly discovered jealousy.

Sherwin had known exactly what to say to set Abby away from Andres. He could feel her distance. She took extra long to brush her hair and polish her teeth. She was too quiet and thoughtful.

Andres waited for her in bed. He knew he appeared composed, but in his mind he was imagining how good it would feel to go to Sherwin's room and bury a fist in the dandy's mouth.

Abby sat on the edge of the bed. Andres reached for her, running his hand up and down her arm. "Your mother will be better," he promised. "Come here."

He said his "come here" with just the right inflection for her to know what he really wanted. He needed to make love to his wife. He needed to know she chose him over that scheming Sherwin.

But for the first time, Abby didn't come to him.

She stood, walked a few steps away, and turned to face him, confessing, "Andres, if something happens to my mother because of my actions, I don't know what I'll do."

Andres heard the fear in her voice. "Abby, you don't know if what Sherwin says is true."

"It *is*. I can *feel* it." She paced around the room, rubbing her arms. "I left without saying anything, and she is the closest person to me."

He'd thought *he* was the closest person to her. Certainly, she was the only one he had. Without Abby, he had nothing.

And yet, she had so much. She had a family that protected and cared for her. She even had money. Trust or not, money would be there, and that would always be an attraction to other men.

For a moment, he considered risking all. He wanted to say *I love you.* These were words that had been gibberish to him before meeting Abby, before *loving* her.

Sitting naked in this bed with the light from the hearth throwing shadows on the wall, he felt the words on the tip of his tongue. *I love you. I need you. Come to bed with me.*

And then what?

Perhaps she was rejecting him because she was aware that she had made a mistake. She hadn't married a man like Sherwin, who could sing and easily be part of the company. She'd married an outsider. A loner. A man who had no family. Not even a country.

"Abby, come here."

She flinched and looked away.

He waited, hurt evolving into anger.

"I thought you would understand," she said, tears building in every word.

"I think I do," he said.

She cocked her head.

"You don't value what I've done," Andres said.

Abby shook her head, as if amazed. "You? We aren't talking about you. This is my mother I'm worried about."

"And you don't know anything except for what Sherwin has said," Andres pointed out, quite rationally, he thought.

But not rational to Abby. "What did you expect him to do? Blurt such news out upon first seeing me?"

"That would be sensible," Andres answered.

"It would not." Abby held her hand up, as if waving him away. "How could Freddie know my true feelings? To him, I eloped as if the opinion of my parents meant nothing. I was there under their roof one day and gone, vanished, the next. You saw my father in Scotland. He was deeply hurt."

"He was angry to have been outmaneuvered," Andres said, feeling as if he had to defend himself.

If he had told her to cut off her right hand, she could not have looked more offended. "*You* — How —" She groaned her displeasure, as if words failed her, but she regrouped. "*You don't know how he felt.* You don't know him as *I* do. He felt *betrayed*. He was *hurt*. *I* hurt him."

"I know that if your mother wanted to tell you she was not well, she could have written," Andres said, and the moment the words were out, he knew they had come across as callous.

Abby went still, her face pale, her red-rimmed eyes narrowing. "You don't know what my parents would do. You barely know me."

Andres climbed out of bed. "Don't know you?" She had become all he could think about. He rose early every morning and worked hard because he wanted to prove to her she'd made the right choice.

He walked up to her, took her by the arms. "I've touched every inch of you," he vowed. "I've been *inside* you. I've heard you cry out my name. I *know* you."

Her jaw hardened. "That is nothing," she said.

Andres almost staggered back. *"Nothing?"* Her charge confused his brain.

"How does what you take from me compare to the hurts and needs of people who nurtured me?" she asked. "Who care about me."

I love you. "I *care* for you." To say more would call for a commitment he feared to make. Instead, he held his breath, waiting for her response.

"Is that all?" She made a self-deprecating sound, as if she found herself part of a ruse. "Care?"

He wanted to kiss her. To force her to understand.

But she pulled away, and he let her go.

"I've hurt them, Andres." The tears were flowing now. She doubled her fist and pressed it against her stomach, as if in pain. "I suddenly can't live with that."

Andres straightened. He heard what she was saying. She didn't want him.

"It's being here, isn't it?" he said, his voice

sounding like that of a stranger. "You've looked at the people here, at your own kind, and you believe you've made a mistake, haven't you?"

Abby was starting to cry so hard that she was hiccuping. "What?" She shook her head as if denying his charge.

But Andres found he wasn't that far from breaking himself.

Abby had tricked him. Without his being aware, she had slipped past walls he'd carefully erected to protect himself. She had shown him a life he'd not dared to even dream of. She'd let him be happy, fulfilled, and now she was telling him it was a lie.

Just as his father had brought him to his house and then shot himself because Andres had not been enough.

However, Abby had introduced him to something he'd wanted without ever realizing it. She'd given him a home and the warmth of her spirit. She'd been a helpmate, a lover, a kindred spirit.

And it had all been a lie.

Of course, he was the fool. He knew better than to trust. He knew it . . . and yet love had come upon him, wooing him, tempting him, deceiving him.

"Go to your mother," he said. "Go back to London."

He turned and started dressing.

"What are you doing?" she asked.

"Leaving."

There was a pause of disbelief. He finished buttoning his breeches and reached for his boots.

"You can't go." Her voice was tight, insistent.

He stamped a foot into the heel of his boot before looking up at her. "Why not?"

She stood in front of him, her unruly curls going this way and that. "We're guests."

That was it? Her only reason for wanting him to stay?

He yanked his shirt on over his head. "Make my apologies," he said. Picking up his coat and neck cloth, he left.

CHAPTER SIXTEEN

Abby couldn't believe Andres had just walked out.

He'd shown no sympathy or willingness to share the blame for the pain she had brought upon her mother. And then he'd abandoned her.

She took a step toward the door.

The distress she'd felt over the information her mother was ill was nothing compared to what she experienced realizing Andres had abandoned her. And it had all happened so fast.

Yes, Freddie's news had upset her. She felt ashamed that while she'd been enjoying herself, while she'd been experiencing a freedom she'd not known before, her mother had fallen into despair. If anything happened to her because of Abby's selfishness, Abby didn't think she could live with herself.

She did believe what Freddie had said.

She and her mother were close, and she could sense the truth of his story. After receiving that first letter from her mother, she had anticipated others, which had not come. Illness would explain the lack of return mail.

But she didn't comprehend why Andres was not more sympathetic. Why hadn't he understood?

Was it because he was so accustomed to doing *what* he wanted *when* he wanted to do it? He had no family. He was free of the burden of guilt . . . but she had thought he would have empathized.

She'd thought she'd meant more to him than that.

Suddenly, Abby realized exactly how much of herself had walked out the door with him. She cared so much for him. She'd fallen in love with him.

And he'd left.

Her temper provided a shield. She doubled her fists, wishing she'd been in her own home, where she could pick up things and break them. What a fool she'd been. *Again!*

It felt good to be angry, and sad, too. She sat in a side chair, crossing her arms against her stomach. It hurt to think Andres didn't care for her. Physically hurt. She even felt feverish, and she realized that this was much worse than what she'd ever felt for Freddie.

Could it be that Andres was jealous over the attention Freddie had been paying to her this evening?

Frankly, Abby had found Freddie annoying all evening long. She'd been polite, but she'd kept a distance. Freddie had been very handsy. And what Andres hadn't seen was the way Freddie had been trying to play with her feet under the dinner table.

It had put her off him completely. However, when he had insisted that she sing, she'd really not had the choice to refuse. She would have appeared rude if she had. So she'd put on a good face and done her best.

She'd noticed Andres standing, alone and apart, silent and disapproving. He hadn't been comfortable in this company.

Then again, Abby could admit she had been too comfortable. She had been flattered to be the center of the evening's activities. And perhaps she hadn't been as mindful of her husband as she should have been. Of course, the squire's daughter, the one whose dress had made her look as if her breasts had been served up on two platters, had done her best to compensate Andres for Abby's lack of attention.

Dame Edith's comments had been mean. The fact that no one had corrected her was even more shameful.

And Abby would be lying to herself if she didn't face the fact that a part of her had been a bit frightened by how harshly they had judged her husband. In a switch of roles, Abby had been included and Andres had been left to fend for himself.

Perhaps she was being unfair to him. The image of the surprise on his face when she'd first started to sing rose in her mind. They were newly wed. Of course they didn't know each other well, and this was really their first fight. They rarely argued at home. She shouldn't have lashed out at him when she was the one who had abandoned her parents.

Abby came to her feet. She needed to talk to Andres, and she had to do it now, before he left.

Taking her cloak out of the wardrobe, she threw it over her shoulders and dashed out of the room, convinced her overwrought emotions had played too large a part in their argument. Both marriage and being in love were new to her.

Perhaps if she didn't try so hard to hide how deeply she had fallen in love with her husband, the scene in their bedroom would not have happened.

And she should have let him make love to her. It would have released tension for them both. Besides, right now, Abby really wanted his arms around her.

Downstairs, a footman stood guard at the door. One glance at Abby and he knew what she wanted. "Are you looking for the gentleman who left?"

"I am."

"He rode down the drive only a moment ago," the footman reported.

"He rode away?" Abby knew she sounded silly, but she was stunned. Yes, Andres had stormed out, but she'd clung to the belief that he would not strand her here.

"A rider just left. It's not such a bad night for travel. Several guests have returned to their homes."

Abby sank down onto the hall steps.

"May I fetch something for you, my lady?" the footman asked.

It took a moment for his words to sink in. She shook her head. "I need a moment," she murmured.

He nodded with empathy, the empathy that she had wanted from her husband.

Why had Andres burned so hot tonight? Thinking back, it was almost as if he'd been testing her. As if he'd searched for a reason to challenge her.

He'd wanted her. Having her in his bed had been important to him. Then again, how insensitive had it been of him to insist on her servicing him?

Abby released her frustration with an angry sound. Men were too difficult to comprehend. Something had been going on in Andres's mind, something she couldn't fathom.

And why must she? She thought of her mother, of Freddie's disturbing words.

"Abby?" Freddie stood halfway up the stairs. "Is something the matter?"

Noting the interest on the footman's face, Abby decided any and all conversations should be away from the servants' prying ears. She stood. "Freddie, I'm coming up." She moved up the stairs, catching him before he came down much further.

"I thought I heard you say your husband had left?" Freddie asked.

Abby blinked, startled that Freddie had been listening for that long. He was wearing a silk brocade dressing gown and slippers.

He noticed her hesitation and had the good grace to act embarrassed. "My room is next to yours," he confessed. "I could hear the row. Not the details," he hurried to assure her, "but enough to know the two of you were not pleased with each other."

She'd not thought she and Andres had been that loud. She blushed and started up the stairs. "It's nothing," she said. "All is well."

Freddie was right on her heels. "But *did* he leave? What of the the bonfire?"

Heading down the hallway, Abby said, "Lord and Lady Landsdowne decided the bonfire might not be a good idea. Apparently there is a bit of hysteria about the French. Andres hasn't been to Spain for years. Even so, the older family members are quite concerned about him." She tried to keep her voice light. "It's silliness."

"Yes, it is," Freddie agreed. He leaned a hand on the doorjamb of her room. "I hope he didn't take offense to it."

Abby shrugged. Freddie was fishing for more information, or did he know more than he was letting on? Suddenly, everything was overwhelming to Abby. She needed to be alone to sort it all out.

"I don't want to talk about it," she said. "Good night."

But Freddie didn't leave her. He followed her into her room, moving right with her through the door.

"Freddie, please, I'm tired —"

He shut her up by placing his mouth over

hers even as he kicked the door closed with his foot.

At one time, Abby had dreamed of being kissed by Freddie with this passionate abandon.

Now, she wanted to gag.

He had his arms around her waist, pulling her toward him. She could feel the bump of his erection against her. Pushing against his shoulders, she struggled to free herself from his grip even as she turned her face.

"Abby, don't be this way," Freddie said, groping for her breast. "We've waited so long for this."

"I'm married." She kept her voice low, not wanting to call attention to what was going on, wanting Freddie to come to his senses and leave her room.

"Yes, and I'll be married soon," Freddie agreed, his teeth brushing the skin of her neck. "You taste so good —"

Abby shoved with all her might, freeing herself. "Stop it, Freddie. This is ridiculous."

Freddie breathed heavily. "Abby, this is the way we planned it. You marry, I marry, and then the two of us could be together."

"You are going to marry *my cousin,*" she reminded him.

"But *you* are the one I love," he declared, spreading his arms as if to take her in them, his dressing gown making the gesture comical. "You are the one I want. My parents will know nothing about this —"

"But I will," Andres's deep voice said from the doorway.

Both Freddie and Abby swung around in shock.

He stood there, his silver eyes reflecting nothing, yet she could feel his hurt, his surprise, as if it had been her own.

"The footman said you'd left," Abby said, the words born of her confusion and distress. The moment they hit the air, and she heard how they sounded, she realized she'd said the wrong thing.

"That must have been someone else. I did go out for fresh air. I needed to think." Disbelief echoed in his voice. He made a small, disparaging laugh. "Apparently, I came back too soon."

Anger that he would believe her capable of being untrue warred with guilt. He shouldn't have walked out. She shouldn't have let Freddie into her room.

"Andres —" she started, taking a step toward him, but he had already disappeared from the door. She started to run after him. Freddie stepped in her path.

Taking her arm, he said, "Let him go. He's angry. He needs to cool his temper."

She had no doubt that her husband was furious, but she wasn't going to wait. She wanted the air cleared between them. She shoved at Freddie but he held on, swinging her around to meet him.

"Abby, have some pride."

"I *have* pride," she shot back. "And whatever I felt for you, Freddie, it's gone. It died when you chose someone else over me."

"That's your temper speaking," he answered. "Your jealousy."

He had hold of her wrist, and Abby had had enough. "It's not. I *love* him, Freddie. I love him in a way I could never have loved you. Do you understand? I don't want you to kiss me or touch me or even *look* at me." The words poured out of her. The truth. There it was. She'd exposed herself. She loved her husband.

She gave a good shake, breaking Freddie's grip and taking off after her husband.

Abby flew down the stairs. Freddie shouted her name, but she didn't heed him.

The footman was still in place, his eyes wide. He pointed down a hall, which, Abby knew, led to a back entrance and a path leading to the stables. "Thank you," she threw over her shoulder as she hurried to catch her husband.

But it was too late. She was halfway down

the path when she heard a horse galloping away. She went to the stables anyway, not willing to take the situation for granted a second time.

A groomsman met her. He was a young man with straw-colored hair and a desire to please. "May I help you, my lady?"

"Did the barón just leave?" she asked, her heart pounding in her chest.

"He did. Borrowed one of his lordship's horses. Paid me to bring you home in the pony cart on the morrow. Just let me know when you wish to leave, my lady."

A numbness spread through Abby at this cruel twist. She stood in front of the grinning groomsman as if she'd been turned to stone.

Andres maddened her. He'd jumped to the wrong conclusion and hadn't even taken five minutes to let her explain what had been happening. Not even a minute.

They'd known each other less than two months — and yet she felt closer to him than any other person on this earth. Obviously, he didn't feel the same about her. How could he believe that she would encourage Freddie, a man she had once loved but for whom she now felt nothing but contempt?

Freddie. He was the reason her husband

had been so insistent that she join him in bed. Andres hadn't been offering comfort. He'd wanted to stake his claim.

Cold, damp night air swirled around her skirts. The fog had come up. She hadn't noticed it as she'd been running down to the stable yard, but now it seemed thick and menacing.

"Is all well, my lady?" the groomsman asked.

"I don't know," Abby answered candidly.

"I'll walk you back to the house," he offered.

"No, I can find my way," Abby said, starting back up the path, her mind focused on Andres's behavior when they'd first gone to their room that evening.

He'd been jealous. But not in a good way. She crossed her arms and picked up her step, her thoughts furious. Her husband had been acting like a dog fighting over a bone — and she was the bone.

Andres hadn't heard anything she'd said about her mother. He'd been more interested in his own pride. He'd wanted her because she was his.

Freddie was worse. He had attacked without so much as a by-your-leave because he'd assumed she'd been his. What had he done? He'd had his ear against the wall?

Had he pleaded with Celeste for the room next to theirs? How tawdry!

Abby opened the back door and went inside only to pull up short at the sight of Celeste waiting for her. Her hostess was in her dressing gown, her dark hair down around her shoulders.

"I almost ran into you," Abby apologized. "Why are you up?"

"I was worried about you. Jonathan is waiting, in case you need him. Is all well? Is there some way we could help?"

Pride warred with unhappiness. Abby had been schooled to pretend everything was fine. Her father had taught her to forge ahead, to not listen to the whispers. You saved your frustration for the haven of your family, but for everyone else, you presented a good face.

Except Abby didn't have a good face to present.

Her anger at Andres fell away as she sank down to the ground in tears.

Celeste dropped down beside her, taking her hand and holding it, letting Abby cry.

"I feel like a fool," Abby confessed when she could speak without sobbing.

"Start at the beginning," Celeste advised, and Abby did.

She told about loving Freddie, and about

Corinne, and Andres's offer. She held nothing back.

In the same way that Andres's confession had freed him, she found the telling cathartic. She left out only one part — her feelings for Andres. They were her secret. Her vulnerability. And she kept to herself her husband's wish for her to make love to him this evening.

Celeste was a good listener. She didn't ask one question.

"There, that's all," Abby said. "I shouldn't be so emotional. I have no right to be. So what if he left? I know how to manage on my own. I can return to London now and see to my mother."

She looked to Celeste, wanting validation of her plan.

Instead, Celeste asked, "Have you told your husband you love him?"

Abby felt tears well up inside all over again. She'd thought she'd cried them out, but there was so much more left. "I don't." But her statement lacked the ring of truth.

"Liar," her friend said softly.

"I can't love him," Abby answered. "I mustn't. He's so handsome and kind and good — but we didn't bargain to love. He chose me because he didn't love me. It's my fault I've lost my heart to him. Besides, how can a man such as him fall in love with me? I'm a troll."

"Abigail, you are no troll," Celeste said. "The idea is preposterous. You are vibrant and beautiful. An Original. Do you know what Jonathan and I thought when we first met the two of you? We thought, 'What a happy couple.' You both complement each other. And when Andres is around you, one senses his contentment."

"But contentment is not love." Abby realized she had to tell all. "After we went upstairs this evening, and I was upset about what Freddie told me about my mother, all Andres could think about was me joining him in bed."

She waited, expecting Celeste to be as insulted and abused as she was feeling.

Instead, Celeste nodded sagely. "That's the way men are," she said. "Let me tell you something my mother told me after Jon and I had a terrible row. She said, we teach men *how* to love. They don't seem to know. They come into this world knowing how to conquer . . . but they don't understand that *claiming* something isn't the same as *loving* it. For too many, love is what happens between the sheets. And it becomes a bit competitive. They keep score like in that game of tennis my husband enjoys so much."

"Score?"

"Yes, if you do this, then I'll do that. But a funny thing happens, Abby, or at least I've found it to be true of Jon, that when a man trusts you, he stops paying attention to who does what for the other. And sometimes the best way he shows you he loves you isn't with words. That would be simple," she added dryly. "No, men show their love by taking care of things around us. By working hard and being certain we are safe. Occasionally there is a man who babbles about love and writes poetry and all that, but most are like Jon — content. He takes his pleasure with me and only me — and expects me to do the same . . . and we are in love."

"You heard what happened over Freddie?"

"It was a bit of a scene, what with doors slamming and Freddie grousing around. I'm certain even Aunt Edith heard it," Celeste said.

Abby closed her eyes, wishing it had not been so. "He's left."

"Are you going to go after him?"

There was the question. "We aren't like you and Jon." Abby sat silent a moment. "And I don't know how Andres will act if I return to Stonemoor. I'm mad for him,

Celeste. In London, I lived a very sheltered life. Andres has introduced me to the world. He'd done so much in his lifetime, and I'm proud of what we are doing to Stonemoor. I envision building it into a grand home, just like yours. And he really is excellent with horses. He will restore his family's reputation. I liked helping him."

"Do you love him?"

Abby raised a hand to her forehead and brushed her hair back with her fingers. "Yes. I love him so much . . . but this hurts, Celeste. His leaving me hurts."

"Then we must teach him to never leave you again."

"How are we going to do that?" Abby asked.

"You are going to London to see your mother. If your husband loves you, if your marriage is worthy of *your* love, he'll come for you."

"He'll misunderstand my leaving —"

"Abby, you don't have a choice. You must go. If you don't and something happens to your mother without the two of you making peace, it will destroy you."

"But if I leave Andres — ?" Abby broke off the thought, heartbroken.

"I'll talk to him."

"What if he doesn't come for me?" Abby

whispered.

"I saw how he looks at you," Celeste answered. "He'll come."

Abby wasn't certain, and yet Celeste was right. Abby had to see for herself that her mother was well, and she wanted — no, needed — to know if her husband had true feelings for her.

"What of Freddie?" she asked Celeste. "I know him as well as I know my brothers. He shall be proud of himself for what he has done." She shook her head. "My poor cousin, having to marry him."

"Be thankful you have finally seen him for what he is. I shall see to Freddie. Jon will take him hunting and give him a good talking to. He won't be a problem. Truly, Abby, he's my cousin and all, but what *did* you see in him?"

"I don't know now." And it was true. Andres had spoiled her. He'd taught her what it was like to be with a man who considered her a partner . . . and that was when she started to believe that perhaps Celeste could be right. Andres might love her.

The possibility was both exciting and frightening. People looked at Andres, saw his face, the many gifts God had given him, and assumed the man needed no one.

She'd thought that, too — but over the

last few weeks, she'd learned he was a compassionate man who needed compassion in return. Nor did he trust easily — and she recognized the expression on his face when he'd found her with Freddie. He had *trusted* her, and he'd felt betrayed.

If he did love her, if he'd been jealous of Freddie's presence, his behavior this evening made sense.

Celeste was right. Abby wanted more than pretending she and her husband rubbed along well. If she returned to Stonemoor now, it would be to a man with a grudge, a man who expected her to choose him over the welfare of her parents — a choice that was too hard without a meaningful commitment from Andres.

"He has to come to you," Celeste said, accurately reading Abby's thoughts. "If you matter to him, he must say the words."

"He may not know how," Abby observed sadly. "Women go to him. He's never had to put himself out for anyone — ever."

"Well, he must for you." Celeste gave her hand a squeeze. "Please, Abby, believe in yourself. You are thoughtful, beautiful —"

"No," Abby denied.

"*Yes,*" Celeste insisted. "You are vibrant, intelligent, everything a man wants in a wife. Don't argue with me. For one moment, just allow yourself to believe."

Abby sat still. She knew her faults. She could list them for Celeste. . . .

"Believe what I say," Celeste insisted.

"If it is true, Andres should be kissing the ground where I walk," Abby answered, half in jest.

"I think he does," Celeste confided. "He just hasn't realized it yet."

Abby shook her head, yet the conviction in Celeste's voice made her pause. "How did you come about all this wisdom?"

"The hard way — through experience. Jon is my second husband. My first was a bitter disappointment. I wanted him to love me. I did everything I could but failed. Truly, Abby, men don't want anything they haven't had to work at gaining. I made certain Jon wanted me."

"What if Andres doesn't come?" That was her greatest fear.

"Then you haven't lost anything, have you?" Celeste said, practical and wise, and Abby knew she had little choice.

The next morning, she left for London.

At the same time, Celeste took the stablehand and the pony cart and drove to Stonemoor.

Abby prayed Celeste was right.

CHAPTER SEVENTEEN

Andres had arrived home in the very early hours of the morning. Sleep had been impossible, so he'd started building a new paddock, throwing himself into the work.

Women had rarely occupied a large portion of his mind. If one had made him unhappy, there had always been more.

That was not the case with Abby. She'd changed him.

He pounded a nail in with more force than he needed and split the board. With a soft oath, he ripped it off the fence post and tossed it aside. He'd been at it for hours. The stable lads were tiptoeing around him. He overheard someone mention Abby's name. They knew she hadn't returned with him.

Andres tried another board and split it, too. He wanted to blame the wood, but he knew better.

He might have lived a lie, but he'd always

been honest with himself.

Yesterday, he had left Stonemoor with high spirits. He'd been proud of what he and Abby were doing here. The windows shone with cleanliness. There was fresh paint everywhere, and his stables were in the process of becoming what he'd envisioned.

Soon Destinada would foal and all the world would see the quality of Ramigio horses. Her baby was going to be a beauty. Andres could feel it.

And now, everything was wrong.

He dropped the hammer and went to the house. He was tired. Exhausted — and he was waiting for Abby.

Perhaps he shouldn't have left the Landsdownes' house party. It had been a tactical error. Instead of leaving, he should have grabbed Sherwin by the nape of his neck and the seat of his breeches and thrown him out the window.

"My lord," Cook said as he walked past the kitchen, "is Lady Vasconia returning today as planned?" Both she and the scullery maid had worried looks on their faces.

Their concern made Andres angry, then he took a look at himself and frowned. He was still wearing his evening dress breeches and shirt — not exactly clothes a man chose for labor. And he hadn't shaved. He probably struck them as some wild creature.

But what could he tell them?

That he didn't know?

Andres would bite off his tongue before saying such a thing . . . because he expected Abby to come home.

Home.

He'd never really had one. Stonemoor was his dream, and as a dream, it had already exceeded his expectations . . . because of Abby.

"She should be here soon," he told Cook and stomped up to the bedroom.

Pouring water into the wash basin, he gave himself a scrubbing. It didn't do much good. The air was cold. He and Abby didn't burn fires in empty rooms, and they rarely had a big one at night. Sleeping together and making love had kept them warm.

The thought of her giving herself to another was like a knife sliding into his ribs. She was his.

But he'd given her up. Walked out of Landsdowne's house without a look backward because he'd truly expected her to follow him. He'd thought she would have been here by now.

As he'd been sawing and pounding, he'd been playing over in his mind the things he planned to say to her. Now it all sounded so contrived. Andres had never had a woman cheat on him. Ever.

That it would have been Abby behaving this way was astounding because, the truth be told, he'd assumed Abby would always be there. She was the one person he'd finally let himself trust —

Andres thrust the thought away. He did not want to think on it. Later, when Abby returned, oh, he'd have some things to say, but first it would be a very cold reception. He might go a day not speaking to her. Let her stew in his unhappiness.

But first, he should make himself look presentable. He picked up his shaving soap. It was hard to mix with cold water. If Abby had been here, he would have had warm water. He wouldn't even have had to ask for it. It would just have been there, a product of his wife's good housekeeping and efficiency.

He pulled off his shirt and lathered his beard. He picked up his shaving strop and sharpened his razor. With a sigh, he tried to put his mind to his tedious task. He'd just taken a swipe along his jaw, shaving it of whiskers, when he heard the sound of a horse and wheels.

Andres rushed to the window. He couldn't

see anything at this angle, but Robin, one of the stable lads, was running toward the drive.

Abby had returned.

Shaving was no longer of interest. He looked at his soapy face. He should finish, and yet he *had* to see her. He *needed* to.

They had things to say to each other, and shaving could wait. He wiped the soap from his face. He had one strip of smooth skin, but he didn't care. He started to reach for the shirt he'd thrown aside, but it was filthy. His breeches were still dirty, too.

Andres didn't want to waste time taking off his boots. He went to the wardrobe and drew out a clean shirt. There was a stack of them folded and neatly put away. His wife had seen to that, and now she was back. She'd returned.

All thoughts of how he would handle her homecoming flew from his mind.

Pulling on the shirt, he started out the door and then thought of a neck cloth. He grabbed one of those, too. His hands were shaking.

His eyes fell on the bed. *She was back.*

Walking out on her, letting her know his anger, had worked. He'd won his point, but at what cost? He didn't believe in second chances. He would not take this risk again

— or let Abby know how much he cared. Love humbled him. Made him realize that he didn't like life without Abby.

If she knew how deeply he cared, she could cripple him.

He left the room, forcing himself to move with decorum instead of racing pell-mell to his wife.

Halfway down the stairs, he heard a woman's voice. It wasn't Abby's. He hesitated, recognizing the voice as Celeste's. Had she accompanied Abby? He waited, listening as Celeste handed her cloak and hat to the maid.

Andres continued down the stairs, tying his neck cloth. He entered the main room off the hall. Celeste stood alone in the center of the room. She heard his step and turned.

"I was almost afraid you weren't home," she said in greeting as she walked over to him, her smile wide, her hands outstretched.

He took her hands, bowed over them. "I thought you had guests."

Abby wasn't here. She hadn't returned with Celeste.

"They are relatives and can entertain themselves." She gave his hand a reassuring squeeze. "I had to be certain your pony cart was returned safe to you."

Andres didn't want reassurance. He wanted his wife. A deep cloud of concern settled over him.

"I'm famished," Celeste said. "Do you have something to eat? I imagine you could stand to eat as well."

"I'm not hungry." He turned from her and walked over to the maid, Ginny, lurking out in the hall. "Have Cook prepare something for our guest."

"Would you like it served on a tray in there, my lord?" Ginny asked.

"Yes, that would be fine," Celeste answered for him. She'd walked toward the door and leaned against the doorjamb.

Andres marched past her into the sitting room. "Where is my wife?" he asked. There was no fire in the grate. If Abby had been here, in this room, there would have been a fire.

"She's on her way to London," Celeste said.

Her words sucked the air from the room. Andres couldn't think. She'd left him. She'd gone with Sherwin.

"It's not what you are thinking," Celeste hurried to say. She walked over to Andres. "She didn't go off with my idiot cousin. She had to go see her mother."

Andres wasn't certain he'd heard correctly. "Why?"

Celeste made an impatient sound. "You know Freddie conveyed the message that her mother was ill."

Andres shrugged, unhappy. "It is what he said. Who knows the truth?"

"She had to go, Andres, to find out. Abby is very close to her parents."

On one level, he understood what she'd said, but Sherwin had taken hold of his mind. "That fop should not have been at your house."

"It was a family gathering, Andres," Celeste said. "He's a relative. If we had known the history behind all of this, Jonathan would have set him straight. As it was, we didn't learn the tale until last night after you'd left."

"How did he even know we live here?" Andres said, asking the question that had been haunting him.

"From me," Celeste admitted with a sigh. "I wrote my mother in London about how much we enjoyed ourselves as your guests. You are a bit of an infamous person there. According to my mother, the women are still talking about you."

Andres made a face. He didn't want to hear this. "They mean nothing to me." He paced the distance from the hearth to the center of the room, and then stopped. "She left me." He had trouble believing it.

"She didn't leave you," Celeste said, coming up beside him. "You left her. She's gone to see to her mother's welfare."

"Without telling me? Without saying one word? What did she do for money? How did she travel?"

The maid appeared at the doorway holding a tray of sandwiches and some cider.

Andres moved away from Celeste, pushing a distracted hand through his hair. "Set it anywhere, Ginny."

The maid did as told and bobbed a curtsey before leaving.

Celeste sat on the settee and began preparing plates of food.

"I'm not hungry," Andres said.

"Of course you are," Celeste countermanded him. "Please sit."

He didn't want to, yet he did not know what else to do. *Abby had left him.*

Celeste handed him a mug of cider. Andres held it without raising it to his lips. She placed a plate on his knee. He could barely look at the food.

"Disappointment is difficult, is it not?" Celeste said cheerily.

"Disappointment?" Andres almost choked

on the word. Was that all she thought he felt?

"You expected me to be your wife returning," Celeste said, "and to be honest, Andres, you are being very pouty about it."

"Pouty?" Andres came to his feet. The plate on his knee fell to the floor. He threw the mug at the fireplace. "My wife leaves me and you call me pouty?"

"Her mother is ill, Andres. When you love someone, you go to them when they need you. Can you understand that?" She answered her own question as she studied him. "You don't understand, do you?"

He didn't know what to say. He was angry and, yes, pouty.

"Do you love her?" Celeste demanded.

The question penetrated the emotions roiling inside him. Celeste sat on his settee like a pagan priestess meting out justice.

"She's my wife," Andres said.

"Do . . . you . . . love . . . her?" Celeste repeated, drawing out each word as if he'd been simple and she'd had to make herself clear.

Andres felt cornered. He felt vulnerable.

Her expression softened. "You poor man," she said. "You are so afraid."

He started to deny it, then realized there was nothing he could say. Celeste saw right through him.

Funny, that Abby didn't.

"Both of you are too fragile," Celeste said. "She's certain you won't come after her, that you don't care."

"She knows differently."

"Does she?" Celeste placed her plate on the tray and leaned forward. "And how does it feel to have your pride and no wife?"

Anger flashed through him. He reached for it. Anger felt better than being vulnerable. "You know *nothing* of us."

Celeste didn't take offense at his tone. Instead, she rose with a sound of resignation. "I know when a man is being too stubborn for good sense. And how futile it is to talk to any of your sex when you are in this state. But understand, Andres, I have come here as a friend. I don't like my cousin. He thinks he is some Captain Sharp. And I am distressed at the thought that one such as him could come between two people who so obviously care for each other."

Her words found their mark. The anger ebbed. He tried to keep hold of it. "If she cared, she'd be here."

"Because it is too much of a risk for you to go there?"

Her challenge hung in the air between them.

"I can't go to London," he said. If he went and Dobbins discovered his presence, he would lose Stonemoor.

But he couldn't say that to Celeste. She'd think worse of him than she already did.

"When we love someone, we take the first step," she said, her expression carefully neutral. "We go to them." She gave him a small, sad smile. "I'll be leaving now," she said quietly. "Andres, please, your pride is not worth losing what the two of you have. I didn't come here to badger you but to assure you that Freddie means nothing to Abby and he never will. You walked out on her, my lord. Now it is up to you to make the first step." She didn't wait for his response but left the room.

He stood very still. He should have gone with her to see that she had safe transportation home, but he couldn't move.

A moment later, he heard the sound of horses riding away, and he was alone.

All of his life, he'd dreamed of a place like Stonemoor, and now he had it. But the dream was hollow without Abby.

Andres raised a hand to his chin and frowned as his fingers brushed the spot he'd shaven, surrounded by his beard. No wonder Celeste had so accurately read him. He was a mess.

"It is up to you to make the first step."

The doubt of his own worth, the sense that he would never measure up to his father's expectations, the fear that Abby could not respect him, collected into a hard knot in his chest.

Could it be that his fit last night — because that was what it had been, a fit — had had more to do with jealousy than he wanted to admit? Could it be that he'd hurt her as much as he was feeling abused? Could it be that Abby thought *he* didn't care?

She had to know he did. . . .

If she had been here, he'd have told her how he felt.

If he went there, he could lose Stonemoor.

Andres sank down onto a side chair, his brain buzzing with a desire to go after his wife and bring her back, and the fear that she wouldn't come back. Then he would have lost all for nothing.

In the end, he decided to write. He would put in a letter the feelings he had not spoken.

Andres sat down to the task. It did not go well. He even attempted writing in Spanish, a language more conducive to what he felt in his heart.

But words failed.

He waited a day, hoping for another solution, watching the road, expecting her to return home.

She didn't.

Andres spent the following day cursing his fates and his wife. He'd never needed anyone in his life. He told himself that he didn't need anyone now.

By the third day, he knew he was wrong.

It was the mistletoe that made up his mind.

In five days' time it would be Christmas. The servants had put up holly and evergreens, decorating in the manner Celeste had done her house. They'd even put mistletoe up, right over the front door.

Cook had told him of the English tradition of kissing under the mistletoe.

Andres had no one to kiss. And he was tired of an empty bed. He didn't like this life he was living. He missed the life he'd had with Abby. Perhaps he didn't *need* her, but he *wanted* her close. He wanted to share the activities of his day with her, to sit across a table and watch her eyes light up when he thought of something amusing to tell. He wanted to tuck her body in close to his and hold her while she slept, protecting and keeping her.

And if it meant risking all he owned to let

her know how he felt and bring her back,
then so be it.

He saddled a horse and left with all haste.

Because when you love someone, you go
to them no matter the cost. He prayed he
wasn't too late.

CHAPTER EIGHTEEN

The trip to London was almost unendurable for Abby.

She wept most of the way, frustrating herself for not being stronger — and yet she couldn't help but sense that she was making a grave mistake.

The Landsdowne coach was well sprung and very good for travel. The servants could not have been kinder.

They made excellent time. After three days of hard travel, she arrived in London shortly after noon. As the Landsdowne servants retrieved the bag she'd brought from the boot, Harrison, her family butler, opened the door.

"Miss Abigail?" He came outside. "Thank God, Miss Abigail, it *is* you."

"Harrison, how is my mother?"

"Sad, very sad. Come in out of the cold and I'll hurry you upstairs to her."

This concern from the usually composed

butler frightened Abby. "Please see to the Landsdowne servants," she said.

"I will, but please hurry. Please. We've waited for you to return home."

Inside the house, Abby took the steps two at a time up the curving staircase that led to the hall where her mother's room was located. The housekeeper, Mrs. George, saw her and rushed to open the door. "We are so glad you've returned," she whispered as Abby whisked by.

A fire burned in the grate. The heavy velvet curtains were pulled against the cold. The air was overheated and oppressive. This was not like her mother. Her mother relished fresh air, always claiming that a little cold kept the blood pumping.

Abby looked to the bed. It was made. Her mother was not there, and Abby felt a small measure of relief. She went around the corner to the small sitting room that overlooked the garden.

Here again the drapes were pulled. Her mother sat in a rocking chair in the corner, her face pale in the room's murky light. She did not act as if she was aware of anyone being in the room with her. She wore a mobcap over her hair and her black mourning gown. Abby had seen her like this one other time — when she had been in mourning for Robert, the oldest son, who had died in battle.

"Mother?" Abby said softly.

Her mother's brows came together. She looked up at Abby, as if not believing her eyes.

Abby walked to the chair and knelt. Her mother's hands were cold in hers. Her mother squeezed her hand hard. "Abby?"

"Yes, Mother, it's me."

Tears poured from her mother's eyes. She fell into Abby's arms, holding her close. "I feared I would not see you again. This was the same as losing your brother. Heath returned from Scotland and said you were as good as dead to us. I can't lose my daughter. I can't lose another child."

"You haven't lost me. Father was very angry." Abby took the kerchief from her mother's hands and used it to wipe her mother's tears. "I'm home now. All is well."

"This is the best gift I've ever received," her mother whispered. "Tell me what you've been doing? Are you all right? Did that Spaniard do something terrible to you?"

He's only broken my heart, Abby thought to herself, but she wouldn't share that with her mother. She had to be loyal to Andres.

Instead, Abby started telling her mother about Stonemoor and the horses. "I appreciated your journal of household advice," she said. "It has rescued me more than once."

Her mother laughed, the sound carefree. Abby opened the curtains, and some of the oppressive gloom dissipated from the room. Already her mother's color looked better. "I had hoped it would be meaningful for you," her mother said.

"I am so sorry to have caused you pain," Abby replied.

"It was the fear of not seeing you again," her mother said. "And also my own regrets."

"What regrets are those?"

"At last I understood how my parents felt when I ran away. I was so frightened for you, Abigail. I didn't know where you were, and when your father returned and said you'd married, I thought my heart was going to stop. I had wanted to be at your wedding. Your father and I have dreamed of it. I now understand why my father cut me off. He'd been hurt. And I was so happy, I was completely callous to him."

"I didn't mean to hurt you."

"We didn't mean to chase you away. *We* of all parents understand eloping. But we were in love, Abigail. From the moment I met your father, I knew my life was tied to his. Everything made sense when I was with him. Certainly he wasn't the man my father wished me to marry. We had no choice but to elope. But you had a choice."

"Did I?" Abby asked. "Father was so set on Lord Villier."

"I would have talked him out of it," her mother said softly.

"And who would Father choose after him?"

Her mother shook her head. "It's the earl of Bossley's son, isn't it? You are in love with him the way I was with your father. In spite of what your father and I thought of him, you loved him."

Abby gave her mother's hand a squeeze. "I don't love Freddie Sherwin."

"You don't?" her mother questioned in disbelief. "You always said you did."

"Because I wasn't thinking clearly. Oh, Mother, this is all so confused, and none of it is your fault, or Father's. I did love Freddie, but he never loved me. Not in the way Father cares about you."

"We knew that." Her mother dabbed her eyes. Her voice had become animated.

"But *I* didn't know. I thought if I confronted Freddie with my feelings, he would see he was making a mistake asking for my cousin. And I believe he does care for me, Mother . . . in his way."

"Is that enough?"

"No. In fact, it is far worse than if he just didn't care. And I think that, on some level, I understood. Then Father arranged for a match with Lord Villier, and well, Andres's offer for a marriage of convenience seemed far more attractive. It took me away from London, away from where people didn't believe I mattered."

"You've always mattered to your father and I —"

"I know that, but to a silly young woman, and that is exactly what I was, a parent's care and love is no match for what other people think of her." Abby rested a hand on her mother's shoulder. "I don't feel that way now. I know I've hurt you and I am sorry for it. Please forgive me."

Her mother's tired face became a wreath of smiles. "We forgive you all. And it is a blessing you are home. Please, don't worry about that horrid Spaniard. I know your father will be able to do whatever is necessary to remove him from your life."

"Mother, I don't want him removed."

"You don't?" Her mother sat back.

"No," Abby said, "I love him."

"Love him?" Her father's voice surprised both of them.

Abby turned. Her father had come around

the corner. He still wore his hat and coat and smelled of London's sooty air. She nodded. "Yes, hopelessly."

Admitting it never ceased to amaze her. Her love seemed to grow stronger with each declaration.

"Well, if you are so hopelessly in love, why are you here?" her father demanded. "And where is the man?"

For a second, Abby was tempted to lie . . . but she realized that this was what had hurt her parents from the beginning. She'd cut them out of her thoughts and her life, and it had wounded them.

"I'm here," she said, "because Freddie Sherwin did something right for once. He told me you were ill. As for my husband . . . I'm waiting to discover if he loves me."

Her mother's empathy was immediate. "Oh, darling."

Her father's brow darkened. "You would be better off without him."

"Would I, Father? I don't think our child would agree."

Abby had surprised her parents few times in her life, but she did so now — and they each had a different reaction.

"Abigail, a baby?" her mother said. The last signs of illness evaporated. Her eyes took on a glow of anticipation.

"This is a devil of a mess," her father said, raising a hand to his forehead. He paced the length of the room. "How can we end this marriage if you are breeding?"

"Heath," her mother admonished. "That's not the way to talk about our grandchild. She's not breeding. She's doing exactly what a woman should do when she is in love."

Her father grunted his opinion. He shoved his hands into the pocket of his coat, his expression reminding Abby of the Stonemoor barn cat when he didn't catch the mouse he was chasing.

Her mother ran her hand over Abby's curls, the way she used to when Abby was a child. "I hope the babe has your hair coloring and your eyes," she said. "And your nose."

"I want him to have something of Andres," Abby answered.

"Does he know?" her father demanded.

Abby hated to admit, "No. This is something I've just realized. We've been so busy at Stonemoor that I didn't notice. However, on my way here, at one of the inns I stopped at, I met a woman who had just realized she was with child. She spoke of the symptoms." Abby felt color rise to her cheeks over talking so frankly in front of her father. "That's when I suspected I was. I have many of the same concerns."

"I always sensed I was right away as well," her mother said. "Almost immediately. Isn't that true, Heath?"

"Do you think it might be a good idea to tell the child's father?" her father asked pointedly, choosing to refuse to take part in good wishes.

Rising to her feet so that she could better face him, Abby kept hold of her mother's hand as she said, "I will tell him . . . when I see him."

"Something is havey-cavey here. Abby, your mother leads with her heart, but you and I always lead with our heads. What are you about?"

"I don't lead with my head any longer," Abby told her sire. "This is my heart, out there for everyone to see. I love him, Father, and I need him to love me."

"And so you are here — ?" her father wondered again.

"Yes," Abby said, "and I hope he comes for me. I want him to care for me as much as I do him."

"What if he doesn't come?" her mother asked, doubt in her voice.

"He'll come," Abby said. She had to believe he would. She must.

Her father grumbled under his breath before saying, "If you are so certain, why go through this exercise?"

"I needed to see Mother. Freddie made her sound as if she was at death's door —"

"Do you think I would let her grow so ill and not inform you?" her father said.

Abby knew he was worked up. There was a time she would have met him passion for passion. But she felt older now, and wiser. "I don't want us estranged. I want my child to know his grandparents." She released her breath and said, "I know you are angry with me, Father. I defied you, but I think that is because I was meant to be with Andres Ramigio."

"You thought you were *meant* to be with Freddie Sherwin at one time as well," he threw back at her.

"I have no argument," she admitted. "I was wrong . . . and if Andres doesn't love me, he may not come for me."

Her father shook his head, as if his anger was churning inside of him. He raised a hand, ready to point a finger and speak his mind, but her mother rose. "No, Heath, no more. Have you forgotten what it is like to be so new in love?"

"Catherine, you have always known my devotion for you."

"Have I? I seem to remember an argument we had a week after we married where I packed my bags and was ready to leave. Do you remember that? You blocked my way, refusing to let me pass."

"You are my wife," her father said. "We were married. You couldn't leave on a whim."

"A whim?" Her mother gave him a sharp eye. "As I remember, you had grown frustrated with lugging along a wife who was crying for her mother. And you weren't going to let me return. Of course, you were very persuasive, sir. Nine months later, we had Robert." Her expression started to crumple at the mention of her son. She forced a smile through it. "I lost one child, Heath. I won't lose another, not when she's made the trip back for us. And this Spaniard, perhaps he is all the things you've warned us about. But then you had a roguish reputation, too — and you turned out rather well."

"I had you, Catherine. That's what made the difference."

"And this Spaniard has our daughter. What is his name, Abby? Not his title, his name."

"Andres. Andres Ramigio."

Her mother tested the name. "Romantic,

359

no?" she said to Abby's father.

He frowned. "I can't like him. He took my daughter."

"And he is giving us a grandchild," his wife reminded him. "Another sign of our love for each other."

"He'll be half Spanish," her father muttered. "Heath Ramigio. It's a silly name for an English baby."

Abby was about to call him out, but her mother beat her to the response. And a nicer one it was.

"He'll also be a remarkably handsome child. Think of it, Heath, he'll be like Abby, my looks and your brains — with a bit of his father thrown in. And who is to say he'll be named after his grandfather? Especially if his grandfather continues to have such a hard head?"

"I've a hard head because I want what is best for my children," was his reply.

"It's not your hard head I worry about, Heath. It's you hardening your heart. You must realize they aren't children any longer. They are adults, and not one of them has listened to you yet. Perhaps your grandson will . . . and I shall encourage Abby and Andres to name him Robert."

Suddenly, the anger left her father. Abby had never seen him cry. Not even at her brother's funeral. He'd stood straight-backed, holding her mother, who'd been consumed by grief — but tears welled in his eyes now.

"I just want to protect all of you," he admitted. "I want you safe. And I didn't do such a good job with my boys. One gone, and look at the other two. I don't want you heartbroken, Abby. I don't want myself heartbroken again."

Both Abby and her mother flew to him. They put their arms around him and hugged him with all they had. He hugged right back.

Her mother used her kerchief to wipe away the tear stains on his cheeks in the same gentle manner Abby had used on her earlier. Her father was a bit embarrassed, but he didn't deny the emotion.

Instead, he said, "If that Spaniard doesn't come for you, Abby, then he is a fool."

"I agree with you, Father. I agree."

The first day home, Abby kept her spirits up. Her mother's health continued to improve. Her trip had served a very good purpose.

The servants all took a moment to let Abby know that they had genuinely been worried for her. It was assumed everything was fine now that Abby was back.

The second day without word from Andres, Abby wasn't as strong in her resolve.

What right did she have to test Andres in this way? She knew he could be fiercely independent. If she had been Andres, she wouldn't have come for her either.

If he did not come for her, did she go to him?

Could she return to her marriage and pretend as if nothing had happened?

Abby feared she lacked that gift.

Jonesy paid a call. She'd heard a rumor that Abby was back, and she fished shamelessly for details about her marriage. Both Abby and her mother managed to keep her at bay, and not one word was said about a baby.

Her mother seemed to understand the doubts Abby was experiencing. It was a good time for the two of them. Instead of just mother and daughter, they spoke to each other as friends, peers.

Abby missed Andres terribly. She missed being her own mistress. She missed the country.

By Christmas, Abby realized her life in London seemed meaningless.

Every year, Abby's uncle, the duke of Banfield, hosted Christmas Day dinner for those who were still in town. Everyone of any importance was there. It was an enjoyable event.

Abby waited until an hour before her family should depart to inform her parents she'd rather not go.

Her father frowned. "Why not? Because of Freddie and Corinne?"

"I have no difficulty being around them," she said, and meant it. She was completely over Freddie. She didn't even consider him a friend. In fact, she felt sorry for Corinne. "I'm just not feeling festive."

"Abby, you can't stay home," her mother said. "It's Christmas."

It didn't feel like Christmas. Abby missed her husband desperately.

"I shall be fine," she told her mother.

"You will not be alone this night." Her father came around to stand in front of her. "Abigail, I shall not have you moping because that foreigner has disappointed you —"

"He has not —" Abby started to defend him.

"Come now," her father countered, cutting her off. "If things were fine between you, he'd be by your side. How much longer will you wait?"

"He's going to come for me," she said, the words starting to sound hollow.

"But not on Christmas Day," her father said. "In truth, I'm a bit disappointed in him. I rather thought he would."

"You did? I was under the impression you preferred to believe the worst of him," Abby said.

"Sherwin would be the worst," her father answered. He placed a hand on her shoulder. "I'm sorry, Abby my girl, for the sadness this is causing you. However, we will not leave you at home, and we must make an appearance to preserve the myth of family harmony. Come with us. We won't stay long. You know anything under Banfield's roof irritates me."

"I fear Andres doesn't care," Abby admitted.

"Don't give up," her mother urged. "When we come home, I shall write a letter to him."

"Please, no, not that." Abby drew a shaky breath. "He has to come to me on his own." It was what Celeste had said. "Only then will I know he cares."

Her parents exchanged a worried look. Abby pretended not to notice, but she did go upstairs and change. An hour later they left the house.

Andres's goal upon arriving in London was to fetch his wife and take her home.

The trip had taken longer than he'd planned. Rain had caused delays. He'd taken a short way around and discovered the road impassable because a bridge had been washed out. He'd been forced to double back, which had cost time he had not wanted to waste.

His one thought was of Abby. He debated the argument they'd had a hundred times in his head. Sometimes he felt he'd been completely justified. Other times, he thought he'd been a fool.

He was so focused and intent on reaching London that he didn't realize it was Christmas Day until he rode down the city's streets and heard people calling out good cheer to one another.

He reached the front step of Montross's house, knocked on the door, and was told they were not at home

"Where is she?" he demanded.

The butler looked him up and down. Servants could be haughtier than their masters in this country, but that was fine with Andres. A Spaniard had more pride than an Englishman, and no one could stare down another like a Ramigio.

The butler shut the door in his face.

Andres was incensed. He stomped back toward his horse. He searched the street.

There had to be a way to let Abby know he was there. He'd climb the walls if he must.

"My lord? Please, my lord?" a woman's voice said from the narrow passage between the houses.

Curious, Andres went around the side of the house. A woman stood there with a cloak over her head, but Andres saw a bit of the Montross livery beneath the heavy wool.

"Please, my lord, off the street, please. We can't have anyone see us," the woman said.

"Who are you?" he asked. He'd been traveling hard and was not in the mood for mysteries.

"My name is Tabitha," she said, bobbing a curtsey. "I'm Miss Abby's maid."

Ah, yes, the one who had tried to stop them from eloping. "She is here?" he asked anxiously.

The maid nodded. "She is, but the family has gone out for Christmas dinner. They are dining at the house of His Grace, the duke of Banfield. Do you know where that is?"

Andres nodded.

"You need to go to her, my lord," the maid said, already backing away.

"Wait," he said. "Tell me more. How is she?" *Does she miss me?*

"I daren't say more, my lord. I'm so sorry.

I've already caused you and Miss Abby so much trouble. But she needs you. She misses you."

The maid turned and ran away — and Andres set off to claim his wife.

CHAPTER NINETEEN

The gathering for Banfield's Christmas dinner was a good one hundred and fifty people.

Abby's aunt had ordered the ballroom set up for the affair, and she was in her element. King George had been declared mentally incompetent earlier that month, and there were rumors swirling that the Prince of Wales might make an appearance in town instead of enjoying his customary Christmas retreat. If so, would he not join the duke of Banfield's festivities?

There was a possibility, or so Jonesy assured Abby as they sat together in the reception room, waiting for the rest of the company to gather.

"Banfield and his wife dearly hope he appears," Jonesy said. "Their star will know no limit in society's firmament if such were the case. Look how crowded it is? All for a bit of Banfield's Christmas goose."

She laughed at her own small joke while taking another sip of her sherry.

The event was a crush. Abby couldn't remember it ever being so full.

Of course, she didn't care about Prinny, as her aunt kept flitting around calling the Prince of Wales, as much as she did the presence of Freddie *and* Lady Dobbins.

Andres's former mistress stood not far from Abby, a spectacular smirk marring her lovely face. Abby smiled back at her, wondering what would happen to Lady Dobbins's beauty if her face froze that way. Then all would see her for the selfish creature she was, and Abby would wager most men wouldn't care about her anymore.

Freddie was on the other side of the room, standing beside Corinne and laughing at everything said to him with the best of humor. Abby barely paid him any heed.

"Sherwin is trying to gain your attention," Jonesy whispered to her. "He keeps looking over here."

Abby shrugged.

Jonesy pulled back, giving Abby a hard look. She looked over to Abby's mother. "Is this the same child?"

Her mother smiled. "Why do you ask that?"

"She lacks our former Abby's anxiousness," Jonesy replied, studying Abby. "She seems sure of herself."

"I am," Abby answered, a bit surprised herself by the transformation. In the past, an event such as this would have made her shake in fear.

But now she had other worries. Besides, she'd been mistress of her own house, had made decisions for herself. Perhaps some of those decisions hadn't worked out the way she'd hoped, but they had given Abby confidence. If she didn't fit in here, there would be someplace else for her.

Nor did she look at the other guests with awe. Yes, her hair was curlier than most, but she was proud of it. Her eyes were blue and not the fashionable brown. Who cared? There was nothing she could do about it . . . and she wasn't interested in people who were so petty.

That was Andres's charm, she now understood. His secret to gliding amongst the *ton.* His good looks were an entrée, but beyond that, he knew how to live in his own skin — and in their short time together, he'd taught her to do the same. To see her strengths and not her flaws.

Or perhaps to see her flaws as strengths —

"What are you smiling about?" Jonesy

asked. "I say, niece, you have come back from the wilds a changed woman."

"I have come back a woman," Abby assured her.

Her aunt's eyes widened and Abby laughed, perhaps a bit too loud, because it drew attention to her. She rose to her feet and reached for a glass of sherry off a servant's tray, but she found herself approached by two notable gentlemen.

The Honorable Piers Robertson was considered one of the finest catches of the Season. Abby had been introduced to him numerous times before, but he'd looked right past her. The other gentleman, Lord Millhorn, was another revered bachelor. Abby had always thought both men too haughty for their own good.

Now she learned there was a different side to them. They set about wooing her. In fact, they ignored other women in the room — such as Lady Dobbins.

Abby didn't understand why they'd singled her out. She was a married woman, and then she realized that could be their purpose. It made her sad. What poor company she was keeping. She missed her country neighbors with their good, honest hearts.

More important, she missed her husband,

and suddenly the thought that *this* was what she was relegating herself to was too much. Ignoring the witticisms of the men who were trying to impress her, she looked around the room.

For the first time, Abby saw how bored Lady Dobbins looked. She barely listened to the conversation of the woman beside her, much as Abby was not listening to the gentlemen talking to her — *and no noticed.* They kept speaking.

Her cousin Corinne appeared miserable as well. She stood tall, lovely, her arms crossed low at her waist, as if she was holding herself together. Freddie barely looked at her. He touched her from time to time, a hand on the elbow, nothing personal. He was busy trying to impress Banfield, who stood on Corinne's other side. Abby had an image of the men speaking *through* her cousin, and never to her.

For the first time, mainly because she wasn't gripped with anxiety over herself, Abby realized that Corinne was intelligent enough to know everything about Freddie. There was a sadness in her cousin's eye that tore at Abby's heart.

All these people talking, and no one valuing each other — save for her parents. They had their heads together, speaking softly.

She realized her father was not watching her anxiously the way he used to do before she'd run off. He appeared relaxed, and she understood that her parents had been just as concerned about her being accepted as she had. In fact, perhaps she'd been so self-conscious because of their worries.

Such a revelation would not have been possible before she'd met Andres.

Life made sense with him. That's what her mother had said about why she'd had to marry Abby's father.

But the words took on a more personal meaning for Abby as she stood amongst her old nemeses and was no longer doubtful of her position.

She was Andres Ramigio's wife . . . and she'd made a terrible mistake in leaving him.

Celeste had been wrong. People who loved each other didn't test their loyalties. They didn't care who took a step toward whom.

Abby wanted to return to Stonemoor. She wanted her husband, and she wanted to leave now.

The Banfield butler appeared in the doorway to announce that dinner was served. All eyes had turned to the servant — but there was someone else there as well.

Andres had come up behind the man. He stood in the doorway, searching the crowd.

For a second, Abby feared her imagination had conjured him.

He was at odds with the present company. He was hatless, and his hair was disheveled. A growth of beard darkened his jaw. Both his greatcoat and boots and spurs were caked with mud, as if he'd ridden hard and fast to reach here.

As if he'd come to find *her*.

Andres's heart hammered against his chest so loudly that he was certain everyone could hear it.

He'd wanted Abby. She was all that mattered . . . but now, he found himself in a room full of the *ton*'s most important personages.

For one terrible moment, he remembered when he'd declared himself to Gillian. He'd done so publicly, in front of many of the same people, and she had rejected him.

Now, his gaze honed in on Abby, and she appeared a stranger to him. Her curls were tamed into a becoming style. She was flanked by prestigious men, honest men who had no hidden secrets, no shameful past. From head to toe, she was the very picture of a woman of substance and grace.

What was he? The bastard son of a disgraced nobleman. A man who had yet to prove himself.

And he loved her so much that pride no longer mattered.

He stood in front of that sparkling company and said, "I need you. I love you."

Conversation stopped. His words echoed in the air.

Abby's response was immediate.

She came running to him. And she didn't stop when she reached him. She threw the full force of her body into his arms. Andres lifted her up, holding her tight. Nothing felt as good as having this woman's body next to his.

They kissed.

Through Abby, he'd learned a kiss could mean many things. It could be simple good morning or good night. Sometimes her kisses meant she didn't agree with him but she was going to allow him his way — for the moment. Other times, her kisses were a trust, a bond, a renewal of those sacred marriage vows between them.

Right now, her kiss threatened to swallow him whole, and in it he understood that she'd missed him as much as he'd missed her. They were two bodies sharing the same soul. They knew that now. She was sorry to have made him come for her. He regretted chasing her away.

He had his wife back. She was more than just a helpmate — she was his conscience, his muse, his destiny.

But they had to take a breath sooner or later.

Slowly, he let her body slide down his, grateful to feel the familiar curves and planes, her sweetness filling his lungs.

"Come home," he whispered.

She nodded. Tears welled in her eyes. His Abby. She always cried when she was happy and sad. He liked her honest emotion.

His fingers laced with hers. He started to lead her away — but then Montross's voice stopped him.

"Here now, you can't just take off."

Andres had forgotten about their audience. The moment Abby had run into his arms, the rest of the world had ceased to matter. "I beg your pardon, sir, but I can."

The moment he spoke the words, he sensed the conflict in Abby. Once again there was that pull toward people she loved.

Fear rose in him. A concern that she could not love him . . . and then she gave his hand a reassuring squeeze. His heart opened.

He saw that she didn't love him less. He just needed to love more.

The realization released years of fears and doubt.

Andres looked to Montross. "She is my wife," he said, "but she is also your daughter, and someday perhaps soon, you will be the grandparents of our children. I would not rip her away from you."

Montross's attitude changed. The tension left him, the bullishness. He nodded his head. "Good, good . . . because I plan on relishing that grandparent role."

For a second, Andres didn't think he'd heard him correctly. Banker Montross, feared by many, had just accepted him into his family.

"I am counting on it, sir," Andres said.

Montross smiled. "Very good, Barón."

The use of his title reminded Andres of the lie he lived. Could a man with so much love in his life continue to keep secrets?

He looked down at his wife. She understood what he was thinking and nodded.

He glanced around the room. There were few friends here. Dobbins was watching him with a sly look in his eye. He was going to take Stonemoor from him, but in Andres's mind, losing the property was worth the price of having his wife back. He knew that now. Furthermore, he didn't want any more threats. He wanted to live his life in the peace of a clear conscience.

"I have a confession," he said, the words

surprisingly easy to say once he'd made up his mind. "I am not a barón. My father was the barón de Vasconia, but I am the illegitimate son. My name is Andres Ramigio, and I am the best horse trainer in all Europe."

Silence met his announcement.

There were several scowls and frowns, but little else. Then again, what had he expected? They would save their true thoughts for when his back was turned.

What mattered was that Montross and his wife crossed the room to stand beside him.

The duchess of Banfield looked around at her guests and announced, in a bit of a dazed voice, "Shall we all move to dinner?"

No one budged, until the duchess grabbed Freddie and Corinne and physically nudged them to the door. After that, people started moving, shooting covert glances at Andres and his in-laws as they passed.

Lady Dobbins was escorted by her husband. Neither looked at them.

The duke and duchess were the last to leave the room. The duchess, Abby's aunt, gave them a weak smile, but Banfield stopped and said, "I say, sister, can't you keep your family in order?"

"Apparently not," Mrs. Montross answered.

Her brother harrumphed his opinion and left them to join his guests.

Andres released the breath he was holding. "I am sorry for being so public with this. I suppose it is not proper manners to announce one's illegitimacy before speaking of it in private." He could have been more thoughtful.

"I already knew it," Montross said.

"As did I," Abby's mother added. "Do you really believe we would let anyone marry our daughter without learning all we could?"

"I have become a commoner," Andres answered. "Of perhaps the worst sort."

"Or one could say there might be a very distinct possibility that my daughter has married an *un*common man," Mrs. Montross said. "I'm not surprised that she did. After all, I did." She smiled. "You will call me Catherine, and my husband, Heath. Welcome to our family."

Her generosity, her understanding, humbled him. He started to put into words what he was feeling, but she shook her head, refusing to hear him. "Please, we are overdue with the welcome."

Before more could be said, Andres noticed that Lord Dobbins had left the sparkling company and was approaching them. Lady

Dobbins poked her head out of the supper room doorway, watching her husband.

His lordship's smile was reptilian. "I hate to spoil such a grandiose Christmas confession," he said, "but we have a problem. I gave Ramigio Stonemoor with the understanding that if he returned to London it would be returned to me."

"*You* are the reason he left?" Lady Dobbins said, hurrying forward. "How dare you? I've had enough of this, Dobbins. I am not some slave girl whose life you can order about to your liking."

"No, but you are my wife," Dobbins answered.

"Who you attempt to control by every means possible! I've had enough, I say. *Enough.*"

"Carla, you are being hysterical," her husband answered.

"Hysterical?" she repeated, her eyes narrowing. "I'm past that, Dobbins. I'm tired of you ignoring me or trotting me out like a pretty plaything." She turned to Andres. "I loved you." She pressed the heels of her hands against her cheeks as if to stave off tears. "You were kind to me. I hadn't realized how much kindness could matter."

"Carla," her husband said, but her answer was to move away from him and head for

Banfield's front hall. They heard her call for her coat and for someone to order her coach to be brought round.

Dobbins swore under his breath. He turned his temper on Andres. "I own Stonemoor, you know. Your being here has returned it to me."

Abby placed her hand on Andres's arm. "You sacrificed everything to come here for me?"

"The price was small," he assured her. "I don't want a life without you."

"And I must correct a misunderstanding Lord Dobbins has," Heath Montross said. "Actually, my lord, you don't own the property. I do. I purchased some of your debts, and the papers concerning that property were part of it."

"You what?" Dobbins demanded.

"You know the influx of cash you needed to meet some pressing obligations?" Heath said. "I was the banker. I admit to doing some sleuthing and learned from my respected colleague Mr. Deeter of your agreement with Ramigio. When he discussed your pressing need for funds, I requested that Stonemoor be included in the exchange. You should pay better attention to what you are signing, my lord." His smile grew grim. "I also want you to remember that no one blackmails a member of my family."

Lord Dobbins's face took on the color of an overripe plum. "They were Carla's debts."

Heath shrugged. "You are not the first man to have a spendthrift wife."

The front door slammed, punctuating Heath's words and reminding Dobbins that his wife had just left.

"What else did I sign away?" Lord Dobbins demanded.

"I would speak to my man of business," Heath politely advised him.

His lordship stood a second longer, and then, finally realizing his threats no longer carried any weight, left, moving toward the front door, presumably to catch his wife.

There was a moment of stunned silence.

Andres faced his father-in-law. "I am in your debt."

"You are a clever man, Ramigio," Heath Montross said. "You have ambition. You remind me a bit of myself, although you are not half as handsome. That was a small jest, son," he said.

"Son" — he had called Andres "son."

The word sounded good.

"By the way," her father continued, "I also have a confession of my own. I lied about the trust. The money is yours, Abby. I was hoping to disappoint your Spaniard and you would have had to return home with me. I didn't see the love then, but I do now. All I wanted was a man worthy of you."

"And you realize Andres is?" Abby asked, very pleased.

"Yes, you have found a good one. Come, Cate, I want my dinner." He took his wife's arm, and they walked down the hall to the supper room.

Andres put his arm around his wife, pulling her close. He kissed her curls, the top of her forehead. "Thank you," he said.

She smiled up at him. "You said you loved me. In front of everyone."

"I'll say it again. I'll say it every day of my life, my *palomita*."

"No, now it is my turn." She placed her arms around his waist. "You've changed me, Andres. You've made me a woman in all ways. My life is richer and fuller because I am by your side. I love you with a passion that grows every day. But more important, I respect you, my love. You've taught me to dream."

"And you have taught me to live," he answered. "You are right, Abby, I was thinking of taking my life that night. I thought I had nothing. Now, I find I have everything I ever wished for and more."

"I love you," she answered.

He hugged her tight. The smell of Christmas dinner floated in the air . . . but he wasn't hungry — at least, not for food.

She caught what he was thinking. Her smile turned wicked, seductive. "Perhaps we would rather return to my parents' house?"

"How many rooms do they have in it?" he wondered.

"So that we can make love in every room?" she asked eagerly. "They have twice as many as we have at Stonemoor."

"Then we must leave," he assured her. "We have a busy night ahead."

And they did.

Later that night, as all the house slept, Andres held Abby in his arms, sated and content with life.

And it was a miracle to him.

"I have a present for you," she murmured.

"There is no need," he answered sleepily. "You have given me all that I want."

"Yes, but I have one gift we shall both enjoy." She whispered into his ear news he'd not expected. *He was to be a father.*

The richness of his life humbled him. "Abby, thank you," he whispered, holding her tightly.

"You had a hand in it," she said, her voice brimming with happy laughter.

"Did I?" He wrapped one of her rebellious curls around his finger. "Before you, I had given up, *palomita*. I had lost my way."

"And I helped you find it," she said, snuggling close to him.

"Yes, my love," he answered. "You helped me find it."

Epilogue

Destinada foaled on a blustery, wet morning in March.

Andres had stayed up all night with the mare, waiting. Abby had joined him for a good portion of the time, although as the hour had grown late, her husband had sent her to bed.

She'd been organizing the linen press, trying to put her mind off what was happening at the stables, when Andres had sent a stable lad for her. "Come quick, my lady. It's time, it's time," the lad had said to her.

Abby had leapt to her feet and come running, leaving behind the smell of clean sheets and lavender for the earthy scents of the stables. So much depended on this foal. Andres had warned her a mare's first foal was often the worst, and any number of things could go wrong with nature.

They'd built a birthing stall onto the stables. It was more sheltered from the elements than the others were. As she marched through the spring mud and stepped out of the wind into the stables, Abby was glad they'd invested the money.

She could hear Andres encouraging the mare in Spanish. The stable lads had gathered outside the stall and peered in to watch. Abby joined them, having to step up on a wood box to see in.

Destinada lay on her side in the clean straw, her labor a sight to behold. Andres stood back, his body tense, as if he readied himself to help the mare at any moment.

"How is she doing?" Abby whispered.

Andres had been so intent on the horse that he'd not realized Abby had arrived. He gave her a quick smile and shrugged. "We shall know soon."

The mare looked distressed, as if not certain what was happening and yet, at the same time, all too aware. Her eye met Abby's, and for a second Abby sensed an understanding between them. All creatures suffered in childbirth.

Abby dropped her hand to rest on her own belly. She was just beginning to show. Andres assured her she would feel the baby's movements soon now. She couldn't wait.

"Am I too late?" her father's voice bellowed from outside. He appeared in the doorway and came stomping down the aisle, trying to rid the mud from his boots.

True to his word, her father had proven he wanted to be a fixture in their lives. Both he and her mother had moved from London and now rented a house in Corbridge. Abby was learning her father had the heart of a farmer, and he'd embraced the stables as a good investment. There could be no higher praise from him.

"You are right on time," Andres called to him.

Her father came to stand by Abby. He shuddered at the sight of the mare. "Women's work," he muttered, and she laughed.

But before she could comment, the foal started to emerge. A thin white membrane covered the two front feet and head. Destinada seemed to have some difficulty pushing her baby out. Andres leaned over, grabbed the foal's feet, and pulled. The baby slid free from its mother.

Abby hadn't known what to expect, or that she would be as moved as she was in watching the birth. The miracle of new life was amazing, but what touched her to the core was how gently her husband helped the mare.

Andres removed the membrane, taking the time to rub the foal's ears, head, and sides.

He grinned up at Abby. "It's a colt." They had been discussing which sex they would prefer. Jonathan had insisted on purchasing Destinada's foal and had been anxious for a stallion. This would please him.

"What happens now?" Abby asked.

"We give mare and foal a moment," Andres said. He came to his feet, pride in his eyes. "He's a good one," he said. The stable lads all added their agreement.

"How can you tell?" her father wondered, voicing the question Abby had.

"He's perfectly formed," Andres said. "Holburn's stallion is well worth the breeding."

"But the foal is a dark bay," Abby answered. "I thought he'd be gray, since both his mother and father are so white."

"He will be," Andres said. "He'll gray out as he grows older."

"Even with that star on his head?" her father asked.

"Yes," Andres said with certainty.

At that moment, Destinada rose to her feet. She gave a shake, the movement going through her whole body like a woman adjusting her skirts. She then turned and, with a mother's insistent gentleness, nudged her colt.

He blinked at her, his wide, wondering

eyes framed by long lashes.

"He doesn't look as if he knows quite where he is yet," Abby said.

"It must be different to be here than from where he was," one of the stable lads agreed.

And then, to her amazement, the colt clambered to his feet. His legs seemed overlong and way too thin, and yet he stood. Destinada nickered her approval.

The colt looked to his audience. He took his first tentative step and then stopped, surprised by his audacity. Even the most hardened of the stable lads smiled approval.

"He's a right handsome one, my lord," Neddie, the lead groomsman, said. They all nodded. Andres beamed with pride.

Within seconds, the colt found his bearings. Destinada had started eating. The colt seemed to follow the sound of her munching and was soon rooting on his mother, looking for his dinner.

The scene was one of maternal bliss. A longing for the child growing inside her filled Abby. Her husband must have felt the same, because he came out of the stall and put his arm around her.

"That is a fine-looking horse," her father declared. "Good breeding. It's what I'm expecting from the two of you," he said, a comment that brought laughter from everyone gathered. Even Abby had to smile in spite of the heat rushing to her cheeks.

"What are you naming the colt?" her father demanded.

"Dinero," Andres answered.

"Dinero? The Spanish word for money? I like that," her father said. "Dinero."

The colt pulled from his mother to look around, as if sensing they were talking about him. "He is intelligent," Andres said with pride.

"Aye, the best," her father agreed. "When do we breed her again?"

"When she is ready," Andres said. "In the meantime, we have the other Andalusians you found. They should be here next month." Her father had become so enthused about the horses that he'd made inquiries. His contacts had located two more horses bred from Andres's father's stables. One was a stallion. They were on their way from Italy.

"I'm going to fetch your mother," her father said. "She must see this."

"I'm surprised she didn't come with you," Abby said.

"She was with her church group." Her father sighed. Her mother had jumped into the daily life of Corbridge and was currently helping to organize a fund to purchase a new bell for St. Andrews's tower. "We'll be back shortly," he promised and left.

The stable hands had to return to their chores as well.

Andres and Abby didn't budge but stood watching this newest member of their stables.

Her husband leaned over and brushed a kiss against her hair. "We have our first success, *palomita.* That colt is beyond compare, and the next one will be even better. We are a success."

"*You* are," she corrected him. "*You* are a success. I'm just the good woman who had the sense to stand beside you."

The expression on his face turned her heart inside out. She knew she had touched him with her words. He reached for her hand, lacing his fingers with hers. "I do not deserve you. You've given me all that I ever wanted."

"What is that? My opinions?" she teased him.

"Your love, your trust . . . your family."

"We were meant to find each other," she whispered. And he nodded.

"From the first moment we met," he agreed. "It is not every woman who knocks me off my feet."

Abby started to laugh, but the sound caught in her throat as she felt her baby's first move. She widened her eyes in surprise. It had been the lightest of fluttering, and yet it had been there, separate and distinct from herself. "I felt him," she said.

"Where?" Andres demanded, already placing his hand on her belly.

"You may not feel it," she started, but there it was again, and she could see by Andres's transfixed expression that he'd felt it as well.

And in that moment, she knew herself truly complete.

Oh, there would be challenges in their future, although she had no fear. They'd already proven they could overcome all odds.

But she also realized that just as Andres had what he'd always wanted — a family, his horses, a place in the world — she'd discovered what she'd been searching for. She was loved by a man who honored her. No matter what life threw at them, they were together. Two would become one.

She kissed her husband, holding him tight — forever and ever.

We hope you have enjoyed this Large Print book. Other Thorndike, Wheeler, Kennebec, and Chivers Press Large Print books are available at your library or directly from the publishers.

For information about current and upcoming titles, please call or write, without obligation, to:

Publisher
Thorndike Press
295 Kennedy Memorial Drive
Waterville, ME 04901
Tel. (800) 223-1244

or visit our Web site at:

http://gale.cengage.com/thorndike

OR

Chivers Large Print
published by AudioGO Ltd
St James House, The Square
Lower Bristol Road
Bath BA2 3SB
England
Tel. +44(0) 800 136919
www.audiogo.co.uk

All our Large Print titles are designed for easy reading, and all our books are made to last.